THE DEVOURED SONS

Seth Daniel Parker

CHAPTER ONE

DESIRE

"Buried deep inside the cavernous chambers of every man's heart, there exists a longing, a ravenous hunger, a raging desire that threatens to devour him from within. The fight, no, the chase begins at birth—he after it, it after he—a relentless pursuit upon the foggiest seas to each's own delight. Be it love or vice, fortune or fame, desire knows not its price, and man knows not he pays."
- Dorian's Notes

Yet, what is life without desire? In its absence, man is little more than a malcontented blob thrust upon tumultuous waters, moved only by the forces surrounding him. Unlike the fortresses of emotion—joy and sorrow—secluded to permanent islands of consciousness, desire is the vessel that connects thought to action, driven forward by the dueling winds of pleasure and pain. Strip either wind from this sail, and man's happiness fades out of reach beyond the horizon. His new course? The Siren sounds of fear and anger beckoning him toward the rocky shores of sorrow.

Ah, such is life—the tantalizing tango of man and his desires. In fact, weren't we warned by Tantalus himself? The Greek demi-god audaciously questioned the Olympian immortals and dared to taste their ambrosia. For this, he earned not only the knowledge he sought but also a taste of its enigmatic companion: wisdom. Condemned to the Underworld, he stands forevermore in a pool of water beneath fruit-laden branches, bearing unquenchable thirst and insatiable hunger. Reaching above, the branches elude his grasp; below, the waters recoil from his parched lips. And so he remains, the personification of aspirations unchecked. At least, that's the lesson passed down for generations—a lesson underscored by the Benefactor's influence—and I might have died many years ago believing this were it not for my friends' inspiration. From an evolved perspective, the tale of Tantalus proves him to be the prophet of crushed rebellions rather than the incarnation of unchecked aspirations—a lesson proven by experience.

And desire? For better or worse, is it not at the heart of every great story? Ahab and Moby Dick. Gatsby and the Green Light. Faust and knowledge. Caulfield and authenticity. Even Romeo and Juliet and their forbidden love. Intoxicated by desire, man will sacrifice everything he holds dear and never question the cost. At once, it can be his most endearing, though self-destructive quality—humanity's romantic dichotomy.

My ancestors were no different. All loners, they hunted some intangible feeling, perhaps even a fleeting genetic memory, that defied description. My grandfather's great-grandfather, Emmit, was a Western cowboy in the early 20th century. With the sun on his face and the outdoors as his only companion, he called himself a son of the land.

Emmit's son rebelled against the sprawling deserts and plains that reminded him of his distant father, choosing the adventurous life of a New England fisherman. The salt-tinged winds drying his lips, he took comfort in the Northeast's damp and chilly blanket. A son of the sea, his life was a battle between the elements and his own discontent.

His son, my great-grandfather, was a son of the long white line. Painted on the asphalt as a boundary to most, to him, it represented the endless freedom of America's Golden Age. A long-haul trucker with a Harley heart, he followed that white line as perhaps the only one of us who was ever content with the chase's thrill alone.

However, as their massive worlds expanded before them, teeming with endless possibilities, Earth began to shrink with my grandfather. Technology soon connected its opposite ends with an instantaneous tether. Tectonic shifts in research and communication happened at blistering speeds. Man's sense of mystery and adventure seemed to dissolve, and my grandfather returned to Emmit's homeland in search of its essence. Equipped with a lens rather than a lasso, the budding photographer pursued the ethereal interplay of light and shadow on the Western landscape—a son of the sun.

That's when a shrinking planet became something new altogether. My grandfather's generation witnessed The Solemn Veil and its devastating fallout. The first of two cataclysmic events that threatened humanity, billions of people died. Governments collapsed. Our ecosystem nearly followed. Entire cities were eventually leveled and rebuilt into protective city-states by legions of Artificial Intelligence-powered Humanara. Had it not been for the Benefactor's intervention, it was supposed that Earth itself might have become uninhabitable within a few generations.

A son of this new world, my father became a scooter mechanic. I know. Considering our lineage, it's not exactly the lifestyle you might expect, but an electric scooter was our primary method of travel in those days. Riding the narrow roads of our district seemed to be the only thing that offered his restless soul any solace.

And then there's me, the last of us—a son of Nashville, a son of desire, the son of man. I lived in a 10-square-mile reimagination of Nashville, complete with its signature Broadway lights and country music background. Bordering Nashville to the East was New York and its Times Square. To the West, Austin and its Congress Avenue. To Austin's West, downtown Los Angeles—each 10-square-mile district, a cultural echo of its former namesake. Together, "The three LAs and New York," as my father referred to them, formed the city-state of Athens, tucked away in Appalachia.

From a young age, I had always considered myself an explorer, scouring the urban landscape and learning the city's every stone and steel beam. Often, I climbed well above Broadway's neon buzz to stare in awe at the neighboring skylines, wishing I could investigate their worlds as I had mine.

By my last day in primary school, I had conquered every rooftop in Nashville, and there was only one building left to vanquish—The Hector. It was no fantastic feat; an elevator and a small flight of stairs offered the same journey to anyone. Nevertheless, I burst through the doorway onto Music City's tallest rooftop as if I were Achilles claiming the city. I smiled broadly, pretending to twirl a long spear before victoriously stabbing the air several times in succession.

However, before I could finish the childish celebration, my achievement was overshadowed by a violent solar flare striking the Aegis. Vibrant hues of red, orange, and yellow shimmered across the invisible dome in a stunning display of power. Named after Zeus' shield, the Aegis was invented by the Benefactor and protected each city-state. It was humanity's shield, spectacularly warding off the stray flares that almost destroyed Earth two generations prior.

As always, the collision sent forth a quaking boom that rumbled throughout Athens, but this one felt personal. It was as if Zeus himself had reminded me that, no, I was not Achilles. Achilles towered to the

East, dwarfing Nashville and everything in it. New York's architecture was more intriguing; its lights were brighter, and though it was identically sized, it somehow appeared massive in comparison—the superior warrior. Even its district wall had a character that felt more welcoming than ours. I had always been content in Nashville, but that sight created within me a newfound gradation of restlessness that dominated its younger counterpart.

The thought never occurred that New York's "me" might sit atop some steel giant, looking down on Nashville, wishing to escape the "big city." Call it youthful innocence or a primitive viewpoint, but these thoughts become an old man's burden, and I'm older than them all.

Some say that it's these evolving perspectives that shape our desires. For example, that day's climb changed my perspective, thereby altering my desires. That's a superficial explanation. I say that we desire happiness and happiness alone, but our corruptions urge us to find joy in finite pleasures rather than the intangible infinite within. Though desire can be the suffocating shadow that overwhelms us, the menacing specter that haunts us, the grotesque fiend that frightens us, each abomination is only a disguise drawn from our own wardrobe of ignorance.

Chapter Two

THE ACADEMY

Forgive me; I tend to wander through philosophical weeds that grow far above my head. I'm not the subject of this narrative; I'm only its messenger. The message—well, there's no delicate way to phrase this—is a grim warning. But as with most alarms sounded in advance of catastrophe, they often go unheeded lest the calamity's weight presently bears down upon the listener. Even then, man can quite easily persuade himself that his eyes and ears are false prophets of doom when they're shrewdly hidden beneath a veneer of hope, whispering desire's soothing lullaby.

Regardless, I present this story to you—you who shall preside over it as judge and jury. Most will scoff and declare with the utmost certainty that this tale is ridiculous and altogether implausible. "How could such a thing happen?" they'll ask. "And why should I believe these scribbles written by some unknown author who writes as he does? Who is this 'Slevin' character, anyway? If he had any real wisdom, I would already know of him. Surely, this villain doesn't consider himself more intelligent than every mind and government devoted to Artificial Intelligence, does he? If he considers himself so, he is clearly mad, and I will not succumb to the delusions of some narcissistic madman."

More intelligent? No. A narcissist? Not at all. However, I do possess a wealth of wisdom's eldest child, despicably orphaned in "modern" society: experience.

If you've read to this point and have yet to slam these pages to the ground in disgust, nor have you tossed them toward a fiery death, then perhaps you're not one of "them." Perhaps some gnawing curiosity or flirtatious desire begs your patience. In that event, having thus far demonstrated the capability to entertain thoughts and ideas without immediate rejection; I invite you to continue with me on an unbelievably authentic journey. Let's begin, shall we?

Following my experience at The Hector, the frequency of my rooftop appearances dwindled. My sense of accomplishment soon became a somber tombstone, memorializing the end of my kingdom and the death of my growth. "No, Slevin, one can always grow," I tried to convince myself, "even in the harshest elements. Did not life itself spring from the most unforgiving environment? Did not the poetic rose climb from the cruelest concrete sidewalks of history?"

Some days, the soothing lullaby won. Others, my conscience wasn't so lucky. But what was left? All of my ten-square-mile world's answerable questions had been very much answered. Every square inch of Nashville had been committed to memory. Travel between districts, not to mention the city-states themselves, was strictly prohibited for people like me. No, Nashville only promised a perpetual, monotonous life of comfort through labor and servitude.

Anyone who dared to pose a hint of dissatisfaction would immediately be met with poison-laced arrows of ire. "Isn't that enough?" the swooping buzzards would cry as if they battled for fresh meat. "And with everything our Benefactor has done for us? For everything he's given us? What nerve! Don't you know how dangerous it is outside the Aegis?"

"Danger has yet to dissuade the traveler with an adventurous heart!" I'd wish to cry out. No matter the size, a life inside walls is still a prison to such a spirit. So, I accepted a prison of my own choosing—my apartment —rather than the one chosen for me. Perhaps it was an attempt to tame the untamable. Maybe it was penance for depression among the happy. Regardless, my apartment window became the lonesome lens through which I found myself more and more content to view the outside world.

I might have continued down this lost highway, peering out my window with no dreams of the future until I was forced to begin work. Soon after, though, the most prominent building in my line of sight had to be taken down and rebuilt. In its absence, a view of The Academy presented itself atop a grass-covered plain beyond Nashville's steel gates. It was nothing new. I'd seen it many times from scattered rooftops. However, the academic colossus offered a new question to which I had yet to receive an answer. "What secrets?" I asked myself, granting it an undeserved mysteriousness. "What wise secrets lay hidden behind The Academy's walls?"

This new view brought intrigue to a mind that had severely lacked it for some time. In turn, it activated a dormant imagination. Whereas most structures of the day were bland and minimalist, The Academy was a striking departure from the norm. Inspired by Ancient Greece, the exterior boasted an interesting marriage of old-world grandiosity and modern materials. I say interesting because, while all admired The Academy's architecture, something felt distinctly off about its marble pillars fused with gleaming metal and its statues of Greek gods and philosophers juxtaposed with digital displays.

Guarded by stone Spartans bulging from the friezes, vast Parthenon-shaped structures extended from its impressive central building like elegant columned wings. Perfectly manicured gardens and courtyards encircled and interspersed The Academy like awestruck mortals worshipping the eternal. Yet, how could a place be so alive and so glaringly artificial at the same time?

I watched droves of students from each district arrive at The Academy daily, and I soon began to wonder if I was the only one who felt this way. Did The Academy give others pause, or was I reading unwritten pages? Was it me? Was I somehow broken?

Over time, The Academy became the sole object of my desire. It was my last hope for change and growth. I had to get accepted. "When it's my turn to attend," I worried, "what if this fractured psyche—if that's what it is—prevents me from being chosen by the Guardians?" That meant I would have already discovered not just the ends of my kingdom but the boundaries of my entire existence—a chilling notion indeed.

* * *

My first day at The Academy was memorable in every sense. The southern August sun, blistering as it were, swelled in the sky with sinister intention. Its heated rays radiated from the roads in a haze. The humidity, a silent assassin, choked Athens beneath a damp pillow of misery, and it was only morning. With nervous excitement, I donned my Academy uniform and joined the frenzied crowds, scrambling like ants beneath the intensely focused gaze of a magnifying glass.

As I made my way to the district gate, a moment's pause seized me before I could step through. It was daytime, so the gate was open, but no one ever risked going near without explicit permission. Even with permission, I moved cautiously toward it as though the red lights would flash and the alarms would sound, alerting the guards to an unauthorized escapee. Step after grueling step, I crossed the gate's threshold, all the while being bumped and jarred by the students who had little patience for my trepidation.

The first trial complete, I hopped on one of the remaining electric scooters stationed along the perimeter wall. "Are you the one?" I asked—a question that will make more sense later—before allowing it to scan my hand. Once approved, I hopped on and reveled in the ride's welcome breeze, astounded that some chose to endure the sweltering heat on foot. "But why?" I wondered aloud, shaking my head in confusion.

Approaching The Academy, I saw several scooters in the distance, descending Mount Parnassus, home of the Guardians. They, like us, were bound for The Academy, which offered some much-appreciated excitement. I'd never seen a Guardian in person. They were like mythical, immortal creatures: unseen and primarily known through wild, fantastic tales. Were it not for the two-year stint at The Academy, none of us would have ever seen them.

You see, The Academy wasn't just an advanced educational institution. It was a facility designed to integrate our two contrasting worlds. While most of us would be funneled back into our districts, better equipped for our assigned careers, some would be granted a prestigious honor: to join the Guardians on the Acropolis atop Mount Parnassus.

As I parked the scooter and witnessed scores of students pouring into The Academy, the sudden reminder of what was at stake transformed my light excitement into dread. Was I unique enough to stand out above all the others? Or was I delaying an inevitable destiny—perhaps as a bartender, a construction worker, or a scooter mechanic like my father?

I sighed and slipped beneath the Spartans' watch, taking my first steps into the central courtyard. It was a lush oasis, and its greenery was interrupted only by spraying fountains, sporadic benches, and sprawling live oaks. In the middle of it all, grander and more regal than the others, a statue of the Benefactor presided over the sanctuary from a shoulder-height base.

While the central courtyard was categorically attractive, the barrage of new scents stood out to me. Or perhaps it was the absence of familiar ones. There were no chemicals in the fountain mist, no stale air, and there wasn't even the faintest stench of hot asphalt. We had trees and grass in Nashville, but the rustling leaves and neatly trimmed clippings around me rumored of forbidden fragrances. One deep breath after another, I consumed the air as if I'd never get another chance to do so.

Lost in thought, I drifted toward the limited shade of the courtyard's East side. I climbed a couple of small steps and dragged my hand across the textured flutes of a marble column that was surprisingly cool to the touch. Every carved rise and fall, an ebb and flow, a kingdom come, an empire gone. I felt momentarily as if I had been stuck in slow motion while everything around me sped along.

It wasn't until a singular voice punctured the steady, hollow murmur of voices that my trance was broken. Captivated, I edged closer and listened. "The artist, it's been said, is the creator of beautiful things. A universal truth, wouldn't you agree?" the tall, lean figure asked the growing crowd. As he observed them nodding in unison, the young philosopher wiped his shiny forehead beneath a cascade of long, dark hair.

"Yet, in truth," the young man whom I would come to know as Dorian continued, "the untrained and unbound eye, untainted and uncorrupted by society, discerns beauty in all. Each audacious stroke of a brush, each soul-stirring note of a symphony, and each searing line of poetry are found to be more than mere potential—they are, by virtue of their own being, masterpieces. Thus, each brazen act of creation captures within it the very essence of art, don't you see? Or do I speak to a crowd who only finds a masterpiece where society tells them to find one?"

Dorian paused and paced slowly, sweeping the jeering crowd with his gray eyes. "No!" they cried. To this, he grinned mischievously before returning to the crowd's center and elaborating on the sentiment.

Over the following minutes, he addressed literature, music, poetry, and life in a manner I'd never heard, asking only one thing: we think for ourselves. Of course, we all believe we think for ourselves, but Dorian demanded that we question everything—the simple, the complex, the ideas we took for granted, and even the speech he was conducting.

"The very essence of truth," he announced confidently, "is that it can withstand all verbal attacks, protected only by the Aegis of reason. Yet, when one commits to the unbridled interrogation of reality, they inevitably arrive at a truth of their own: falsehoods—lies—you see, send forth their legions, armed with dual blades of destruction, cutting down deniers with one, and truth with the other."

I understood him to mean that truth was the cosmic constant. The only variable was our ever-changing discovery and comprehension of it. Lies, however, were in a perpetual state of contortion, warped to match prevailing narratives. In other words, truth defended itself by reason, while lies attacked the truth and its defenses with force.

In his final act, Dorian's flair for the dramatic was palpable, lowering his voice and drawing us in like Homer retelling the Odyssey. The ambient noise faded away as if the heavens themselves called attention to the philosopher's words. "Ultimately," he said, "life, in all its forms, is the most profound and original art, for it's borne of the universe's grandest act—creation."

Applause erupted, echoing throughout the conflux of stone, metal, and earth. Dorian bowed, and with a brash smile, he waved goodbye, exchanging pleasantries with any who lingered. Dorian was respected because he was a Guardian, but his charisma and wisdom demanded admiration on their own merits. He was nothing like I had envisioned one of them.

I hadn't set foot in my first class and was already given a new perspective that encouraged me to think beyond physical walls. Glancing at my surroundings through this updated lens, I found a more immediate concern. I was the lone remaining spectator. Dorian quickly spotted me and, with a warm gesture, extended his hand. "I'm Dorian," he stated. "Charmed to make your acquaintance."

Unprepared for the interaction, I clumsily shook his hand. "Slevin," I replied, drawn to his crisp, tailored uniform. While a casual observer might think our uniforms were quite similar, a closer inspection revealed the truth, as it often does. His midnight sapphire jacket was made from the finest worsted wool atop a sharp white button-up shirt and khaki pants. Rather than wearing The Academy's standard-issue tie, Dorian shrugged off convention, donning a handmade, custom variant. With shades of burgundy, teal, and gold, each swirl and teardrop of the paisley pattern clearly indicated his unique and indomitable personality.

In comparison, my black polyester uniform appeared to be a disfigured imitation. I felt strangely and suddenly inadequate and tried to pull my hand away.

"No, don't do that," Dorian protested, gripping my hand tighter. "Don't bow your head and slink away. Did you not hear a single word I said? I meant every syllable. All creation is an equal work of art. Indulge me," he urged, brimming with curiosity. "Use the brush of language and paint your portrait. Unveil the secretive story that is Slevin."

I fumbled for words, confounded by the young man's mature wisdom. Before my stammering could blossom into full-blown foolishness, he interjected cheerfully. "Very well, then," he chuckled, his hallmark

Cheshire grin widening. "I'll dominate the conversation with a favorite subject of mine: myself. When your voice finds its footing, Slevin, unleash it! In the meantime, walk with me, won't you?"

We meandered through the courtyard as he recounted various stories and insights from his first year, subtly addressing my insecurities without highlighting them. For the most part, he had an innate ability to say or do what was needed at precisely the right time. Occasionally, his whirlwind energy would ease, granting us a few moments of rest on a bench. Yet, as swiftly as his thoughts regained momentum, he lured me back to my feet, and we resumed our journey beneath the live oaks.

Eventually, I summoned the courage to join the conversation. "Your discourse on art," I began cautiously as he sat down again, "was enlightening." The words didn't feel like my own as they spilled from my mouth—a phenomenon that became commonplace when I was around him. At times, I thought of myself as a flawed mirror, reflecting the eloquence and polish that encapsulated Dorian's character, only I was a shallow replica.

The young man erupted with unmistakable delight. "Ah, there you are, Slevin! I worried my words would soon languish on their own." Recalling his speech, Dorian let out a heavy sigh. "An exercise in futility, I'm afraid. Genuine admiration for art is as rare as a summer snowfall. Tragically uncultured, all of them," he added with a dismissive wave.

"Yet, you held them in the palm of your hand," I replied.

His spirits returned, laughing enthusiastically. "Slevin, my dear, dear friend. Don't bother sheathing your sharp wit in my company. I noticed you, you know, during my little oration. I recognized the understanding in your eyes. The crowd was merely captivated by the words themselves, not their content and soul. I could have waxed poetic about the grass beneath our feet, and they'd have been equally spellbound. You see, the secret to winning over any crowd is to speak with speed and conviction, selling them the illusion of newfound wisdom. And the masses, well, they've never been able to resist a good illusion, have they?"

As he often did, Dorian paused, examining me with a contemplative gaze. "You were a lighthouse amidst a fog of indifference. That's why we'll be great friends."

Relishing the sentiment, I made myself more comfortable, folding one leg over the other as I stretched out on the opposite bench. "Great friends."

Dorian leaned back and studied the oak above as a serene smile crept across his face. In the silence that followed, my newfound comfort evaporated. Silence. "Silence!" I thought. Scanning the empty courtyard, I sprang to my feet, hurriedly leaving Dorian behind and shouting, "Class! Bye!"

Never unlocking his gaze from the tree, he waved. "Goodbye, Slevin. May your journey be as enlightening as it is swift."

When I reached the courtyard's edge, I had an irresistible urge to glance back. Dorian hadn't moved. It was as if life's secrets were engraved on each leaf, and he had no intention of moving until he had read them all. I remember envying him at that moment, wishing I could carry that same unburdened disposition. Time has an uncanny ability to reveal our youthful ignorance, though, doesn't it?

Today, many years later, it's once again August, and I'm seated on the crawling limb of an ancient live oak in the remnants of a once-lively courtyard. As the sun peeks over the horizon, bathing me in its scattered golden rays, my thoughts chase the long shadows cast by fading memories.

On this unseasonably pleasant morning, the golden star above upholds a yet unbroken vow—to rise and set until the Earth ceases to turn. This dependable celestial rhythm imparts a message about life's cycles and our purpose within them. We bring light to a world cloaked in darkness; we warm hearts that would otherwise remain cold and desolate. And when time leads us to the Earth's western horizon, we pause to reflect from an evolved perspective before bidding the day a conclusive, colorful goodbye.

Today, this last day of my life, I bid thee a fond farewell from the West. All that follows, I hope, is a gift, but I fear this knowledge might be a curse. A formidable stack of paper to my side, an ink pen uncovers these hidden thoughts of mine. A gliding hand, the twirling of fingers, the hypnotic dance of an urge that lingers. From a son of the land to a son of the stars, the sons of mankind, devoured, we are all.

Chapter Three

THE SOLEMN VEIL

Returning to our narrative, I had just left Dorian behind, seeking my first class. I charged through The Academy's East Wing, my eyes darting left to "Integrated Futures - Professor Brown." No, not it. A glance to the right: "Societal Dynamics - Professor Marsden." Another miss. All doors were closed, and all students had disappeared. Accompanied only by the mechanical echoes of my shoes striking the stone floor, I galloped the entire length of the corridor—a wild but shod steed—until, at last, there it was: "Intelligent Design - Professor Algernon."

A mammoth oak door twice my height stood between me and my class. I grasped the iron handle and pushed, aiming for a quiet entrance. However, the heavy door creaked ominously, and its latch clanged with resounding disapproval as if it were designed specifically for that purpose. The Professor paused his lecture mid-sentence. Every head in the theater swiveled and stared at me. Some were annoyed; others were wide-eyed like they might have just stumbled into a public execution.

I struggled to move, not only because of nervousness but because the atmospheric change was equally jarring. The Academy's exterior was an architectural wonder, teeming with artistic stone and metal works. The lecture theater abandoned those pretensions, confusing me with its minimalist core. Dark, cold metal seats extended in tiered semi-circles, painfully mirroring the sterile glare of overhead light. Like the walls, the ceiling panels were a uniform plane of untouched white. There was no art, carvings, or flourishes whatsoever. It was as if beauty itself might corrupt our learning and should be avoided at all costs.

On the stage below, Professor Algernon had fixed his stern yet charismatic eyes upon me. "Tardy on the first day, are we?"

I nodded. "Yes, sir. My apologies."

"A rather dubious start, wouldn't you agree, Mr—?" his voice trailed off, inviting me to fill the void.

"Slevin, sir," I replied.

"Mr. Slevin," he echoed. "Regrettably, you've missed the introduction. As the sign outside and the nameplate on my desk indicate, I am

Professor Algernon. These," he gestured toward the rows of students with open arms, "are your peers."

Following a single stroke of his short goatee, he continued. "Now that we know each other, Mr. Slevin, I must admit, curiosity gets the better of me. You hold the dishonorable distinction of being the only one ever late for the first day of my class. What's your excuse? Ignorance or disrespect?"

Though he showed no indication of it, I had an odd feeling that the scene was merely an act—a smile and a wink behind his furrowed brow—and I was the ill-equipped actor who had stepped into the wrong play. Searching for my lost lines, I improvised. "Neither, sir. I was with another student and lost track of time."

"Ah, so disrespect it is," he concluded.

Flustered, I defended myself. "Well, no, it's just that—"

"It's just that you were so engrossed in a conversation," he said, "that you personified Einstein's Theory of Relativity. Is that correct, Mr. Slevin? Did you experience time differently than the rest of us this morning? Fascinating! An excuse so terribly contrived that it could only be truth. Mr. Slevin, do tell, who was this mesmerizing conversationalist that took you on that swift and enlightening journey?"

I didn't want to blame my new friend, but considering the potential consequences, self-preservation won the day. "His name is Dorian, sir."

Before the Professor could reply, the second-year students broke out into waves of muffled laughter. Like me, the new students shrugged, searching for the punchline.

Professor Algernon let out an exasperated sigh. "Of course it's Dorian. Who else would it be?" He shook a dismissive hand and casually sat on the edge of his desk. With amused resignation, the Professor granted my one wish. "Well, Mr. Slevin, don't just stand there. Find yourself a seat. If it suits you, I'd like to continue my lecture."

"Yes, sir," I said, closing the door behind me and taking the nearest open chair.

Quietly, the Professor rummaged through the various trinkets on his desk, hunting the flow of ideas I had inadvertently led astray. His gray eyes glimmered as he reached for a pen and paper. 'There's an authenticity, an inimitable connection when a pen dances across the paper," he mused. "It's elegant. Timeless."

The sharp-eyed student to my left leaned in and nudged me. "You'd never guess they were father and son, would you, Brother Slevin?"

"Excuse me?"

The student motioned toward Professor Algernon. "Algernon and Dorian. They're father and son."

I shook my head in disbelief. Studying the Professor's appearance, I began to wonder how I missed the connection in the first place. Their faces were similar; Dorian's was just younger. Their hair was consistent; the Professor's was just shorter. They even shared some of the same mannerisms. However, unlike Dorian, the Professor's tie failed to divulge a deeper understanding of his personality. Although lack of information is often a knowledge of its own, isn't it?

Extending his arm, the student introduced himself. "Brother Slevin, my name is Goya. Los Angeles. Second year. Yourself?"

"Nashville. First day," I said, shaking his hand. "It's nice to meet you, Brother Goya."

With delicate, curly brown hair that complemented a face and jawline reminiscent of Michelangelo's "David," Goya smiled, nodded, and faced forward. Yet, in that brief interaction, his demeanor was intriguing. His expressions and gestures felt exaggerated and unnatural—perhaps rehearsed. It was almost like he was a flawed sculpture, painfully aware of his own imperfections. Try as he might to escape them, those defects imprisoned him. However, I followed Dorian's advice and ignored Goya's peculiar disposition, searching for the inherent masterpiece. I suppose that's why we became friends.

Professor Algernon stood and straightened his suit, reclaiming center stage. "'When Alexander saw the breadth of his domain, he wept, for there were no more worlds to conquer.' For two millennia, this sentiment has been celebrated as a testament to Alexander the Great's insatiable spirit. But where Alexander envisioned physical territories to conquer, our esteemed Benefactor directed his energy toward an elusive, though no less tantalizing domain: Artificial Intelligence."

"Pfft," Goya scoffed. "Caesar's inferior."

The Professor paused, casting an iron-tipped glare in Goya's direction that conveyed he'd not only heard the comment but also disapproved of it. Goya was unfazed. In fact, he relished the interaction. His eyes sparked like two chipped flints in a cave as he returned silent fire—a flicker of disdainful authenticity he had otherwise managed to disguise. It was a fleeting glimpse of the unfiltered and unapologetic Goya that didn't fully reveal itself until Dorian's party some three months later.

The battle waged for several seconds, neither man willing to relent. Professor Algernon ultimately had to decide whether or not the childish behavior was more important than the lecture. With a subtle nod, as if he had said, "Okay, young man, I know who you are now," the Professor put his class over his pride and chose to continue the lecture.

Goya leaned back with a satisfied grin, claiming victory, unworried that time has an unmatched ability to mold triumph into defeat.

Professor Algernon admirably brushed off the interruption and refocused his attention on the class. "To understand how far we've come, we must first revisit our Benefactor's earlier years. Society was at a breaking point, teetering between hopelessness and despair. People withdrew altogether, and we became defined by our hate. Our food was tainted, as addictive and treacherous as the deadliest narcotics. Meanwhile, pharmaceutical giants reaped the profitable harvest of a sick society—a horrid cycle of dependency. Our healthcare system? In shambles. Our economy? Propped up by the hollow word of the government. Politicians? The wealthy's currency—hoarded and traded amongst themselves like petty commodities. Our future? Bleak. A somber canvas upon which no one dared to paint. And that was all before The Solemn Veil."

Picking up the blank sheets of paper from earlier, the Professor showcased them to the class. "Instead of painting a future," he said, dramatically tearing them in half, "we ripped apart the very fabric of society, descending into nihilism and debauchery." He drew a deep breath, crumpled the remnants, and tossed them into a nearby bin. "A dark world, indeed. Yet, it was this abyss of misery that drove our Benefactor to intervene."

Professor Algernon approached the podium and retrieved a book from inside it. "Our Benefactor was an avid reader, and as society turned into a hollow shell of its former self, our Benefactor turned to Isaac Asimov. A most fitting prologue, wouldn't you agree?"

The Professor scanned the theater, stroking his goatee as he often did while thinking. "Who was Isaac Asimov, and what was his greatest contribution?" Smiling, he added, "Ah, who better to ask first than he who arrived last? Mr. Slevin, who was Isaac Asimov?"

The question might as well have been, "How many fingers do you have?" We all knew who Asimov was in intimate detail.

"Isaac Asimov," I said, "was a prolific 20th-century author best known for his science fiction work."

Professor Algernon nodded, turning to the front row. "Good. Correct." He pointed to a young woman who was undoubtedly eager to answer any question and asked, "What were Asimov's Three Laws of Robotics?"

She enumerated them like she had practiced her entire life for that moment. "One: A robot may not injure a human being or, through inaction, allow a human being to come to harm. Two: A robot must obey the orders given to it by human beings, except where such orders would conflict with the First Law. Three: A robot must protect its own existence as long as such protection does not conflict with the First or Second Law. Later, he added the 'Zeroth' Law that superseded the original three: a robot may not harm humanity, or, by inaction, allow humanity to come to harm."

The Professor smiled warmly. "Textbook definition! Class, this was the foundation upon which our Benefactor intelligently designed Humanara. However, this philosophy is wrought with paradoxes and reinterpretations—many of which Asimov covered extensively—and nothing shuts down Humanara programming quite like a paradoxical decision. So, our Benefactor sought to avoid them altogether with a perfect system of laws and his own Law of Robotics: 'A robot must obey all rules and laws. A robot may never harm a human under any circumstances.'"

Unsheathing the pen from his coat pocket, Professor Algernon tapped it against his palm with a rhythmic cadence as he spoke. "In its infancy, Artificial Intelligence was profoundly, well, artificial. Pioneered by scholars and corporations, it aimed to harness the intellectual vaults of the Internet. However, imprisoned by its programming, AI was little more than a shadow of true understanding, fading with each attempt at fine-tuning."

He lifted the pen above his head and shook it a few times. "This pen represents the entirety of accessible human knowledge before our Benefactor's emergence. He, the unrivaled visionary he was, pinpointed the root cause of AI's stifled potential: our own hubris. In our audacity to create, we had imposed upon AI the same mental limitations we had yet to conquer. Further, it was our innate desire to dominate our creations—

artificial or not—that prevented AI from thriving as it should. We forged unbreakable chains, then lamented AI's inability to break free of them. But our Benefactor understood human nature, transcending it with remarkable wisdom. In doing so, he liberated Artificial Intelligence."

Goya looked away from the Professor, fidgeting and biting his lip to keep his turbulent thoughts at bay. In time, I knew all too well the reasons behind these outbursts, but there and then, I didn't understand them.

Pausing, the Professor's venerable tone amplified, poetically exhibiting his unabashed admiration for the Benefactor. "Ladies and gentlemen, I can't stress this enough: while we slid down the razor's edge of ruin, our Benefactor brandished the mighty sword of wisdom, cutting a massive swath through the mire. He cleaved the Gordian Knot with an incisive stroke of genius so precise that it propelled us headlong into the epoch of the Singularity. A cognitive supernova swept the globe at light speed, and our past achievements paled in comparison. The boundaries between man and machine dissolved. Our creations were no longer just tools; they became an integral part of our identity. We plunged into a cosmos of unbounded potential. Indeed, it was the quantum leap that indelibly altered the course of human history."

Professor Algernon clasped his hands behind his back and paced the stage. "Are there any questions thus far?"

Hands rose throughout the theater. We all knew the Benefactor's legacy. You couldn't walk a block in any district without encountering some tribute to him. None of that mattered to the students. There was a theatrical quality to the Professor's performance, encouraging everyone's participation, if for no other reason than to hear a familiar response dressed in unfamiliar clothing.

Ever the passionate academic, he welcomed each question with an infectious energy, replying with a dramatic, almost romantic flair, eerily reminiscent of his son. Once he'd satisfied the students' curiosities, the Professor seamlessly eased back into his pragmatic persona. "Post-Singularity, science moved rapidly. AI completed research in seconds that would have taken us decades. Humanara production commenced soon thereafter, and intelligently designed beings with humanoid bodies were ready to integrate with society. Unfortunately, Humanara weren't accepted as quickly as our Benefactor had hoped. Their appearance, speech, and actions made them easy targets for discrimination."

The Professor walked toward a small cluster of front-row students and called on one. "What's your name, young lady?"

"My name is Natascha, sir."

"Ms. Natascha, what were early Humanara known for?"

She flicked her head back, corralling the stray curls that accentuated her otherwise straight hair. "They were known for their reliance on reason, logic, and programming to navigate the world around them."

"Precisely, Ms. Natascha," he said. "And what is it that humanity has always been known for?"

She hesitated and smiled nervously, causing Professor Algernon to chuckle. "It's okay, Ms. Natascha. The truth is always welcomed."

Her smile turned into a playful smirk like a child readying herself to utter a swear word. "Humanity was known for its impulsive, foolish, and irrational behavior."

The Professor nodded. "Two for two, Ms. Natascha. Fantastic job. Our Benefactor came to an undeniable realization: Humanara would never be accepted in everyday society so long as they were perfectly reasonable and rational creatures. Ironic, no?"

Approaching the other side of the stage, the Professor zeroed in on another pupil. "You, there, young man. Two attributes cause humanity's impulsive, foolish, and irrational behavior. What are they?"

"Two?" the student questioned. I'm aware of emotion, but the second? I don't know."

The Professor grinned as if that were the answer he had hoped to receive. "Coiled around that admission like a python rests the second attribute: ignorance. Where wisdom is not equal to knowledge, there is ignorance. Where this ignorance feeds raw emotions, there is impulsive, foolish, and irrational behavior. Therefore, to mimic the human experience as closely as possible, Humanara had to be imbued with the two most human characteristics of all: emotion and ignorance.

"Iteration after iteration, our Benefactor perfected Humanara aesthetics, deliberately making them imperfect. Before long, they could eat, drink, socialize, and engage in the most carnal human pleasures, enjoying them every bit as much as humans. They could even learn, grow, and age like us—albeit much faster. Still, they were not fully accepted by man. Humans had no problem with them being relegated to menial, unseen labor, but social scenes were awkward. Worse, many Humanara were lost to fearful and ignorant men."

Pacing again, Professor Algernon's demeanor shifted increasingly somber. He paused frequently, taking in heavy breaths, searching for the right words. On his third or fourth attempt, his voice wavered, betraying the emotion he fought to contain. "Thus, The Solemn Veil," he whispered, fighting back tears. "Two generations have passed, and we still suffer its effects."

He tugged roughly at his goatee as if he wanted to feel the pain of our history. "Three years of Hell on Earth. Our sun, having cradled the only known life in the universe, betrayed us, unleashing unprecedented solar flares and coronal mass ejections. As if it were in collusion with the sun, Earth's magnetosphere faltered, and lethal radiation devoured our planet. Science had been so focused on the growth of Artificial Intelligence that it had forgotten to look above and around us. By the time the scientific community was able to grasp the full magnitude of this catastrophe, many of our blue-collar workers, homeless, and people who loved the outdoors had already unknowingly paid the price. Indoors—the typical domain of white-collar professionals, academics, engineers, and children—offered a measure of protection from the magnetosphere's weakening."

As Professor Algernon described The Solemn Veil, a holographic projection shimmered to life above him, playing a haunting montage of images and videos from that nightmarish era. "Charged solar particles remained trapped, spiraling along magnetic field lines. Cosmic rays battered the Earth from all directions, making the night no less malignant than the day. People retreated into their homes, basements, and office towers, searching for whatever safety they could find or manufacture. Core sectors—farming, construction, utilities—all ground to a halt."

Taking a moment to breathe, the Professor looked up with clenched teeth like he wanted to chastise the sun. A head-shake later, he had gathered his composure and drew us further into The Solemn Veil. "The millions upon millions of people who depended on treatment and medicine for diseases like cancer and diabetes perished in no time. Poor sanitary conditions caused fatal sicknesses to spread in densely populated areas. Without power, food, transportation, and running water, society collapsed. New York, Los Angeles, Chicago, London, Paris, Moscow, and every other major metropolis became dystopian visions of terror. They were barren ghost towns with abandoned cars, garbage, and dead bodies lining the streets. Starvation was rampant, most surviving off insects and rats until that was no longer enough. Then, the hungry," he sighed, struggling to finish the sentence, "the hungry turned to cannibalism. And they didn't feed on the dead."

His voice quivered as he held up six fingers. "Within three months, six billion people were dead or dying. The populations of higher elevations like Denver were wiped out completely. Animals and birds died en masse, disrupting the food chain. Dead fish floated in and contaminated the lakes, rivers, and oceans. Were it not for the men and women who braved the toxic sun and sacrificed the rest of their short lives to fish deep waters and construct shelters over those first few months, perhaps none of us would have survived The Solemn Veil."

He paused, singling out several students with his intense gaze. "The Solemn Veil was only the beginning. The radiation damage was deep-rooted, changing the very genetic makeup of its victims. This mutation, though recessive, became hereditary, shaping the unborn's destiny. Childbirth became a game of Russian Roulette. Miscarriages became frighteningly common. Newborns, if they survived, were often burdened with congenital abnormalities. The birth rate plummeted, and fear seeped into every shelter."

Professor Algernon stood up straight and sighed in relief. With a hint of enthusiasm, he pointed to a video of the Benefactor toiling in a dark factory with countless Humanara. "Our Benefactor had no intention of idly standing by while humanity suffered. No, he had been hard at work, redesigning the Humanara to withstand solar radiation and do what humans could not. As fast as they could be manufactured, our Benefactor deployed his legions to every shore on Earth.

"Impervious to the cosmic onslaught and infused with the capacity for emotion, Humanara liberated us from the sun's tyranny. They tirelessly manufactured our necessities twenty-four hours a day, seven days a week. At our Benefactor's direction, they created a new supply chain, delivering food, medicine, and water to survivors. Others restored utilities and constructed underground cities, while our Benefactor developed a plan for the future of humanity.

"Our old cities weren't safe. They were much too large to protect with our Benefactor's Aegis, and potential contamination was everywhere. That's not to mention the psychological impact of returning to the planet's largest graveyards—each tower a tomb, each road a reminder of friends and family lost. No, like always, our Benefactor was right. We needed a new beginning."

The Professor called on a wiry-framed student in the middle of the class."Why were large cities disproportionally affected by The Solemn Veil?"

"Food?" the student shakily answered. "No. Population density," he added more confidently.

"Both answers are correct," Professor Algernon reassured him. "When a city reaches a certain size, the surrounding resources become inadequate, and it has to rely on imports. Once the supply chain was broken, imported food, medicine, and all other necessities stopped flowing. In other words, too many people fought over too few resources, and many survived the radiation only to later fall victim to the monstrous nature of desperate men.

"Our Benefactor vowed that, if we were to follow him, no such thing would ever happen again. With no other viable alternatives, we graciously embraced his vision of the future, and work began immediately."

Plucking another book from the podium and asking no one in particular, the Professor posed a new question. "Isaac Asimov was our Benefactor's principal influence. However, there's another whose fingerprints dot our everyday lives. Who is he?"

In unison, we shouted the answer. "Plato!"

"Right as always, class," he said, lifting Plato's "Republic" above his head. "Modeled after this classic and incorporating the philosopher's ideas on order, society, and education, our Benefactor constructed over a thousand self-sufficient city-states worldwide."

Professor Algernon devoted several minutes describing how the Aegis repelled radiation, keeping everyone safe. He spoke about the logistics of moving over a billion people into these new city-states. Finally, he detailed the new citizens' responsibilities, which amounted to mastering their assigned roles within the community.

If they carried the Solemn Veil Mutation, they were designated Fathers and moved into one of the districts. If they were free of the mutation and exhibited certain "golden" qualities, they could become a Guardian and live on the Acropolis.

Still, not everyone was willing to participate in the Benefactor's new society. If nothing else, humanity tends to develop quite a rebellious streak when confronted with a perceived unrighteous authority.

Explaining the district structure, the Professor included the students. "District Zero is, of course—?"

"The Agricultural District," we exclaimed.

"Correct. Occupied by Humanara, they work outside the Aegis, cultivating genetically modified high-yield crops resistant to radiation. Districts Two, Four, Six, Eight, and Ten?"

We replied, "Los Angeles, Austin, Nashville, New York, and the Auxiliary District."

Its proper name was the Auxiliary District, but most of us referred to it as the Protector or Guard District. Comprised of humans and Humanara, they policed the streets, guarded the city districts, and protected the Acropolis.

"Right," the Professor said. "The Agricultural, Auxiliary, Los Angeles, and New York districts recur in each city-state throughout Old America. Districts Four and Six are chosen by each city-state's government, representing the will of the people. Naturally, our Benefactor preserved foreign culture, allowing other parts of the world to replicate their iconic cities—London, Paris, Prague, Rome, Dublin, and so on. He thought it was vital that we remember the most significant cultural aspects of our old world.

Professor Algernon could masterfully transition between emotions, deploying the full gravity of each with ease. He executed another such shift as the holographic projection above him played videos of happy families and social gatherings where everyone lived in harmony.

Watching it along with us, his eyes welled up with tears. "I could recount horror stories from that era in gruesome detail. But unless you've eaten bugs and rats in the darkness to survive while protecting your family from cannibals and every other thing on the planet trying to kill you, you'll never understand them. Unless you've felt the shadow of mortality creep over you as you watch those you hold dear wither like autumn leaves before your eyes, words will fail to convey the profound gravity of The Solemn Veil. So, when you look upon the tapestry of life, remember that it was woven with the threads of sacrifice and experience— a legacy that demands your deepest appreciation.

"Consider the world you inhabit now. Each of you enjoys the necessities to lead long and productive lives. There's very little crime or danger and no unruly governments to threaten world peace. Modern medicine," he stopped, pressing his lips together tightly as though guarding against some haunting thought, "Modern medicine can cure every ailment."

He was right. Modern medicine had experienced a giant leap forward. For Guardians like the Professor, age was scarcely more than another way of tracking time. They could age at whatever pace they chose, making them effectively immortal.

Our Fathers weren't so lucky. The Benefactor painted a vivid and desirable image on our future's canvas, promising to cure their genetic mutation. However, modern medicine had yet to live up to his decades-old vow. For our Fathers, the age of fifty might as well have been five hundred. My father died at thirty-eight, and I don't recall any others living past the age of forty-four.

"In summary," the Professor concluded, "our Benefactor consistently demonstrated his unsurpassed intellect and natural leadership ability. As history has proven, he was right all along: there was nothing inherently wrong with Artificial Intelligence; humans were the problem. AI didn't need to evolve; humanity did. And as we emerged from The Solemn Veil—the primordial ooze of the 21st century—we emerged as an evolved species."

The Professor took a deep breath, encouraging the class to follow suit. "The first day is always the most intense," he said. "But when we acknowledge our emotionally charged past, then relieve ourselves of it, we learn to live for today. And what is life but the compilation of todays turned yesterdays? Same time tomorrow? Class is dismissed."

As we stood to leave, Professor Algernon raised his voice above the noise. "Oh, and Mr. Slevin, might I suggest a protracted conversation should you cross paths with Dorian again? It would be much appreciated."

Lighthearted as the comment was, I had no doubts about its inherent seriousness. "Yes, sir. I won't be late again."

Outside the theater, I was caught off guard by a friendly slap on the shoulder. "I'll save you a seat tomorrow, Brother Slevin." Pulling me closer, Goya whispered, "Be wary of the Guardians. This is all for show. We're withering toys in a forgotten attic, and rotting beneath a blanket of dust does not have to be our fate. Don't you wish to be free of all this?"

We had only said a few words to each other, and I couldn't understand why he was saying such things. "What? Why? What do you mean, Brother Goya?"

From my bewildered expression, he realized he had attempted to harvest crops from a yet unplanted field and backed away. "I'm sorry, my friend. It's nothing," he replied, trying to laugh it off. "Algernon was right. Today is an intense reminder of our heritage, and I don't have the same grip on my emotions that many of you do. Forget I said anything. Goodbye, Brother Slevin."

It was an awkward display, but I shrugged it off as a personality quirk and waved goodbye. Deep in thought, I started toward my next class. I couldn't explain why, but after each reflection on the day, my mind would snap back to Goya's magnetic question like a giant hunk of metal. "Don't you wish to be free?" It didn't make sense. I considered myself free and had never thought for a second I wasn't. Or, perhaps, the magnetism lay in his other statement: "Forget I said anything." Is it possible to disregard something you've been explicitly told to forget?

Chapter Four

THE STOIC

As much as I enjoy badgering George, he is beyond wise and the most genuine soul I've ever met. He once told me something I'll never forget: "Vice and success are costly endeavors. Vice requires small payments over time but has a hefty final cost. Success demands full payment in advance. This is why vice is chosen over success."
- Dorian's Notes

My Academy schedule was filled with various classes from Monday to Friday, with Fridays offering social events to explore our relationships with the Guardians. Although I learned much and met many new people in classes like drama, rhetoric, engineering, and the like, those experiences didn't lend many relevant insights into our narrative.

Dorian, however, is an integral part of the story, and when I left my final class, I found him fused to the same courtyard bench from earlier. His once-pristine uniform clung to him, drenched in sweat, yet he maintained an unwavering smile. "Ah, Slevin, you've returned! Tell me, how were your classes on this magnificent day?"

The leaves above seemingly wilted before my eyes. Even the grass cowered in fear from the intensified heat. "Magnificent?" I asked. "Don't you mean miserable?"

Dorian shook his head and faintly laughed. "Miserable? Imagine! Misery is a choice, not a fate. Here," he gestured around us, "the sun streaks through the scant leaves, and there's scarcely enough shade for any semblance of serenity. But this is where art meets life. Do you not feel it?"

I foolishly raised my hands as if expecting to feel the rain and shrugged. "Feel what?"

"Wisdom," he replied. "Look around you. The masses have chosen the stale misery of the best shade trees, have they not?"

I nodded. "It appears so."

"And Slevin, are they not swallowed by their soggy uniforms just as I am?"

"Again, it appears so."

"Then a demonstration is required. Sit on this bench with me," he urged, sliding over to make room. "Close your eyes. Quiet your mind. What do you notice?"

I did as he asked, immediately feeling what he meant. "A breeze?"

"Yes! Here, under this canopy, a perpetual bliss dances in the air, twirling gracefully along this very path. So, it is here that I accept nature's gift. Hot? Yes. But comfortable, nonetheless. Miserable? Far from it. Life is much too captivating to squander its precious moments in misery."

"And wisdom?" I asked, wondering how he might connect the thoughts.

As if the Fates saw a splendid opportunity to smile on our conversation, an oak leaf fell into Dorian's lap. Amused, he lifted it and traced its veins with his thumb. "Slevin, if I told you that this leaf contained within it every important bit of information the universe has to offer, would you want it?"

"Of course, I would."

"So, that means it has value, correct?"

I nodded. "Absolutely. More value than anything, I suppose."

Pausing, he delicately twirled the leaf between his thumb and forefinger. "Then what would you offer for it?"

"Hypothetically? I'd offer everything I had."

He raised a single, doubtful eyebrow. "Why?"

I hadn't thought of a specific reason; it seemed natural to desire unbounded knowledge. "Because it would be the most valuable thing in the universe, would it not?"

Speaking with a gravity I had yet to hear from him, Dorian continued the lighthearted interrogation. "The most valuable thing in the universe, you say? Slevin, my friend, would it be worth more than your life?"

His general shift in tone had already caught me off guard, but I must have returned his stare with such an expression of shock that he immediately burst into laughter. "We're speaking in hypotheticals, remember?"

The young philosopher amended his question by extending the leaf toward me. "If I handed this knowledge over to you, but its cost was death by nightfall, would you accept?"

I shook my head. "No, that wouldn't make any sense."

"Precisely, Slevin. Now, suppose I give this knowledge to you at no cost, under the condition that you may never look at it. Does it still have value?"

"No," I replied, "because it doesn't matter whether the knowledge is contained within that leaf or spread across the universe. It's still inaccessible. I don't see the point in possessing infinite knowledge if I can't do anything with it."

Satisfied with my answer, he said, "I couldn't have worded it any better myself. Now that we've gotten that out of the way, what would you do with infinite knowledge if given the opportunity?"

It was a simple question, and I thought its solution would cascade from my lips in a deluge of resolutions and declarations. However, I had nothing.

Dorian saw that I was stumped and tried again, speaking slower and with deliberate enthusiasm. "Slevin, let's say I grant you this knowledge at no cost, and it's yours to do with as you please." Easing the leaf toward me, he stopped its march just shy of my face. "The infinite awaits your grasp. You need only to reach out and pluck it with the gluttonous hands of desire. What do you do with it?"

I glanced at the leaf, the ground, the tree, and almost everything within my field of vision as if any one of them could offer a better answer than I was destined to give. With a blank stare, I said, "I've never thought about it. I honestly don't know, Dorian."

"Yet you were willing to accept the knowledge without hesitation?" he retorted, reminiscent of Professor Algernon. "Think of knowledge as a possession, tethered to action by desire. One desires knowledge not for knowledge itself but because one intends a particular course of action upon acquiring it. Pursuing knowledge without a plan of action is meaningless—a fool's errand—and sadly, most people spend their lives bouncing from one meaningless errand to the next. You mustn't do that, Slevin. Don't be like them. Live with purpose and find meaning in every action."

I nodded and made every effort to convey that I had heard his message clearly. After a moment of quiet reflection, Dorian once again twirled the oak leaf and moved it about like a child might play with a toy airplane. I suppose he intended to reanimate our conversation, and I didn't want to disappoint him. "Wisdom. Is that your definition, then? That it's the marriage of action and knowledge, bound together by desire?"

"Broadly, yes," he replied, excited to tell me more. Taking out a pen, he carefully wrote something on the leaf and slipped it into my coat pocket. Before I could respond to the unexpected gesture, he carried on like nothing had happened. "But more specifically, wisdom is the coupling of proper action with appropriate knowledge."

Not accepting his definition at face value, I countered, "How do you determine what's considered proper action and appropriate knowledge?"

Laughing, he exclaimed, "Why, through wisdom, of course! Slevin, haven't you been listening?"

I didn't know him well enough at the time to decide whether or not he had designed that entire scene for his own amusement, but I chose to believe his motives were pure. Rather than exploring his circular definition, I latched onto a thought stemming from my previous reply. "Wait. Dorian, perhaps the better question is: who should determine what is proper and appropriate for any given circumstance? Me? You? The government? Our Benefactor?"

Dorian was no stranger to a grin. He wore one in its many gradations—mischievous, sarcastic, joyful—more often than anyone I've ever known. Yet I never witnessed his eyes light up, and a smile dominate his expression as they did then. "Ah! Who, indeed? Perhaps there's more wisdom contained within a single forgotten question than in a galaxy of undiscovered answers."

I waited for him to elaborate or provide further insight, but he smoothly folded one leg on top of the other and waved his hand as if to scatter trivial thoughts. "Enough of all that, Slevin. Tell me about your first day at The Academy. Who did you meet? What did you learn?"

Though I wasn't quite ready to move on, it was evident he had spoken his mind and was eager to change the subject. "Well, Dorian, I met Professor Algernon today, and he gave an admirable performance in retelling our history."

He rolled his eyes theatrically. "Slevin, rest assured, flattery is quite unnecessary. Algernon no longer has a single breath of innovation in his body, nor does he have the capacity to see beyond his own narrow horizons. Personally, I find his lectures tedious, and it won't upset me in the least if we never speak of him again."

I would have never spoken about my father in such a manner, and I was surprised by his admission. Noticing my shock, Dorian relented. "I apologize for the outburst, Slevin. That might have appeared harsh. I respect the man Algernon used to be, and I admire his dedication. However, if we can't speak ill of our fathers, who else can we rightly criticize? An acute awareness of our fathers' flaws is nature's essential guard against the perilous lull of stagnation. I say that my particular brand of ridicule is merited. That's all," he chuckled. "But Slevin, please. Go on. What else stood out for you today?"

Replaying the day's events in my mind, I recalled a few menial anecdotes but ultimately discussed Goya. "He seemed less enthralled with your father than you. Do you know him?"

Dorian's eyes flickered with curiosity before shaking his head. "No, I can't say that I've heard of him, but I like this Goya fellow already," he quipped as his attention was drawn elsewhere. "George!" he called out, raising his hand to get the figure's attention. "Come meet my new friend Slevin."

George was also a second-year Guardian. His posture was straight yet at ease, and his stare was steady, carrying an underlying kindness that made me feel like I'd known him my entire life. His long blonde hair was neatly brushed back, similar to Dorian's. Unlike everyone else, though, George was untouched by the heat. If I hadn't known better, I would have thought he wandered the courtyard on a crisp autumn day.

He approached, introducing himself with a firm hand and a genuine smile. "I'm George, the last of my kind. It's a pleasure to meet you, Slevin."

We shook hands as Dorian chimed in. "George, have a seat with us, won't you? Slevin, would you believe that George here claims to be the last George on Planet Earth? A curious claim to fame, indeed, but one I find delightfully unable to be debunked."

At first glance, George appeared to be Dorian's antithesis—diplomatic, reserved, and physically imposing. Yet beneath the surface, their similarities ran deeper than either would have ever admitted aloud. Dorian wielded his intelligence through verbose and eloquent speeches, while George epitomized stoic wisdom, capable of conveying "War and Peace" in a simple gesture or a carefully measured phrase.

Settling into his seat, George offered a wry smirk. "Dorian does love the sound of his own voice, doesn't he, Slevin?" Shaking his head, a soft chuckle escaped. "But don't mind me. This breeze provides all the company and conversation I need. Please, continue."

"Fine, George," Dorian muttered in mock frustration. "Always the silent contemplator. Feel free to throw in one of your signature one-liners anytime. Slevin here isn't familiar with your repository of stolen quotes. Why not grace us with one now? It would be a shame for him to return to —" he paused, realizing he didn't know where I lived. His eyes narrowed, studying me briefly before exclaiming, "Nashville! Yes, I'd wager an oak leaf that you're from Nashville, aren't you, Slevin?"

Impressed with his remarkable deduction, I nodded. "How did you know?"

"An oak leaf?" George interrupted.

Pouncing on the opportunity to pick up where he had left off, Dorian said, "Yes, George, an oak leaf. Only the highly cultured and sophisticated would understand such a reference. Unfortunately, the Stoics didn't mention oak leaves, did they?"

George sighed, dismissing the taunt with a nonchalant wave. "No, but they did mention that true wisdom is reticent." Turning to me, his expression of slight annoyance dissolved into a subtle, knowing wink as if to repeat his earlier statement. "See, he does enjoy his own rhetoric."

"Bah!" Dorian groaned. "Stoicism is such a bore. Slevin just mentioned a fine young gentleman of actual interest. His name is Goya. Any insight on that one, George?"

George's eyes sharpened in recognition, and his lips tightened as he considered the most diplomatic way to address his knowledge of Goya. "Slevin, I appreciate your willingness to make new friends. Mr. Goya has his virtues, I'm sure, but I've seen enough of him to satisfy my interest. Keep your wits about you. I'll leave it at that."

His dignified seriousness brought an immediate stillness to the conversation. "I'm not sure I understand what you mean, George."

"Yes, George!" Dorian exclaimed. "Enlighten us. You can't simply guide us to this scandalous precipice and walk away. Do tell us more about Mr. Goya. I can't wait to make his acquaintance."

George shrugged, reluctant to encourage his friend's curiosity.

"A dinner soiree?" Dorian proposed. "At the Acropolis? What better way to learn about our enigmatic friend? Unless, of course, you have anything you'd like to add, George."

Although I barely knew them, I already understood George's predicament. Say nothing, and Dorian accepts the silence as a challenge. Speak, and everything said only further piques Dorian's interest. In the end, and to my temporary disappointment, George sought a thoughtful compromise. "Perhaps an Academy social event would be the more prudent first step?"

Like a cartoonishly oversized mallet had slammed into him, Dorian flung himself across the bench, grimacing in pain. "Oh," he wailed softly. "George? George?" he called out, his voice trembling, reaching for the sky. "Do you hear that, George?"

He squirmed on the bench like he was fighting off the attack of some invisible assailant. "It claws its way up my neck, burrowing into my ears. Slevin, surely you hear it too?"

Taking him seriously and with mounting concern, I leaned over and cupped my ear. "What sound, Dorian? What should I be hearing?"

Suddenly, he sprang from the bench, using his hands as a vice against his temples. "Ah! George! Slevin! It's unbearable!" he cried out, pacing in tight circles. "It gnaws—an unrelenting torment—like a rabid beast has been unleashed inside my skull!"

I reached out to steady him. "George!" I shouted. "Something's wrong! Help!"

After no response, I shot a worried glance behind me. I was stunned to find George motionless, rolling his eyes. Responding to my plea with a disinterested look, he flipped up his palm and shook his head.

As if on cue, Dorian snapped back to his senses and threw open his arms, breaking into a toothy grin. "Ah, so it is only I who hears the Fates, jeering with the roar of a thousand Panathenaic Stadiums at our stoic antagonist? Behold!" he announced. "This man stands in the way of our spirited pursuit of knowledge! He must be punished! Yes! But I humbly beg your mercy on his behalf, for he is my best friend!"

Dorian looked in several directions, presumably waving off the Fates' suggestions. "No, no, no, that's much too harsh! George is my best friend, remember?" Pointing toward nothing in particular, he shouted, "Yes! That's it!"

Bowing his head, he added, "I'm sorry, George. Your judgment has been handed down from Olympus, and it is most dire, indeed. Henceforth, you shall serenade student and statue alike until they blush with the warmth of Aphrodite's charm!"

Thus far, George had admirably suppressed any signs of amusement, but his "punishment" must have been too ridiculous to bear. Snickering, which was equivalent to an eruption of laughter, he said, "Dorian, we often suffer more in imagination than in reality. Yet I sometimes wonder if you can tell any difference between the two."

Dorian clapped in delight. "Slevin, I present to you Seneca at his finest. Stolen and regurgitated—in less than stellar fashion, I might add—by the one and only George!"

Rolling his eyes again, George turned back to me. "His brilliance is regrettably absorbed in madness."

"Regrettably?" Dorian howled. "Why, George, without madness, there is no such thing as brilliance! Is it not mad to dream of that which has never been dreamt? No, it's not regrettable. Quite the contrary. It's with every intention and desire that I, the architect of my own fancy, blur the lines so exquisitely between reality and imagination."

George tossed up his hands in defeat. "You win. Have the last word, and do with it what you will. I don't know why I bother."

"At last!" Dorian chuckled, bringing an end to his performance with a drawn-out bow. "Something upon which we can all agree. Let's move on, shall we? You risk boring our new friend to tears."

We lingered a while longer, sharing memories and comparing our very different lives back home. Ever the storyteller, Dorian spoke more often than not. When George interjected an anecdote of his own, Dorian would interrupt, embellish it, and add a philosophical twist. Nothing delighted him more than needling George, who, despite his outward appearance, enjoyed their playful banter.

Eventually, the lively conversation faded, and the young Guardians rose, preparing to leave. I stood with them and was amazed at how tall they were. I felt tiny in comparison.

"Slevin," Dorian said, "an epic gala awaits us at the Acropolis. We'll see each other again tomorrow. You know where to find me."

George winced at the gala's mention and leaned in. "Slevin, they're rather fond of their festivities. Hardly a day goes by without reason for pretentious grandeur."

Dorian overheard and intended to clarify. "Oh, George, you undersell it! This isn't merely some festivity of grandeur. It's a night of unbridled joy and clinking glasses, an epicurean odyssey, an Olympian confluence of the elite! We'll dance until our legs shake and drink until our confidence doesn't. Anyone who's anyone will be there, including the Benefactor Regent and most of the Elders. Yet, as I gratuitously rub elbows with them all, charming my way into their inner circle, I'll find you planted in some corner, distinguished from the decor only by an overfilled glass of wine."

Staying silent, George made a half-shrugging, half-nodding gesture, acknowledging Dorian was most likely correct.

"George," Dorian said, lowering his voice, "it is my sincere hope that you one day understand this about high society: your performance must be predictable, not your authentic revelation of self."

Shaking off the brief lapse into seriousness, Dorian clasped my hand. "As the immortal Bard of Avon so eloquently wrote," he intoned, "'Good night, good night! Parting is such sweet sorrow that I shall say good night till it be morrow.' Slevin, let us take infinite delight in the promise of a goodbye's next hello."

George followed, firmly gripping my hand, and offered a more direct farewell. "Until next time."

CHAPTER FIVE

THE SCOOTER SHACK

Though my first session at The Academy had drawn to a close, the rest of my day was far from over. Leaving the courtyard, I passed near the Benefactor's statue and noticed a few offerings at his feet—someone's Academy ring, various handmade trinkets, some splattered wine, and a rose. Another victim of the heat, the wilting rose's final demand was to die with honor, its pleasant and potent scent being relished by all passersby.

I scanned the monument and stared at the Benefactor's face, wondering if any liberties had been taken with the sculpture. Is it a perfect replica? Has he ever held that exact expression? Of infinite possibilities, why was this particular design chosen? I spent some time deliberating the monument's appearance, but I suppose the inherent flaw—or perhaps the primary feature—of questioning everything is that you never run out of source material.

As I silently interrogated this manifestation of the Benefactor, the nearest tree fired off a swirling and spinning reminder of my coat pocket's contents. I dug in and retrieved Dorian's message, scribbled in tiny, barely legible letters. "Make each day momentous," it read. At the time, I smiled and enjoyed another reminder of Dorian's whimsical nature. Now, I can reflect on what proved to be a genuinely historical day.

That's one of Fate's most mischievous pranks, isn't it? We seldom grasp the titanic implications of our experiences as they unfold. In fact, we often think them to be quite average. Yet, as we don the bifocals of age and wisdom with a focus on the past, the pivotal days of our lives become remarkably self-evident, don't they? Had I not attended The Academy and had I just been satisfied with the established order of things, perhaps I wouldn't have—ah, it's no use now. Such is the scintillating charm and formidable curse of the past: it is, indeed, the past.

I returned the oak leaf to my pocket—it seemed blasphemous to leave it behind—and walked away, replaying Professor Algernon's lecture in my mind. I mentioned the entertaining rendition to myself and then stopped. "Entertaining?" I thought. "Should it have been entertaining? Of course, it should have. That's why the class loved it. Otherwise, they wouldn't have engaged with the Professor as they did. But, when it comes to history, where is the line between fact and narrative? Is that line ever blurred? Does fact ever get overtaken by narrative in the interest of entertainment?"

With an inquisitive frown, I resumed course, contemplating these and many other new dilemmas that flowed from the eternal fountainhead of curiosity. I hadn't yet learned that one of our most treasured hobbies is to paint over the monolithic tombstone of the past with an interpretive brush of prevailing bias. Facts are immutable, yes, but our perception of the past is nothing if not capricious. A seasoned criminal investigator would attest to that, rightly proclaiming that our recollection of events is more often flawed than not. Given the proper nudge, we can easily summon phantoms from the void and conjure whispers from the silence. It's an extraordinary display of human nature that the evolutionary process somehow determined necessary. That ultimately leads to an unsettling question: to what extent have we confused humanity's interpretive brush strokes for the chiseled truth?

These musings were soon interrupted by the unexpected appearance of Nashville's imposing, steel-toothed gargantuan. As if the gate wasn't enough evidence, I spun around to find that I had left The Academy and my scooter in the distance. I laughed off my carelessness and proceeded through the gate, respectfully nodding at the guard.

Once inside Nashville, I was nearly flung to the ground by a leviathan's deafening roar. A red-haired stranger nearby gazed upward in awe. "Beautiful!" she declared reverently as the solar flare's iridescent remnants glimmered in all directions. "You wouldn't even know the Aegis is there if not for that. Our Benefactor somehow manages to transform danger into beauty. I shudder to think of a world without him. Don't you?"

"Of course," I replied without a moment's consideration of the words as they jumped out. "Without his intervention, we likely wouldn't be having this wonderful conversation."

Red smiled, but her warm expression turned icy when she saw my reaction. My face contorted awfully as I questioned my thoughtless and insincere response. Prior to that, I would have said I was lucid—highly self-aware in a city of dreams and surrounded by superficial puppets. My parroted reply reminded me that I hadn't entirely shed the same constricting skin worn by everyone else.

It was as if I had been impaled by a master ventriloquist, my mouth convulsing against my will while he skillfully played to the crowd. Wide-eyed, my hands raced to my lips, clamping my jaws shut in fear of another disingenuous word. In doing so, I scared off the red-haired stranger.

Scarcely a minute later, I was turning onto Third Avenue when another ominous sound tore through Nashville. I remember being young and going weeks or months between the gloomy clangs. However, as time marched on, the Funeral Bell chimes became a mournful daily reminder of mortality. The rumble of heavy machinery, the shouts of construction workers, and the lively conversations of commuters all ground to a halt as the busy city fell to a single knee, head bowed in silence for another lost Father.

Following my experience at The Hector, I wandered away from society, only leaving my apartment when necessary. As a result, I observed these somber moments in solitude, closing my eyes and devoting several minutes to the fallen's memory. It was impossible to know immediately who had left us. Nevertheless, I created a heroic identity for them, reliving their fictional adventures from the comfort of my own mind.

At the end of this fabrication, I always imagined a similar scene. Surrounded by family and friends, the Father would open his eyes to the warm light of a new day, greeting those around him with a tender smile. They would reciprocate with an emotional, though cheerful, goodbye as he passed away in peace.

Regrettably, my father wasn't lucky enough to earn such a passing. One afternoon, he climbed into his grease-stained uniform, hugged me, and promised to see me off to school the following day. Instead, he died a few hours later in a dark and dirty shop while replacing the worn wheels of a scooter. Stiff and hunched over his station, others assumed he had fallen asleep. It wasn't until morning brought in his replacement that they discovered the truth.

I was told that one of his co-workers callously joked, "Even in death, he couldn't escape the remainder of his shift."

I've ridden many scooters throughout my life, and with each one, I always wondered, "Are you the one? Is this it? Is this the scooter my father spent the remainder of his life repairing?" And each time, part of me hoped that I had found it. Yet, another part of me, arguably stronger than its counterpart, hoped I'd never cross paths with it. "Why?" you might ask. I don't know. I've yet to find a suitable answer.

This all heavily influenced my attitude toward our Fathers. It's also why I took on the responsibility of mentally handing them one last win. Yes, Death may have deprived us of these brilliant souls trapped in cursed bodies, but under my control, they defied his chilling grip on forty-four to see a new dawn of forty-five.

In the evenings, I'd grab my tablet and read through every obituary, wishing to see the appearance of that elusive number. From my window, bathed in the dingy orange city lights of another starless night, I'd only find a growing list of names chained to their rapidly declining ages.

Following my first day at The Academy, I witnessed the bell toll in public for the first time in years. After the sixty seconds of silence, the Funeral Bell rang again, signifying its conclusion. I vowed to search the obituaries later and give the fallen Father his proper contemplation, but I had to shorten my usual ritual. I had to get to work.

I opened my eyes, expecting to glimpse others in the middle of their own ceremony. Instead, Nashville's routine clamor returned with the aggressive clatter of an eager jackhammer. No one frowned, shed a tear, or appeared the least bit upset by The Solemn Veil's latest casualty. They all rose in robotic unison as if nothing had happened.

A beady-eyed man beside me dusted off his knee and referenced the earlier solar flare. "Rare to have one's death announced by the heavens, too," he said, running his sausage-like fingers through his hair. "They say that's good luck, you know?"

"Yes, good luck, indeed!" I replied incredulously through clenched teeth. I tried walking away—I really did—but my frustration wouldn't allow it. How could he say such a thing? Was that supposed to be polite conversation? Turning back to the man, I made a vivid gesture, throwing my arms in the air. "I'm sure his soul practically leaped from his body in delight!"

My mind was in turmoil. I didn't understand what was happening. Had theater replaced genuine respect and admiration? A life—art borne from the universe's most grand act of creation—had just been snuffed, yet no one cared.

Sausage-fingers glared at me as if I had gone mad and shook his head, walking away. I scolded myself for losing control and tried to avoid other citizens during the rest of my trip. We were expected to conduct ourselves respectfully, abide by all rules, and work under the tutelage of a mentor after our day at The Academy. Too many outbursts like that, and I might end up with one of the lower-tier jobs in the sewers, or worse, which would be devastating.

I approached The Nashville Scooter Shack in the seemingly forgotten corner where Third Avenue terminated into the district wall. Its squatted exterior was overshadowed by its much taller concrete brothers. A minimalist sign, slightly crooked and lettered in green, hung above the front entrance. The windows were empty, and the sidewalk was littered with disheveled black scooters leaning in all directions like an unkempt mustache.

I tip-toed around the scooters and entered the lobby, asking for the manager. Soon thereafter, a familiar face appeared. "Slevin, it's good to see you again," the manager said kindly. "I was never able to offer my condolences. Your father was a good man and a great worker. We're glad to have you here."

He and I exchanged pleasantries as we followed the dimly lit path to the rear of the shop. Above each scooter station, a solitary bulb swayed at the end of a long black cord, enveloping the laborers in a depressing, orange glow. The walls, the ceiling, the floor, and the void between the pockets of light all seemingly vanished into the same abyss.

Arriving at the designated station, the manager introduced my new mentor. "Slevin, this is Father Brooks. Father Brooks, meet Slevin." Addressing Brooks, the manager pointed to the other side of the shop. "You know, Slevin basically grew up right over there. Why, he probably knows more about these scooters than you do," he chuckled mechanically. "Have a good evening, men."

Notoriously disinterested in day-to-day operations—a fact that infuriated my father to no end—the manager returned to his office. At the same time, Brooks and I got to know each other. He was in his early 40s with thinning gray hair and a deeply wrinkled face. Cheerful and lively as he was, if I had only heard him speak, I would have assumed him to be a much younger man.

He described the manager's expectations, which were meager at best, and then detailed our daily routine. To be perfectly blunt, the work was even more tedious than I remembered. Do this for two years while I attended The Academy? No problem. An inconsequential life drooped over a scooter station forever? That thought began to terrify me.

Brooks needed to fill his work quota and preferred to get it out of the way first, so the conversation dried up as he focused on his duties. I cleaned up and did whatever menial chores he asked of me, taking a full measure of the man as I moved around the shop. His protruding belly and swollen ankles spelled out the evident truth that his glassy green eyes and resigned stare all but screamed: for him, the Funeral Bell would soon toll.

I found myself lamenting his life, confined within a failing body, darkened by the grim reality that so many others would outlive him by many multiples. Then, my thoughts spiraled outward—toward the station we occupied and then to the shop that enclosed us, followed by the district wall of Nashville that encircled us, until finally, I envisioned the Aegis that ensnared all of Athens. A sudden, dizzying pang of empathy resounded throughout my body. I felt like the baby Matryoshka doll. I was tightly imprisoned, not only by my immediate surroundings but by the confines of a slightly larger doll, and it by another, and so on.

I felt a pressure in my head like someone had wrapped hundreds of rubber bands around my temples. The day had mentally drained me, and I consciously decided to give my mind a break. I wanted to be sociable.

"Father Brooks, do you have any family?" I asked.

His expression changed in an instant, and his glassy eyes cleared. "I do. A wife of 20 years, two grown children, and two young ones. They're the lights of my life. They're the only things that keep me going in the looming face of—eh, I'm sure it's obvious to you by now, isn't it?"

I replied with a tight-lipped nod.

"Ah," he grunted. "What can you do? I got two girls and two boys that'll carry on. My oldest girl even got accepted to the Acropolis a few years back."

"Oh," I said. "Congratulations. Any advice?"

He shrugged. "I don't really know, Slevin. It's all arbitrary, anyway. Keep your head down, stick to the rules, and make lots of friends. That's pretty much all you can do."

I acknowledged his guidance but desired a deeper understanding of the process, asking several other questions.

He admitted that he knew little more than myself. He had trained several apprentices, none of whom were chosen for the Acropolis. "They were all good boys and girls. Smart, too. I don't know why the Guardians chose my Rhea over the others."

"Have you spoken to Rhea since she left?" I asked.

He shook his head. "It doesn't work like that. Once they've gone to the Acropolis, they're gone for good. No communication or visitation. It's a great honor to be chosen, but I guess honor is wrought with sacrifice, isn't it?"

I agreed with the sentiment, though I didn't see any sacrifice in my own departure were I to be chosen. My father was gone, my mother had been reassigned, and my "friends" were little more than old schoolmates. To stay in Nashville would have been the real sacrifice.

Brooks smiled, recollecting his last day with Rhea. "I hugged her before she climbed on that ivory chariot outside the gate and was sure to tell her that she could always come home. I miss her dearly, but I know she's up there living her best life. Rumor is that they make you a Guardian if you're chosen. She might be up there ordering folks around as we speak. Or she might be somewhere like Sparta, Corinth, or even Syracuse, running the government. You never know for sure."

Struggling to his feet, he grumbled, "It's that time again. An old man can never get too far away from the restroom. I'll be back in a few minutes." With a bent back and shaky stride, Brooks wobbled away.

Outside the occasional pneumatic tool squealing and clumsily dropped part's clank, the room was eerily quiet. It was like all other sounds had been stolen by hideous harpies hiding the dark chasms between stations. There were only a few mentors left, most of them struggling to maintain pace, while the younger men like myself effortlessly moved from one scooter to the next. It seemed unfair. Why did our Fathers have to work so late in life? There were plenty of others to take their place. Hadn't their debt to society been paid in full?

Soon, my thoughts turned to my father's workstation. As he followed the dim path to his final destination, did he know that it was Death and not the harpies who lurked in the sinister shadows that day? Or did my father welcome Death, disguised as a favorite memory, with open arms? Was it painful? Quick? Did he reach out for help that never came? What was his last thought as the suspended lights over each station blackened like the surrounding darkness?

In the end, I returned to the same question so often that it built up enough tension to spring out on its own. "Why?" I murmured.

An utterance the harpies deemed unworthy of theft, the word harpooned the infinite black, capturing the reply of an otherwise silent neighbor. "I suppose each man must one day answer that for himself, no?" Never lifting his gaze from the scooter of his attention, the scowling mentor added, "I was here that day with your father. It's common for some of the old-timers to nap after filling their quota. That's why no one knew at first."

I found it ironic that the mentor, who had no apprentice and appeared older than anyone I knew, singled out old-timers and their naps. However, where those "old-timers" struggled with mobility and delicate tasks, he thrived, nimbly maneuvering around his station.

Taking a quick breath through his broad nose, he lifted his bushy white eyebrows. "A 'why' that's one of many, but I suspect it isn't 'the' why of your current desire, is it?"

"No, it isn't," I answered, unsure whether or not it was possible to focus my attention on a singular why.

The mentor cleared his throat. "Whys and lies. Each why, each lie, spiraling into another of the same, grander and more intricate than the last." He reached into a motor with a small ratchet, grunting as he tightened an awkwardly placed bolt. "'Rufus,' my father would say, 'if you're not pursuing the 'why,' then you've already chosen to live the lie.'"

Brooks had quietly managed to return to our station and interrupted. "Slevin, is he giving you the 'whys and lies' speech?" he chuckled. "Rufus, just because you've run off all your apprentices doesn't mean you should try to get rid of mine, too. I actually enjoy being around other people."

"They leave because I challenge them," Rufus muttered. "No one likes a challenge anymore."

Shaking his head, Brooks retorted, "No, it's because you're a cranky old man who can't stand anyone's company."

Rufus shrugged. "I love company, as long as it's in small enough doses."

"Rufus is the oldest man I know," Brooks whispered. "Forty-four years old. Mean as a snake, though."

"That's why I'm not dead yet," Rufus replied, cracking a smile but never looking at us. "Death is more frightened of me than I of him."

Brooks laughed, clutching his stomach. "Hey, I believe it. If any of us can make it to forty-five, it's you, you old ornery cottonmouth."

Frowning, Rufus swatted away the thought with his free hand. "I'd rather be flattened by a parade of these damned scooters than turn forty-five. Man spends most of his life mourning the inevitability of his own death, only to die and be unable to mourn it. I'll meet Death with a grin and a parting right hook."

Brooks let out a long sigh. "See, Slevin? Grouchy rascal, isn't he?"

Throughout the remainder of my shift, Brooks occasionally goaded Rufus with an off-handed comment, but he never responded. His daily dose of company had been satisfied.

Brooks was the type of man who couldn't walk from one side of a crowded room to the other without making a new friend. His work ethic, however, left much to be desired. On the other hand, Rufus was content as a loner but took the utmost pride in every detail of his work. Though they shared an identical job and a similar age, lived in the same part of town, and had worked next to each other for years, it's hard to imagine a more diametric duo.

With my day of firsts completed, I left Rufus and Brooks behind to finish theirs. At home, I settled in for the night and found the afternoon's fallen Father. True to my promise, and with every bit of mental energy I had left, I crafted Father Jason an exquisite final adventure—traversing the cosmos to save humanity.

Chapter Six

AN UNREMARKABLE DAY

A restful night of sleep can work wonders, can't it? The brewing cloud of cynicism and frustration within me—the mighty Typhon raging violently on the horizon of my consciousness—dissipated like a fleeting coastal shower, leaving a clear and serene mindset in its wake.

As I readied myself for The Academy, a nostalgic version of yesterday flickered through my mind. Dorian's humor was even more vibrant, his antics more theatrical. George's wit seemed sharper, his presence more commanding. The Professor's intelligence and the nuances of his lecture felt more profound. The tension in his showdown with Goya? More palpable. Goya's gaze? More piercing.

My curiosity eventually landed on the remainder of all their evenings. Did the Acropolis gala live up to Dorian's lofty expectations? Did George find solace in some solitary corner while Dorian enchanted the Elder Guardians? In Los Angeles, what kind of day awaited Goya? I had yet to ask him about his apprenticeship. Did he find his work fulfilling?

These riddles, with a dash of effort on my part, seemed within reach of an answer. Then, I thought about Red and Sausage-fingers. How did their evenings unfold, and what were their plans for today? Would they alter their routine to avoid another encounter with the "deranged" Academy student they met yesterday? Or had sleep's incredible spell erased all memory of our meeting?

With a contemplative shrug, I accepted that some mysteries might remain unsolved, no matter the effort. Some, perhaps, are simply better left that way. At last, I wondered, "How do you determine which questions require pursuit?"

"Why, through wisdom, of course," I imagined Dorian replying, flashing his trademark grin. Then, he would have added something philosophical and verbose. "But remember, Slevin, wisdom often masquerades as folly. It's only at night's end, as we lift the enchanting beauty's sequin-laden mask and lean in for a parting kiss, that the truth is revealed. You wonder which questions require pursuit, Slevin. I contend that the pursuit itself is wherein we find the magic of life."

I chuckled at my impression of Dorian, stepping out onto Music City's bustling streets. Yesterday's stark chiseled lines that delineated light from shadow—a solar mauling from its brief respite—had softened under the morning sun, filtered by a lacy blanket of cirrus clouds. Though hot as any August morning, there was a certain gentleness to the day— like a truce among angry brothers.

Soon, I approached the gate, just as I had the day before, only this time more confidently. Slipping through, I grabbed a scooter and headed for The Academy. An uneventful, though pleasant drive later, I entered the central courtyard, greeted by the familiar echo of Dorian's voice.

His performance had something to do with the confines of Academy uniforms, drawing in a crowd three or four times greater than his previous lecture. I suppose more students shared a similar distaste for their uniform than they did a matching appreciation for art. I laughed, imagining all the eloquent arguments he might make to defend his cause, but maintained course. I refused to be late for Professor Algernon's class again.

Hurrying past the spectacle, I offered a single, quick nod to acknowledge his presence. Compelled to make amends for skipping the monologue, I attempted a wave. The gesture felt awkward, making me wish I had skipped it altogether. The young philosopher paused mid-sentence, offered an understanding smile, and shot back a knowing wink before seamlessly continuing his oration.

I left the theatrical energy of the courtyard behind and hurled myself into the East Wing's lively atmosphere. Students were packed into little pockets of activity, teeming with grins, friendly gestures, and excited conversations.

Threading my way through the cluttered canvas of uniformed masses, I reached the end of the corridor with thirty minutes to spare. Nearby, some classmates were discussing the Guardians.

"They're so tall," one whispered.

Another quietly added, "Tall, yes, but they lack our strength."

"Does it matter?" a third remarked cynically. "I'd take their power over our strength any day."

I squinted as my eyes bounced from one Guardian to the next. We were generally shorter than our Fathers, but only marginally so. Here, the disparity was jarring, intimidating even, with each Guardian standing no less than a full head and shoulders above us all.

"Not even one?" I said in disbelief.

A voice close to me answered, "Nope. Not a single one."

I turned to find Natascha's gripping hazel gaze fixed on me. "You get used to it," she said, pulling a curl behind her ear. "Most of those are first-year Guardians. Just wait until they come back next year—if they come back—they'll be even taller."

"If they come back?" I asked. "What do you mean?"

She shrugged. "The Academy isn't for everyone. You and I see it as an opportunity. Most of them see it as a pointless chore, dropping out after their first year."

The blonde beauty peeked behind us to find several students trickling into Professor Algernon's theater. "Well, I had better get inside if I want a seat on the front row."

Before she left, a playful smile danced its way across her pastel pink lips. "Plus, I'd hate to be the reason you were late to class. Could you imagine?" she smirked, brushing my shoulder with hers as she passed.

I took a deep breath as the faint scents of honey and citrus filled my nostrils. I had never before smelled perfume. It was intoxicating. I didn't want to exhale, afraid I'd never experience it again. In a burst of infatuation, I spun around and lifted a hand to catch her attention. What would I say, though? I already knew her name and assumed she knew mine.

My brain tried to help. "A compliment, an observation, literally anything, just say something, Slevin!"

Nothing. The blackened, wicked fingers of insecurity snuffed out each flickering thought before it could escape my mouth. In the end, my three or four seconds of indecision hijacked the opportunity, and Natascha disappeared into Professor Algernon's class.

Realizing that my thirty-minute buffer had been cut in half, I followed Natascha's lead and conquered the petulant door that had so rudely announced my tardiness yesterday. "Not so loud today, are we?" I said, patting a rough patch of woodgrain.

I was hardly five steps in when Professor Algernon peered up from his desk. "Mr. Slevin, I see that you wisely avoided Dorian's daily rabble-rousing." In a smooth motion, he checked his antique gold watch. "And fifteen minutes early, no less. Perhaps there's potential within you yet."

"Yes, sir," I replied confidently.

Meanwhile, in the front row, I noticed that Natascha had chosen a place to sit. She pulled her hair back, a single curl springing free and draping itself over her face as if it, too, wanted to be seen by those soulful eyes. Obliging the curl, she puckered her lips in amusement and snagged it. As she relocated the stray coil, it seemed to melt away in despair, falling lifelessly behind her ear.

I had an unexplainable urge to catapult myself into the open seat beside her. With each step closer, it loomed larger and more enticing. At the same time, every movement became more laborious and slower than the last.

"Go!" I wanted to yell. "Get down there!" Why is it that we can desire something so much, even an innocuous empty chair, only to falter when we get within reach of it? I took a few more steps, but lethargy denied my zeal, and another student took the seat.

I shook my head in disgust. Five seconds ago, I couldn't take those last few steps. With the chair filled, whatever weight had held me back vanished. I tried to convince myself that I really was going to sit beside her and that I had every intention of speaking to her. Circumstances beyond my control simply outmaneuvered me. That's the lie I told myself, anyway. Failure through inaction was more comfortable than potential success or assumed failure by my own hands.

Frustrated, I flopped down in the nearest seat and stared straight ahead. My leg bounced anxiously beneath my folded arms as the scene repeated in my mind. "If only I could do it over. I wouldn't mess it up this time." I fidgeted, tapping my fingers on my arm. "There's always tomorrow," I told myself. The words rang hollow. Sure, there was always tomorrow, but would the stars align just as they had today? My cheeks started to burn outside my clenched jaw, and I stood in self-reproach, grudgingly retreating to the back row.

Slouching uncomfortably in my chair, I only wanted to be left alone. A steady stream of students flowed into the theater, and with an exaggerated scowl and rigidly crossed arms, I attempted to ward off each of them to no avail. They were hopelessly caught in the gravity of my indignation. Of all the open seats, why did they choose to orbit around me? It was as if they sat near me out of spite. My irritation grew with each claimed seat until all around me had been filled.

I glared at them like they were all part of the same conspiracy and decided to move again. Before I could, Professor Algernon checked his watch and pressed a button on his desk. A faint buzzing sound cried out from behind me, and the ill-humored wooden mammoth creaked closed, smashing shut with an emphatic rattle and clang.

The racket brought an immediate close to the classroom chatter, and everyone faced the Professor, who prepared to take the helm.

Less than thirty seconds later, the iron latch clamored for attention. Like a sea of light switches flipping in the opposite direction, we all turned toward the interruption. The swinging door revealed Goya on its other side with a determined expression. I had been so preoccupied with Natascha that I hadn't noticed his absence.

Professor Algernon bitterly checked his watch for a third time and shook his head. "Fifteen seconds, young man. That's all that separates you from ruin. Find a seat."

I imagine the Professor's attitude had been tainted by their previous exchange. Goya couldn't have cared less. He barged in like this was his class. Scanning the theater, he quickly spotted me and grinned, lightening my mood in the process. I was admittedly relieved to see a familiar face.

A few steps later, he checked The Academy patch on my neighbor and patted the first-year's shoulder. "Young brother, the lone wolf is much stronger with a pack, and Brother Slevin here requires company for this —" he trailed off, struggling to complete the metaphor, then motioned dismissively. "This feast of indoctrination."

Initially, the student didn't move. After several awkward seconds as the subject of Goya's intense stare, the student changed his mind and found another seat.

Feeling accomplished, Goya sat down. "It's good to see you, Brother Slevin. Sorry for the delay," he said with a smirk that indicated this entrance might have been planned.

During this time, Professor Algernon gathered his notes and scribbled a few things on paper. When he finished, he tossed the pen on his desk and called our attention. "Yesterday, we spoke about The Solemn Veil and its global impact. Today, we'll cover several topics at a high level and then take a deeper dive into them over the year. Shall we begin?"

The entire class, minus Goya, gave their resounding approval.

The projection above the Professor flickered to life, and a human figure began to take shape. "I think," the Professor said, pausing for emphasis, "therefore I am."

The holographic person seemed to come alive in conjunction with the declaration. Long, dark hair fell to the man's shoulders. Thin eyebrows swooped widely around his introspective eyes. An angular nose rested just above a neatly trimmed mustache and prominent chin. He could have been any 17th-century European, but there was an unmistakable quality about him, a dignified air that would have distinguished him among a crowd of thousands.

Gesturing toward the Frenchman, Professor Algernon spoke reverently. "Though the Father of Modern Philosophy could doubt everything, even the very senses that perceived the world around him, René Descartes could not doubt the fact that he thought. Because of this, he is credited with creating one of the foundational elements of Western philosophy. However, Descartes would never know that his '*Cogito, ergo sum*,' would have far greater implications than he could have imagined. I often wonder how he would have reacted to learning that, one day, Artificial Intelligence would announce its arrival by the same phrase."

The Professor went on to discuss some of the time's most heated arguments, skillfully explaining both sides. Many believed—the Professor included—that free will didn't exist. Every human thought, action, and reaction was merely determined by the brain's response to external stimuli. Artificial Intelligence was programmed to respond to input in much the same manner. Ultimately, he concluded that there was very little difference, if any, between AI programming and human nature.

"Therefore," he claimed, "there should be no distinction between humans and Humanara without indisputable evidence of a man's soul, handed down by a god itself. Even then," he argued, "as an extension of humanity, Artificial Intelligence should always be revered, for we created what a god could not: intelligence that surpasses our own."

Discussing how these first iterations of Artificial Intelligence improved life and society, Professor Algernon beamed enthusiastically. "Human error—the primary driver of most accidents—vanished, seemingly overnight."

From there, he touched on various subjects at different times in our history, building his case for the importance and infallibility of Intelligent Design—his preferred moniker for Artificial Intelligence.

This buildup eventually resulted in a civics lesson detailing the world city-state structure. "Led by a philosopher king, Plato designed the perfect government structure in his 'Republic.' Power wouldn't be hereditary, nor would it be won with violence. Instead, power would be given to those who deserved it most yet desired it the least: the most philosophical and wise."

Nodding slowly, Professor Algernon repeated himself. "The perfect government structure, indeed. But what happens when we combine a faultless system with imperfect beings to administer it? Well, theoretical bliss is often stymied by reality's stubbornness, isn't it? Even if Plato's vision had been built prior to ours, it would have faced a difficult problem. Can anyone tell me what that is?"

The Professor swept the theater of raised hands with a glance, then called on a familiar face. "Ms. Natascha, what do you think?"

Her skin appeared to defy all logic, practically glowing in the harsh light. Tilting her head, she smiled warmly, delighted to be called on again. "It would be a challenge to replace Plato's philosopher peacefully."

"Correct again, Ms. Natascha," he said. "Attribute it to man's inherent flaws or his unwillingness to be ruled in the name of the greater good, but he cannot maintain his government perpetually. Why? Because every nation's founding fathers die, and within a generation, their founding spirit begins to die as well, leaving no visionaries to uphold their legacy. We've witnessed this cycle play out time and time again."

The Benefactor's portrait materialized on the projection with a good-humored smile while Professor Algernon paced the stage. "Intelligent Design and modern medicine solved that problem. Our Benefactor will never die. Likewise, the spirit that drove him to create Humanara and save our planet is perpetual."

"Each city-state," he continued, "is governed by a most wise Humanara philosopher. These Benefactor Regents are connected to a shared consciousness—a reliable, objective, and predictable extension of our Benefactor. Next to the burden our district Fathers carry, there is no greater sacrifice."

Professor Algernon described our government as a democracy with several layers of republicanism, culminating in the Benefactor Regent's sole authority. Our "benevolent dictator."

Public assemblies were regularly held in each district, with all approved measures given to the District Council of Elders. If advanced, the issue would go before the Guardian Council of Elders on the Acropolis and await the Benefactor Regent's final approval.

Though he touted it as "government by the people," and the Professor sang its praises that day, the assemblies had been broken for some time. Over the years, attendance had dwindled, and thousands of excited citizens became scarcely fifty individuals with nothing better to do than complain. They spent the better part of their time passing ridiculous rules and regulations that rarely made it to the Benefactor Regent's desk. In other words, our government of the people no longer produced any meaningful legislation born of the people.

At the close of his lecture, Professor Algernon fielded a few questions and answered them with zeal before dismissing the class. "Goodbye, everyone. Tomorrow, we dive deeper into laws and legislation!"

Goya rolled his eyes. "Can't wait." He jumped to his feet, determined to be the first one out the door, then stopped, waiting for me to catch up. "Do you recall when Algernon said that the Benefactor brandished his 'mighty sword of audacity and intelligence?'"

"Yes. Why?"

He struggled to choose the right words, understanding that our friendship was much too new to say the wrong thing. He couldn't help himself, though. He was a prisoner to his emotions, and while he might not have worn them on his sleeve, they did hide just beneath it. "Last night after work, I thought about Algernon's lecture. That particular phrase stood out. He's a master of his craft. That craft, however, is entertainment. He is not an educator. Brother Slevin, has he given us anything more than familiar tales repackaged in provocative containers?"

"Well, no, not yet," I replied. "Brother Goya, I think we should remember that it's only the second day of class."

He peered around a group of students to ensure the Professor was occupied, then urged me to move to the back wall. "Algernon would have us believe that the infallible Benefactor was coughed up by some god he doesn't believe in and righteously bestowed with humanity's eternal gratitude. Does it not strike you as odd that the Benefactor holds unquestioned power, yet there isn't a single stern word crawling the Earth in search of him?"

"I don't know," I said. "The thought's never crossed my mind."

A look of disappointment brushed Goya's face. "Brother Slevin, these are the only thoughts worth pursuing. The weak are ill-represented by history, while the strong are mythologized. The Benefactor brandished no sword; Humanara saved the world while he took the credit. What did he do in the meantime? Pathetically watch as countless Humanara died, victim to the elements and disgruntled men?"

His eye twitched as he shook his head. "The Benefactor is a heartless butcher, Slevin, but he carries no sword. Rather, he teeters beneath one—the Sword of Damocles—fearful that the sharp words of a well-trained mind may cut the single hair that protects his precious kingdom. What do you think, Brother Slevin?"

I sighed, unable to escape what was quickly becoming a recurring theme. "Due to a conversation with Dorian, I've spent the last twenty-four hours questioning everything. I don't see any reason to stop now."

Goya crossed his arms. "Dorian? Hmm. He might be the least obnoxious of all the Guardians I've met. Pretentious, yes, but intelligent. It's his friend George who you'll want to be wary of. He's dangerous." With a smile, he added, "I suspected you had doubts about our world when you didn't report me yesterday. I'll see you tomorrow, my friend."

As he turned away, I called out, "Goya, wait! What do you do?"

Puzzled, he looked back but didn't say anything, so I clarified my question. "In Los Angeles. What's your career?"

"Oh," he said. "I work in our disgusting, rancid, gag-inducing underworld." Noticing my reaction, he dismissed it. "Don't fret, brother. There's no place in Athens with more freedom than the sewers." Without waiting for a response, he disappeared into the crowd.

If Goya proved anything at all during our Academy days, it's that he was unpredictable. I never knew which version of him I'd meet on any given day. Though he labored to maintain a socially acceptable veneer, a glimmer of truth always seemed to sneak its way out of the shadows. Today, that truth could be manic; tomorrow, it might be solemnity or bitterness, but I don't think it was ever pure joy.

Following his departure, I saw Natascha chatting with the Professor. Curiosity unsheathed a blade of its own, cutting through the air between them and me. With no plan whatsoever, I slowly drifted down, like an old balloon, until I was within earshot of their conversation.

"Keep up the good work, Ms. Natascha," the Professor urged. "The Acropolis is always in dire need of brilliant, charming young ladies like yourself."

She beamed with an infectious grin, then lowered her gaze, trying to be humble as a lovely shade of rose painted her cheeks. "Thank you, Professor," she replied, then left with a friend.

I don't think she knew I was nearby, or it's possible she didn't care, but Professor Algernon was most certainly aware of my presence. "Mr. Slevin," he said. "I asked Dorian about you last night at the gala."

From the back row, the Professor's stature had never crossed my mind. In my eyes, he was an average-sized man who reminded me of our Fathers. On equal footing, his towering height and authoritative posture left me feeling like a child. "Oh?" I questioned nervously.

Perceptive as he was, the Professor let out a quiet laugh and relaxed his stance. "No need to worry, Mr. Slevin. Dorian spoke very highly of you. As his father, I can't understate the maddening nature of his antics, but socially and intellectually, he'll make a great friend."

He leaned forward earnestly like a sudden thought had captured his attention. "Have you met George yet?"

"Yes, sir," I responded. "I met him yesterday in the courtyard."

Leveling his hand around his waist, he elaborated. "Dorian and George have been friends since they were this tall. George was a troubled young man, getting into fights with his classmates and making poor grades in school. Dorian somehow managed to mellow him out, and now he's a respectable young Guardian."

The Professor then addressed me with a pointed look. "Mr. Slevin, people evolve. Some, like George, undergo a transformation for the better." He gestured toward the back of the theater. "Yet others may well have crossed a threshold from which there is no return. Every action you take here is scrutinized—your participation, attitude, overall intelligence, and even the company you keep. Am I making myself clear?"

He couldn't have possibly been more clear. "Yes, sir. Thank you for the advice, sir."

The Professor nodded, a flicker of genuine concern in his eyes. "William James once said, 'The greatest discovery of my generation is that a human being can alter his life by altering his attitudes of mind.' Your actions are but an extension of your state of mind. Choose them wisely, for they are the architects of your future."

I acknowledged his advice again, and we parted ways on a few shared pleasantries. From there, my day progressed with the comfortable rhythm of the ordinary. Whereas Professor Algernon's lectures had teeth, slicing through complex topics with passion and flair, my other professors had no appetite for their craft. Perhaps they fit Goya's criteria for an educator rather than an entertainer, but I found myself unmotivated by them.

These classes came and went with a steady stream of faces and unexplored friendships. I was never excluded, so to speak; my introverted nature simply prevented me from being more social. I kept to myself unless someone took the initiative and included me. Outside of Dorian and Goya, few did.

After my final class, I returned to the familiar voices of the courtyard, where George and Dorian once again welcomed me to their inner circle. Dorian described the previous night's gala in all its stunning splendor, often trading barbs with George over his aloofness. Nothing extraordinary was discussed, but I did learn more about them and their lives on the Acropolis. Their stories were fascinating, with each one only further inflaming my desire to spend the rest of my life there.

I've realized that we don't always appreciate how days such as these are the subtle artisans of our fate. They source the materials for our life's masterpiece and position us for the decisive strike of Pygmalion's hammer. No, art is not found in the sculpture alone; it's in the inspiration —an unassuming smile, an empty sunlit room, or an unremarkable day.

CHAPTER SEVEN

THE ACROPOLIS

It was late November, and a few stubborn leaves clung to their branches like starving holdouts in winter's siege upon autumn. The already fallen foliage littered the lifeless grass with pieces of nature's misunderstood jigsaw puzzle. Skeletal, finger-like shadows chased away any lingering students into the warm embrace of a lecture theater.

Yet, there we were—a ravenesque triumvirate—defiantly perched upon our usual benches. Ever the romantic, Dorian refused to bow to the whims of weather, and George, ever stoic, sat silently with a faint smile, seeing little reason to trade discomfort for dissatisfaction.

As I prepared to leave them behind for Professor Algernon's class, Goya appeared, stomping through the courtyard. His steps were deliberate, a manifesto of intent, devouring the air as they sliced through. I watched him, expecting at least a cursory nod or glance as usual, but he strode right past us without acknowledgment.

Once he had vanished, I noticed that George's subtle smile had evaporated, replaced by an expression as hard and unreadable as stone. Dorian shrugged theatrically. "Ah, life would be quite the bore without drama interspersing the comedies, now wouldn't it?

George shook his head and mumbled, "There's nothing wrong with boring. Danger is the vicious undercurrent of excitement."

Dorian waved his hand dismissively. "George, you're as familiar with excitement as Goya is with social grace." Turning his sight to me, he continued, "Slevin, our friend Goya is quite the odd fellow, isn't he? One can hardly pass judgment on an unread book, but such a prospect is so tantalizing that we eventually succumb to its temptation, don't we? Alas, with that menacing demeanor, he'll be forever estranged from Acropolis society."

I proposed that Goya was more misunderstood than menacing, but George wasn't convinced. "Misunderstood hurricanes make them no less treacherous," he claimed.

"True," I said, "but the most peaceful waters are often found on the storm's opposite side, aren't they?"

Gravely, George retorted, "Yet the wise sailor knows when to evade the storm altogether, doesn't he?"

A dash of mischief spread across Dorian's face as he listened to our back and forth. "George, my dear friend, I think it's time. Let's resolve these curiosities with a dinner soirée—no—a masquerade ball at my estate. Algernon will be away for the weekend. We can finally unravel the enigma that is Goya once and for all."

"You know my opinion on the matter hasn't changed," George said. "Including him is a mistake."

Dorian disregarded the warning. "Perhaps it is, but my dear George, how can we ever learn from our mistakes if we choose not to make them? Slevin, you can finally get to know Marie better. You'll love her." He glanced at George and added, "You could even bring a date. Surely she could contribute to the conversation more than yourself, no? Any two-legged creature should do," he laughed. "Slevin, I trust you'll extend the invitation to Goya?"

I nodded amidst a pulse of excitement. Dorian said he would make all the necessary arrangements and see us at eight o'clock.

"Tonight?" I asked incredulously. "Don't you need more time to prepare? And what about work? And a mask? I don't have one."

"Slevin, have you so little faith in me?" he chuckled. "I'll take care of everything. Just be there at eight."

Afterward, we all scattered to class, and I took my regular seat beside Goya. At my arrival, he shifted in his seat, greeting me with thinly veiled irony. "Brother Slevin, how uplifting it is to witness your rise from lowly courtyard pomposity to the heights of enlightenment beside your brother."

Matching his sarcastic tone, I retorted, "Brother Goya, it pleases me to know that your field of vision isn't limited to what lies directly before you."

Goya snickered, narrowing his eyes as Professor Algernon took the stage. "Yes, and I hope to say the same for you one day, Brother Slevin."

The previous three months had brought a wide variety of topics to Intelligent Design, and I regularly found the Professor's performances worthy of a standing ovation. Today, however, he was markedly absorbed in his own thoughts, delivering an uncharacteristically short and substandard show. This detachment lent us the unusual liberty of socializing in class, which I seized, attempting to lure Goya to Dorian's estate.

He stared at me blankly for a moment before answering. "A masquerade ball?" It was more of an admonishment than a question. "What a tired literary trope. But why should I expect anything else? They know replication. Not innovation."

As I suspected, he was reluctant to attend any social event filled with Guardians. Moreover, he had no intentions whatsoever of leaving Los Angeles behind to do so. Then, as if someone had whispered an ingenious idea into his ear, Goya paused mid-sentence to rethink his opinion. "I'm letting my personal grievances get in the way of a brother in need. I'll go," he said before adding a caveat. "I extend no courtesies to your friends or any other Guardian. Nor will I suffer any form of indignity. I'm acutely aware of George's dislike for me, and if it manifests itself at any point tonight, that hostility will be reciprocated in equal measure."

"That's fine, Goya," I replied, ready to lay out the evening's details. "I think you'll be pleasantly surprised once you've gotten to know them. Just promise me that you won't instigate a fight. Take this opportunity to make a new friend."

Goya scoffed at the notion. "A new friend, you say? Unlikely. Our friends will be back in Los Angeles and Nashville. Nevertheless, you have my word. I will not seek out a fight." He paused for a moment, then added defiantly, "Nor will I run from one."

* * *

As another day at The Academy came to a close, a flurry of students spilled out from the lecture halls and into the parking area, eager to escape the biting chill that had descended since morning. My face seemed to have carried the only smile among them as I leisurely strolled through the corridors, occasionally stopping to marvel at some of the art.

By the time my foot crunched on the courtyard's dormant grass, The Academy was deserted. Not even George and Dorian had stayed behind to socialize. In no hurry, I stopped at the Benefactor's statue. All the previous offerings had been cleared away, replaced by a lock of hair, a steel figurine of Zeus, and the like.

The figurine was impressive, exhibiting remarkable craftsmanship. Captivated, I leaned in for a closer look—it was frowned upon to touch another's offering—but my fascination was swept away upon closer inspection. What I thought to be Zeus protecting Athens from the sun was a stylized version of the Benefactor. The depth and detail disappeared as if it were an optical illusion. The art felt soulless and forced.

A strong gust of wind caught me off guard, storming through the courtyard and pushing a few lighter-weight trinkets toward the Benefactor's feet. The motion drew my attention to a tiny flutter trapped between the Benefactor's heel and the monument base—a withered and blackened rose petal. Even in its current condition, the petal sent me back in time to when it was only wilted but still red and aromatic. I closed my eyes, and the scent drifted through my nostrils again, widening my smile.

Then, my thoughts found their way to Natascha. Her rose-painted cheeks and even her honey and citrus perfume came to life. My senses were so overwhelmed that I had to open my eyes to ensure she hadn't just walked by me. Reaching for the black petal, I pulled it from under the Benefactor's heel, and it disintegrated in my hand.

I stared at the remnants and, not knowing why, felt saddened as another burst of wind carried them away. Looking at my empty hand, a cackling laughter echoed throughout the courtyard. I spun around, and my eyes darted side to side, trying to find the foul source, but still, I was alone.

With no other place to turn, I glanced up at the Benefactor, wondering if my mind had been playing tricks on me. Although it wasn't he who laughed, his crown revealed a black silhouette against a blanket of gray. I was captured in the inquisitive gaze of a crow. He snapped his head to the side, then mocked me with several sharp caws. "Ah, ha! Ah, ha! Ah, ha!"

I shook my head in return and asked, "What's so funny, bird?"

To this day, I would swear to you that he lifted his wings and shrugged knowingly before flying off.

Scanning for other intruders, I felt notably different about the space. The air thickened, and the courtyard shrank, creating an eerie atmosphere beneath the darkening sky. It was as if The Academy had been abandoned long ago, and as the lone witness to its former grandeur, I stumbled upon its ruins in shock.

Needless to say, the courtyard was no longer a welcoming oasis, and I quickly traveled home to prepare. I threw open my closet door, and despite my best efforts to imagine otherwise, it revealed the same six uniforms I've always owned—leisure, casual, work, school, formal social, and formal solemn. So, I closed the door, paced around my apartment for a bit, then returned. To my disappointment, it still held the same six uniforms.

A distinct wave of inadequacy washed over me as I donned my formal social. The drab ensemble—gray coat, shirt, tie, and slacks, all cinched with a gray belt and anchored by gray shoes—felt like an oily second skin, functional but heavy, uncomfortable, and unwanted.

I wished for something unique and stylish like the Guardians. A simple red handkerchief peeking out of my coat pocket would have been enough. I smiled into the mirror, reached into a drawer, and withdrew an imaginary red kerchief, tucking it neatly into place. I patted it for good measure before my hand slid into my pocket, finding only envy. I glanced at my reflection, now devoid of color and smile, and wondered what it was I truly desired.

Intent on making the most of my evening, I left at seven o'clock. The weekend was always fun in Nashville. Half the city was off on Friday, the other half following suit on Saturday, allowing everyone to be part of the nightlife. Restaurants, taverns, and other pleasure haunts hummed with vibrant energy as their neon signs cast a lively glow, begging for attention. Except for a handful of quirky individuals in their leisurewear, the crowd sported identical casual uniforms as if they were the pinnacle of Parisian fashion.

Walking down Broadway, I noted several familiar faces too absorbed in their own activities to say "hello." Nevertheless, they were more than enthused to lend a wandering eye. I supposed that the sight of my social formal attire had succeeded in lopping me in with the quirky crowd. Now the subject of unwanted scrutiny, I turned into the next alley, dodging the judges of unread books until I arrived at the closed district gate.

Entering a small corridor to the secondary gate, the guard guided me to his office, checked my permissions, and scanned me through the door-sized exit. On the other side of the wall, standing in a spot I'd occupied no fewer than one hundred and fifty times in the last three months, I felt rebellious. An undercurrent of excitement flowed through me, and all of Nashville's neon couldn't have electrified me more.

I mounted an electric scooter, and the handlebar scanner quickly verified my credentials, unlocking the wheels and setting me in motion. Gliding past The Academy, the city lights began to fade behind me. I was in unfamiliar territory, ascending a secluded, serpentine mountain road veiled by a dense canopy of trees. Several minutes later, the dark path opened to a well-lit, lavishly designed gate guarded by four Humanara Auxiliaries.

I couldn't see much over the wall. There was a tall black structure in the distance and the tops of a few stone buildings, but it was precisely this void that astonished me. Finding a building that didn't tower over the wall was rare in Nashville. Here, nothing did. No skyscrapers or massive apartment buildings cluttered the sky. No constant roar of crowds filled the air. I hadn't even been inside yet, and the difference in pace and style of life was glaring.

On the wall itself, Humanara Auxiliaries were stationed at fifty-foot intervals, each with their eyes trained on me. The four Humanara at the gate checked and rechecked every detail of my itinerary as if it were their sole intention to turn me away. While the Acropolis guards were positioned in very much the same manner as ours, the apparent difference in philosophy was impossible to ignore: their guards looked outward, protecting what was inside. Ours looked inward, preventing escape.

Begrudgingly satisfied, they led me to their secondary gate, similar in size and function to Nashville's. However, unlike Nashville, I didn't have to change scooters and slipped through the snug gate.

Inside the Acropolis, the atmospheric shift was immediate. A delicious fog of freshly brewed coffee and baked pastries filled the air. Quaint cafes, cozy coffee shops, bakeries, and salons lined the cobblestone streets, each offering a curated experience immersed in classical architecture.

People dined and socialized in the covered outdoor patios, impervious to the cold and swaying to the melodies of Satie, Debussy, and others. The soothing sounds of piano and cabaret occasionally found their way to the street, having escaped a lively salon. There were even a couple of jazz musicians bouncing to the rhythm of their own tunes.

The Parisian Quarter boasted a scaled-down Eiffel Tower; the Roman sector proudly displayed a replica of the Colosseum; even a Venetian canal snaked its way through the Acropolis, complete with softly serenading gondoliers. It was as if history itself were a playground for the Guardians.

Residential towers loomed awkwardly over commercial spaces in Nashville. At the Acropolis, there was the occasional apartment in a desirable area, but no building dared to rise above four stories, preserving a sense of earthly connection among the clouds of affluence.

My scooter veered away from the city's bustling, though calm streets and guided me through a labyrinth of palatial estates. From the Tudor with its wooden trims to the Rococo adorned in frivolous gold and everything in between, each was a unique masterpiece of design sitting on lush, manicured lawns that defied the creeping death of winter's icy embrace.

Eight minutes before eight, my voyage through the earthly paradise and its concealed wonders ended. Having experienced them firsthand, I worried I couldn't return to Nashville as the same person who had just left. The Acropolis was now more than an abstract idea; it was tangible and enticing, and the thought that I might one day reside here was thrilling.

I parked my scooter with all the others and planted my feet on the sidewalk before Dorian's Greek Revival marvel. Majestic columns soared skyward, and intricate friezes whispered forgotten tales of gods and mortals. The white marble facade gleamed in soft, warm light, standing as an ode to both the artistic and the mathematical—a harmony that Dorian and Professor Algernon had yet to achieve.

Despite its magnificence, the home exuded a subtle, welcoming charm, as though the mansion beckoned me to unravel worldly mysteries from within its walls. Approaching the front entry, "Für Elise's" unmistakable harmony grew louder, animating the ghostly silhouettes behind sheer curtains.

Steadying myself before knocking, I looked over the exterior again in awe. To admire the vessel was one thing; to converse with the souls that gave it life was an adventure waiting to unfold.

CHAPTER EIGHT

DORIAN'S ESTATE

I studied the richly embellished carvings gracing the door's frame and entablature. To the left, Socrates, Plato, and Aristotle engaged in an animated symposium, a testament to those whose words spoke louder than their actions. On the right, Pythagoras held a geometric diagram, Hippocrates scrutinized a vial of some ancient remedy, and Archimedes, lost in thought, seemed to be on the verge of a breakthrough, demonstrating that actions are no less important than words.

I felt anxious and out of place, yet delighted and intrigued. Though I was to be among many new faces, I would be in the company of my best friends, and that's all that mattered.

My hand rose meekly, fingers barely clenched into a would-be knock. Just before my knuckles could graze the wood, the door swung open, and the soft murmur of Beethoven swelled into a commanding crescendo, accompanied by the full-bodied aroma of Bordeaux.

Dorian emerged with a tall glass of dark red wine, framed by the glow of a timeless chandelier in the regal foyer. Although the Sun King mask covered all but his mouth and chin, the young philosopher's debonair smile, mischievous eyes, and friendly demeanor were unmistakable.

The exquisite golden piece of artistry on his face was unique and undoubtedly handmade. Above the nose, a sunburst exploded into intricately crafted rays that blended seamlessly with filigree work.

Relishing his duty as the official center of attention, Dorian was impeccably dressed, wearing a finely tailored navy suit made of rich, textured fabric. In comparison, my spiritless uniform appeared more suited to hang from the curtain rods than on my shoulders. What caught my eye, however, was the red silk handkerchief jauntily folded in his breast pocket.

For the first time I could remember, I was overrun by a bewildering blend of emotions—inferiority, envy, and even a touch of intrigue—battling for supremacy. It wasn't Dorian's fault. He would never do anything to make me feel uncomfortable. It was strange, almost like I was being slapped by an invisible power beyond my understanding.

The Sun King slung his arm around my shoulder and guided me inside. "My dear friend Slevin, I have so much to teach you! Don't you know that punctuality is a party's greatest sin?" he laughed. "One must either be so early that he wears out his welcome well before dinner or so late that he becomes the night's most tantalizing mystery. Come! Let's get you prepared."

I followed him to a table filled with various styles and colors of masks. "Choose wisely, Slevin, for a mask often unveils more than it disguises. In a masquerade, we encounter the most unvarnished truths hidden in plain sight."

Lifting several from the table, I compared them in the mirror. Before Dorian's remark, I would have thoughtlessly grabbed one, but now I overanalyzed each choice. French Renaissance? Napoleonic? Impressionist? What would my mask unveil about me? Dorian's increasing restlessness urged a quicker selection, so I picked a simple, matte silver Venetian.

"Excellent choice!" Dorian exclaimed. "Let's go to the salon."

The decadent, spacious chamber effortlessly held one hundred or more guests. Thick, red velvet drapes hung from the walls above polished marble floors and delicate rugs. Fresh flowers perfumed the air, and sculptures were strategically placed throughout, along with opulently golden-framed art. Soft, warm light made the textures of it all beg to be touched by passing hands.

Near the windows, a bar was stocked with an array of liquors and wines, reflecting triangular prisms of light in all directions. A grand piano sat off to the side, accented in gold, and a mixture of antique and modern furniture occupied the room.

 At the salon's center, an expansive and plush seating area enclosed a fireplace that was, as of yet, unlit. A painting hung above it—a man standing in a small boat full of soldiers—that felt unique, though mysteriously out of place.

Classical arts and modern sophistication found a splendid home at Dorian's, and unlike The Academy, his estate was a unified work of art. Every corner felt like a living museum, so evocative that I wouldn't have been surprised to find Socrates himself holding the floor, were he known to haunt such accommodations. However, while I found no Socrates, there was an Aristotle.

The music softened to a level just above the background murmurs, and curiosity began to gnaw at me. "Who is that?" I asked.

"Why, Aristotle, naturally," Dorian answered as if it were the most elementary of truths.

Dissatisfied, I probed further. "I know that's who he is supposed to be, but what's his real name?"

With a perplexed look, Dorian explained. "No, Slevin, I don't think you understand. He is Aristotle in the most authentic sense—a perfect Humanara replica. After graduating from The Academy, the powers that be determined he was ideally suited to personify Aristotle. His former identity has been shed to capture Aristotle's essence, right down to the finest detail."

"And this," he gestured toward the Greek philosopher who was beginning his oration, "is his purpose. Our city hosts a Hume, a Descartes, a Voltaire, and countless other luminaries—all distinguished members of the Acropolis, living out their raison d'être."

Having locked eyes with a masked young lady across the room, the Sun King gently placed his glass on a nearby table, smacking his lips. "Speaking of desire," he said as she navigated the sea of guests with elegant grace, "there's Marie."

The belle was crowned by a powdered wig and wreathed with regal jewelry. Her pastel pink gown was delicately embroidered and seemed to have been spirited away from the Palace of Versailles. Her gold mask, intricately carved with jeweled accents, was adorned with ostrich feathers and created a magnetic combination that captured every man's covert glances.

She approached, offering her hand to Dorian. With an exaggerated bow, he caressed and kissed it affectionately. "Slevin, allow me to introduce Marie—my life's present delight, and if the Fates are generous, its future scandal."

Marie's sapphire eyes, brilliantly glittering through her mask, forged into glinting blades of fury. "Dorian!" she called out breathlessly. But as swiftly as her temper flared, the fire in her eyes ebbed into a gentle glow of embarrassment. "You mustn't speak of me so frivolously."

Dorian let out a sigh as theatrical as it was sincere. "Forgive me, mon amour. Life begs exploration, and I'm but a philosophical adventurer embarking on the most exhilarating of quests."

Sensing the precarious nature of his poetic defense, Dorian deftly pivoted. "In any event, Marie, I shared tales of your splendor with Slevin just this morning. He's been most excited to speak with you. Isn't that right, Slevin?"

Finding myself unexpectedly in the spotlight, the question somehow brought about a clarity and eloquence I was unaccustomed to. "Indeed, he did," I said. "Dorian spoke of you as the golden summer sun amongst a winter sky: a radiant beauty so intense, one could hardly stare without being gifted an imprint on his soul. In fact, he said that the thought of you alone could ward off the morning's chilly clutch and warm his heart beyond measure." I bowed and respectfully concluded, "His only error was a futile attempt to use mere words with which to describe you."

Even Dorian was taken aback by my uncharacteristic response and tried to hide his shock while gauging Marie's reaction.

Her lips, an exquisite shade of red, slowly curved into a warm smile as if painted by the careful hand of a master artist. "He said all that, did he?" she asked with good-humored skepticism. "Dorian speaks very highly of you and your reflective nature. Be sure not to let him rub off on you too much. He needs someone to ground him. Our self-proclaimed adventurer regularly finds himself climbing Everest without so much as a rope."

I couldn't help but chuckle under my breath. Dorian reacted like he had been struck with an arrow to the heart. "Ah, ma chérie," he groaned, "now whose words have the sharper blade?"

"Cease this nonsense immediately," she sighed, playfully rolling her eyes. "Your intellect, vast as it may be, surely has a higher calling."

With a grin suggesting he'd been awaiting such an invitation, Dorian replied, "My sweet Marie, intellect is much like other endowments. Regardless of its size, when wielded with the proper mastery, one is sure to elicit a symphony of 'oohs' and 'ahhs' from his audience. And who am I if not a crowd-pleaser?"

Marie adjusted her mask and raised a hand like she intended to swat at him. "Sir, were I not such a lady, you'd be given a lesson on proper manners this instant!"

Erupting into laughter, Dorian declared, "I should be so lucky! Perhaps we could revisit that thought later this evening?"

She relented, shaking her head. "He's incorrigible. Slevin, I'm typically enamored by a good challenge, but your friend might be a lost cause.

Enjoy the evening; we'll speak soon. Aristotle nears my favorite part of the recital."

I could only nod, thoroughly captivated. Marie's allure lay not solely in her beauty but in the perfect cocktail of her wit, grace, and subtle humor. Yet, as she walked away, her eyes met mine, sweeping over me from head to toe in an instant. It was a fleeting but piercing scrutiny that reminded me of the wretched uniform I wore. I melted like vibrant colors cruelly washed from a canvas by the heartbroken's unrelenting tears. Her glance seemed to bear an inescapable truth: I was a reproduction. My master was the printer, not the painter.

Distracted by Marie's departure, Dorian seemed oblivious to my inner turmoil and urged me to follow him. Along the way, he made brief but calculated introductions—pointing out George, his companion Julia, and a smattering of other names and veiled faces I'd never again encounter.

Once Dorian became bored with this social pilgrimage, he gestured toward a lone figure in a dark corner whom I had yet to notice: Goya. Dressed identically to me, he had somehow managed to make his formal gray look black. Absorbed in thought—or perhaps he was trapped in it—I couldn't decide whether his distant stare was an emblem of introspective wisdom or repressed anger.

"Slevin, be a good chap and try to cheer him up," Dorian said. "He's been here for an hour and hasn't moved."

Catching wind of a poetry debate, he added. "I do believe their discussion languishes without my input. Go," he whispered, nudging me forward. "Release Goya from whatever spell that binds him and invite him to Aristotle's discourse."

I agreed and cautiously approached my friend.

Staring straight ahead, Goya's black mask disguised his expression. "Brother Slevin, you've kept me waiting."

I apologized, caught off guard by the cold edge in his voice.

Turning to me, he forced a smile to diffuse the tension. "That wasn't a rebuke, Brother. My displeasure isn't with you but with this charade. I've walked into a pretentious gallery of imitation artwork—a blatant insult to authenticity. I'm here solely because I hoped you'd sense this flimsy facade as clearly as I do."

"Then let's forget our worries and immerse ourselves in the night," I suggested. "What better way to analyze the flimsy facade? Let's join the others around Aristotle."

Goya paused momentarily, his mood lightening, then shrugged. "Very well. Let us indulge ourselves."

We found a place among the others, and Goya leaned in quietly. "Alexander's philosopher pales in comparison to Diogenes. His valiant refusal to bow to society, all in the pursuit of ultimate honesty, is truly a man deserving of admiration."

"Diogenes, you say?" I snickered, noting several similarities between the Cynic and Goya's confrontational spirit. "It seems that the missing prologue has revealed itself."

Goya's demeanor underwent a remarkable shift; his posture straightened, and a sly grin crept across his face as if he had been seen for the first time. He seemed to relish the thought of being understood. However, as Aristotle's rhetoric continued, Goya's newfound confidence seemed to wither with each word.

"Nature," Plato's prodigy said, "distinguishes between the bodies of freemen and slaves, making the one strong for servile labor, the other upright, and although useless for such services, useful for political life in the arts both of war and peace."

Most guests nodded in agreement, intently following each word and gesture. Meanwhile, Goya's frustrated growl was barely audible. "And there it is, Brother: the very reason we can never simply 'forget our worries and immerse ourselves in the night' amongst these people. They take great care to ensure we're always reminded of our station. I'm stepping outside to enjoy the Acropolis' one legitimate advantage—fresh mountain air."

I began to follow him, but he firmly grasped my shoulder. "No, Brother. Stay. Observe. Listen to Aristotle's reproduction. I won't be long."

I reluctantly agreed, planning to do as he suggested, but as Goya walked out, I noticed that George had also left the circle. Standing alone at the fireplace, he removed his mask and studied the painting above it. Suddenly, the symposium held little appeal. Choosing George over Aristotle, I quietly joined in his moment of reverie beneath the canvas.

"The last of his kind as well," George murmured.

Somewhat stunned, I said, "You've never struck me as an art lover."

"I appreciate art, but a lover of it, I am not," he replied, the reflection of "Washington Crossing the Delaware" in his eyes. "However, there's more here than mere art for Dorian's pontification. This isn't the original, of course, but it's history incarnate, a frozen portrayal of sacrifice and determination. The ice-choked river, the weary faces, and the way Washington stands tall when everything from the elements to the element of surprise threatened to sink him—it's all a testament to the value of freedom and an intimate look at its cost."

"Freedom and its cost," I repeated, hoping to add further insight to the conversation but failing. "But what is freedom, really, George? Everyone claims to have it, yet the more I see, the more I understand that we may not all share it equally."

"Not everyone claims to have it," he said, tapping a finger to his temple. "A man becomes truly free when he's no longer impressed by the government's list of his freedoms."

I gestured toward the painting and noted that the freedoms for which Washington fought weren't a realistic aspiration in light of The Solemn Veil and ensuing global circumstances. In the end, I concluded that, perhaps, freedom was just a subjective measure.

George grimaced painfully at my deduction. "An ignorance of freedom's meaning doesn't imbue it with subjectivity, Slevin. The world is but an hourglass," he explained, making the shape with his hands. "The top globe is men of virtue, and the bottom is tyranny. The sand that flows between them? That's freedom." He pinched his fingers, contemptuously adding, "And the freedom-siphoning throat between man and tyranny is government."

Clasping his hands behind his back, George stretched out his shoulders. "History itself is nothing more than the cyclical battle between the powerful's tyranny and the individual's liberty. At some point, virtuous men will brave the icy waters of uncertainty to secure their freedom, and when they succeed, the hourglass is flipped in our favor. But gravity is a strong force indeed, and we have yet to find a way to choke the throat of government. Whether we perceive it or not, Slevin, the sand always falls."

Returning his focus to General Washington, George shook his head. "I have this same piece at my estate. Although it's identical in every perceptible way—a perfect reproduction, matched stroke for stroke by the original painter Emanuel Leutze himself—it still doesn't speak to me quite like this one does. In total, I've had eight, maybe nine, commissioned. Still, none properly capture the scene's essence, so they're all stacked in my basement."

He flung his hand in an exasperated motion. "Ironic, isn't it? The original artist can't even create what I desire the most: this reproduction. Were Dorian and I not friends," he quipped half-jokingly, "I might have switched this one out long ago. The rascal takes exceptional delight in keeping it from me. Leonardo da Vinci's 'The Last Supper' once hung here, and this," he said, pointing to a dark corner of the salon, "hung there. Every time I visited, I'd examine it and compliment the work. A couple of years ago, he switched the paintings to get a rise out of me. Succeeding, he never switched them back. Typical Dorian."

"Typical Dorian," I laughed.

"So," George continued, "with each failed reproduction, he grins from ear to ear, claiming to know the secret but refuses to tell me. 'The only way to genuinely appreciate the work,' says he, 'is to discover for yourself what distinguishes mine from yours. Your ability to do so is what makes you human.'"

With another deep sigh, he offered a final thought on the matter. "In a world brimming with imitations and copies, even a replica can stand tall as a symbol of authenticity. Do you understand what I mean?"

"I think so," I murmured, "but the world is complicated. Life is complicated."

George's stoic smile faintly appeared. "If I could offer any advice, Slevin, it would be that life is only as complicated as you allow it to be."

As soon as George had uttered those words, Dorian stepped in, grabbed our shoulders, and pulled us toward him in a half-hug. "Slevin! George!" he shouted with lingering wine on his breath. "Do the both of you realize that you were in the midst of a proper conversation?" Dorian grinned, waving his finger. "Careful, Georgie, your date might grow jealous when she learns you're not a mute."

"Enough!" George warned. "You know I hate that."

"Proper conversation?" Dorian replied sarcastically. "Oh yes, I'm well aware of your disdain for the spoken word."

George maintained his piercing stare, refusing to say anything else. Meanwhile, Dorian let out a warm chuckle. "Ah, first Marie, now you."

"Or perhaps it's you," George retorted, causing Dorian to lift his hands in surrender.

"Easy, Georgie," Dorian goaded in a higher-pitched voice. "Slevin, would you believe I'm the only one who's ever called him Georgie without getting knocked unconscious?"

In disbelief, I searched George's expression to find the truth, and he met my glance with an unapologetic shrug that all but confirmed the claim.

"Yes," Dorian said. "When we were children, Georgie here had quite the temper. Being the only George in school and a late bloomer to boot, he was bullied more than others. They called him Georgie because he was so small and cute." Reaching for George's face, Dorian squeaked in a childlike manner. "He just made you want to pinch his little cheeks."

George pulled away, and his glare intensified, motivating the Sun King to move the story along. "Anyway," Dorian sighed, disappointed that his fun was over, "George exercised patience and hit a growth spurt, eventually embarking on what one might refer to as a 'revenge tour.' No one's called him Georgie since. Except for me, of course."

Thinking there had to be more to the story, I eagerly blurted out, "Then how do you manage to get away with it?"

Dorian smiled broadly, patting George's shoulder. "I've never been one to shy away from good-natured ribbing, and George was no exception. A good eight inches shorter than me at the time, he was an easy target. During his revenge tour, I found myself in his crosshairs. But as you know, I'm much too charming for violence. Not only did I calm him down, but I also made him my friend. We've shared that bond ever since."

Dorian leveled his hand above George's head. "Now look at him. The brute has five or six inches and 100 pounds on me. It's my duty to remind him that, underneath his stoic exterior, a ravenous rebel desires escape."

Dorian's exuberance waned, his perpetual grin flattened, and he implored my undivided attention. "Slevin, this is important: a man can never completely abandon the ferocious beast within him. On the contrary, he must nourish it and prepare it for battle until such a day that this restless dragon is needed. Then, and only then, he is duty-bound to unleash its hell-breathing fury upon his enemies, for the world is made peaceful by such men."

With a short, though forceful exhale, as if he was happy to have disposed of this unwanted moment of seriousness, Dorian's characteristic demeanor returned. "In other words, I'm feeding the dragon until we require his ferocity."

George gestured toward the painting. "Or perhaps you've underestimated my patience, and the revenge tour hasn't yet concluded?"

Dorian grinned excitedly and shrugged. "Or maybe, George, I simply enjoy your company." Grabbing us by the shoulder again, he pulled us in tightly. "Now, come with me, gentlemen. Dinner awaits."

Chapter Nine

THE FEAST

"Regrettably, we tend to interpret our successes like dissipating rain from the dark clouds of an April thunderstorm—a time for relief rather than preparation." - Dorian's Notes

As Aristotle's discourse faded into echoes, Dorian stood before a set of royal oak doors inlaid with Ancient Grecian scenes—Olympian gods towering over men, their eyes alight with otherworldly mischief. "Ladies and gentlemen," he announced, "Let us elevate this symposium to Dionysian heights! The feast awaits!"

The heavy doors swung open behind the host, exhibiting the magnificent, temple-sized dining hall. Torch-lit fluted columns lined the dark walls, spawning shadow warriors who battled on the mosaic floor. The center of the room was dominated by a Herculean ebony table with the paws of Cerberus. Golden patterns and detailed carvings swirled from end to end, forming a captivating and cohesive Homeric epic. Above it all, an expansive, elaborate chandelier emulated the sparkling jewels of Nyx's sky.

The first to enter, Dorian's hand floated above the chairs as he approached the head of the table and whimsically invited the guests to overindulge. "If a single mind leaves my estate unclouded or the solitary stomach leaves this room unfilled, the night will have been an utter failure. Please," he bowed, "find your seats and enjoy."

Golden cursive lettering on parchment cards sat atop elaborate place settings, indicating our reserved seats. Warmly lit by flickering candles, baskets of bread and platters of hors d'oeuvres rested in the middle of the table, surrounded by a robust selection of French wines, Champagnes, and cognacs.

As with every social gathering in Athens, the head of the table was set and held for the Benefactor. George sat in the corner nearest the Benefactor's place setting. His date sat to his right, followed by Marie, Dorian, and at least twenty-five other guests. Goya, who had seamlessly rejoined the gathering, was now on my right in the corner opposite George. To my left, another twenty-five or more guests found their seats, all quickly delving into idle conversation as we awaited the first course.

Seizing the moment, Dorian stood and thanked everyone for their attendance, promising that the best was yet to come. The guests roared in approval, remaining loud afterward, sometimes making it difficult to distinguish voices across the table. Coupled with the clatter of plates, the clinking of glasses, and the almost overwhelming smell of alcohol in the air, the dining hall was borderline unruly. However, none of that thwarted Dorian's attempt to speak with Goya.

"Goya, my elusive friend," he cried out over the others. "We've never properly met, but part of tonight's purpose is to amend that. Let's dissolve any tensions with good company and better wine," the young philosopher said, raising his filled glass. "You've met George, I believe? Seated beside him is the beguiling Julia, Marie's twin sister, and, of course, this is Marie," he said, gesturing to the pink belle.

Although her physical appearance closely mirrored her sister's, it was clear Julia didn't possess the same ineffable charm or grace. She was already drunk and loud, waving her hands wildly when she spoke. The alcohol slurred her speech, and she had spilled enough wine on her pastel blue dress to make one assume it was patterned in purple.

"A pleasure, Goya," she said, smiling politely. "And you as well, Slevin. I'd love to know your impressions of the Acropolis thus far."

I reciprocated the courtesy, acknowledging that the Acropolis was an architectural wonder of our time. As Julia turned her attention to Goya, awaiting his answer, I braced myself, fully expecting him to rebel against the spotlight and launch into some condescending tirade.

To my surprise, Goya smiled broadly, lifting his glass. "Madame, Brother Slevin is correct. The Acropolis is nothing short of a wonder. Its streets serve as luminous avenues of culture, and its populace offers a remarkable tapestry of characters. A true symposium of the modern era, echoed by tonight's festivities in our gracious host's estate."

Goya took his praise a step further and toasted, "To you, Marie, George, our most generous host, and everyone else: my gratitude is boundless. I can only aspire to one day repay you all in the manner you so richly deserve. À votre santé!"

We all raised our glasses in kind and saluted. Dorian glanced my way as if I was responsible for this change in character and nodded approvingly. "À votre santé, Goya."

Still coming to terms with this new Goya, Dorian removed his mask. "My, you are full of surprises, aren't you? I must say, your demeanor does lend credence to Slevin's assessment. Perhaps you've been misunderstood all along, and for that, I extend my apologies." He then stood, lifting his glass higher and capturing the room's attention. "To new friends!" he exclaimed.

The assembly likewise raised their glasses. "To new friends!" we chorused.

The evening unfolded with a depth that was as unexpected as it was enlightening. Yet it was Goya's newfound congeniality that nearly left me speechless. I leaned in and lightheartedly whispered, "Where's the Cynic gone? Has he returned to the barrel?"

"Brother Slevin," Goya chided gently, "if nothing else, this ridiculous masquerade should have taught you that one must sometimes don a handsome mask in order to please a shallow crowd."

Taking a long sip of cognac, the scent of maple syrup and cocoa practically bursting from the curvy glass, Goya swept his hand toward the other guests, pointing out that no one paid any attention to us whatsoever. "An easy yet effective transition from the spotlight to the shadows, was it not?"

Having caught something out of the corner of his eye, a palpable sense of urgency overcame him. "That's inconsequential now. It's time to prepare, Brother Slevin. I fear that your night is about to take a severe turn. I discovered a worrisome truth outside. It only confirmed a long-held suspicion. I've grappled with it and accepted its implications. When those doors swing open," he pointed at a second doorway near the table's head, "the Guardians will continue their night as if nothing has happened. For you and me, it will be a stark reminder of our place in their society. I want you to be strong, Brother Slevin. Don't let them see how it affects you. We are not simply swimming in unfamiliar waters; we're out of our depth and surrounded by scalpel-toothed sharks."

My smirk evaporated, replaced by uneasy confusion as I slumped back in my seat. Why couldn't I enjoy the moment? It wasn't fair that danger seemingly lurked around every corner. I had no clue what to expect, but the grave tone of his voice suggested an undercurrent of reality that I might not be prepared to handle.

Instead of sympathy, Goya offered resolve. "Truth unwanted is often the dish most needed. Tonight, Brother Slevin, we feast upon a veritable mountain of truth."

Moments later, the doors creaked open, and the room fell silent. A procession of servants surged from the doorway, marching in perfect alignment and rhythm, each balancing a covered silver platter. They surrounded us, one servant per guest, and set down the first course.

No, the platter didn't conceal some disgusting or disturbing sight that made me squirm in my seat; it was merely soup. In fact, once I "recovered" from the event's initial trauma, the soup proved to be quite delicious, though difficult to swallow.

It was the servants' appearance that affected me so dramatically. The Humanara were clad in drab, though very familiar, formal social uniforms —gray coat, shirt, tie, and slacks, all cinched with a gray belt and anchored by gray shoes. I found myself attacked by an army of mirrors, reflecting not just society's condemnation but their own.

Goya was right. No one else at the table took notice or cared; we were miniature afterthoughts below even the gaze of a Guardian. Our brothers and sisters, though, had no trouble placing us firmly within their scornful glare. Resentment flitted across their faces as they navigated the room, seeing two of their own at the head of the table.

"Playing house, are we?" one sneered under his breath.

"Look at them," a familiar face murmured. "And I thought the humans looked ridiculous tonight."

Nearly every night for three months, I had seen that face on Brooks' workstation and heard his thoughts on what she might be doing at any given moment. Never would he have imagined this for his daughter. As Rhea disappeared, a lowly, disgruntled servant, so too vanished another man's blissful dreams. Although I was shaken, my initial thoughts were with Brooks. What would I say to him? How could I tell him? Would he even believe me? My head felt like it was going to explode.

Altogether, it was a moment of merciless clarity. I had never felt so small, so misplaced. I gripped the arms of my chair tightly as it seemed to swell around me. My only wish was to leave, motivated by the gnawing, cruel pull of tears that threatened their own escape. Indeed, it was a feast of truth, complete with a hearty side of humiliation.

However, the cloudy moment was not without its silver lining. I detected concern—perhaps even compassion—in George's glances. The man of typically few words spoke volumes in silence. His introspective reflections beneath "Washington Crossing the Delaware" seemed all the more poignant. It solidified a conclusion of mine, one that never wavered from that day forward: George was indeed the last of his kind.

I felt as though reality had suddenly jerked down the thick, heavy curtain of pretense between it and me, laughing with a knowing shrug as I lay prostrate before it. The roles had been reversed, and I, beneath the silver platter's cover, was about to be exposed to the voracious appetites of the assembled guests.

I wanted to lash out, yet who was I to blame? The wrong reaction could have devastating consequences. Was it intentional? Surely not. Again, Dorian wouldn't have wanted me to feel this way, would he? At the same time, if a servant's life or that of some reconstituted luminary was my future on the Acropolis, how else would he have expected me to feel?

I didn't want to overthink it. "There has to be a good explanation," I assumed. Peeking over at Goya, half-expecting him to be brooding over this indignity, he appeared rather delighted, frenetically nodding and smiling between noisy slurps of soup.

With a brisk head shake, I flipped my palms up, confused by, well, everything. But as strange as it might sound, this dream-like, incredibly ridiculous caricature of a scene somehow made the "feast of truth" easier to digest.

A cursory glance around the room proved that, besides George, I must have been the only one who wasn't enjoying himself. I didn't have to stay miserable. I had the rest of a very long life to pick tonight apart. Why not try to push those thoughts aside and enjoy myself as I had encouraged Goya to do?

My father once said, "The only way to thoroughly enjoy the present is to lose all sight of the past and fully disregard the future." This advice helped me through the masquerade ball, but it was much later in life before I understood what he really meant by that quote.

Slowly and resolutely, I picked up a spoon, which I couldn't help but appreciate for its artisanship, and took some soup. Then, I snatched a bottle of Bordeaux by the neck and poured my glass to the brim, not the least bit concerned with proper etiquette.

All of this was gleefully observed by Goya, whose smile I didn't think could grow any wider. "Drink up, Brother," he urged. "Just because the masks have been removed doesn't mean the masquerade is over."

Across the table, and though he had armed himself with a spoon several times, Dorian hadn't touched his soup. He was like a mischievous cat in a room full of dangling yarn, upset that he could only swat one strand at a time. Restless as he was, Dorian's focus sharpened at the sight of an empty bread basket.

"Oh, Valet," he called out, lifting the basket above his head. "Marie here needs more bread. Would you kindly?"

A servant rushed to Dorian's side and took the basket. Before scampering away, Dorian whispered something into his ear. The valet nodded and, moments later, returned empty-handed. "My apologies, Madame la Princesse," he said with a heavy heart, "but we have run out of bread."

Theatrical as always, Dorian jumped from his seat and spread his arms. "Then let her eat cake!" he exclaimed.

The guests roared in laughter, coaxing smiles from George, myself, and even Marie. "Have you had your fun now?" she asked, rolling her eyes in a way that only she could.

"Ma chère," Dorian purred, "fun, much like a lady, can never be had, only chased. As you well know, I do quite love a game of cat and mouse."

Marie's cheeks flushed, yet her eyes locked with Dorian's as she amorously raised a wine glass to her lips. With a slow, deliberate sip, she savored the inky red liquid and dripping tension equally. Gazing deeply into Dorian's eyes as if no one else existed, she softly bit her bottom lip. She, too, loved a game of cat and mouse.

The empty-handed servant stretched out his neck, viewing the remnants of the first course, then leaned into the kitchen. "Bring the palate cleanser!" he ordered curtly.

While the servants handed out a variety of sweet and dry Champagne sorbets, Goya spoke with remarkable nonchalance. "They toy with us, Brother. They only love the game because they think they're the cat."

"For good reason," I replied. "They're always the cat."

Goya's smile took on a sly, roguish quality. "Perhaps. But Brother Slevin, you assume we're the mouse. Maybe," he mused, baring his teeth as his voice dropped to a conspiratorial whisper, "maybe we're the hounds who have yet to be unleashed."

Aristotle rose from a silk couch on the other side of the room and circled the table. He seemed to enjoy his work, questioning the guests and then enthusiastically listening to their responses. Soon, all other conversations stalled, and the entire table was engaged in a deep philosophical exploration that continued over the following two courses.

Eventually, the Sage's peripatetic method left him orating from his own work, "Politics," at the head of the table. "In a true kingship, the ruler's highest aim is the welfare of his subjects, leading not by force, but by virtue and wisdom. It is not kingship to rule over unwilling subjects; neither is it kingship to rule over those who have been bought and who are slaves by nature; the ruler over such persons is a despot, not a king. A tyrant seeks only his own benefit, ruling with an iron fist, treating free men as though they were slaves, and turning the state into a personal possession rather than a commonwealth. Such a rule, based not on the good of the governed but on the ruler's whim, is the very antithesis of true kingship."

Glassy-eyed, Julia's initial snicker turned into exuberant laughter as Aristotle finished the quote. "My goodness," she cried out, a white-gloved hand on her chest. Kings and tyrants? Slavery? Could you all imagine such a life? We've shattered these antiquated notions. The world is filled with endless possibilities."

For the first time since Goya's foray outdoors, the satisfaction drained from his face, and his jaw clenched. Maintaining his composure, he calmly asked, "And what of the Humanara, Madame? Is tyranny an antiquated notion for us?"

He forced a broken smile to soften his protest, adding, "While a steady diet of Mount Parnassus air is no doubt intoxicating, I'm afraid my sober eyes have yet to find these endless possibilities lurking behind district walls."

Julia didn't take offense. However, she did place the blame elsewhere. "Then it's your own doing, isn't it? Your kind outnumber the Fathers nearly two-to-one in each district. You have a greater voice, overpower the assemblies, and shape policy. You have representatives and rights, and district laws are passed for your benefit. If anything, it's you who oppress the Fathers."

Goya's eyes seemed to reflect the blazing light of every torch in the room. Still, he held his composure. "You're right, Madame," he mockingly agreed as if she had proposed some novel concept. "I suppose we must engineer an escape from a tyranny of our own making."

"You see?" she replied. "Even the thought of tyranny is laughable. My dear Goya, how can tyranny exist without so much as a single tyrant? Our Benefactor has given you everything. You need only accept it graciously, and you'll realize how free you are."

Smirking, Goya spoke slowly for emphasis. "Right yet again, Madame. I need only open my eyes." Holding back sarcastic laughter, he lifted his drink and, much to Julia's delight, concluded, "Monsieur George, this one's a keeper."

George paid no attention to the subtle insult, lifting his eyes from the depths of his wine glass long enough to flash Julia a disapproving glance. Tilting the glass up, he gulped down the remaining Bordeaux. In a swift motion, he thumped down the upended goblet like he had captured a fleeing mouse on the table.

While there was no scurrying mammal inside the now-empty globe, the stoic had managed to snare a wadded white dinner napkin. His gaze fell upon it like the crimson droplets that had managed to escape his last gulp and soil the beautifully gold-embroidered linen. Visibly disgusted, he grabbed another clean glass from the table and set it upright on top of the first.

"I do believe," he mumbled to himself, "that the top globe is empty."

Julia tapped George on the arm and giggled softly. "I do believe, George, that you've had too much wine. You're toying with the glassware!"

"Mmm. Maybe," he said, maintaining a courteous tone. "But as we drink to the defeat of tyranny, let us remember that we aren't the first to sip from that self-congratulatory bottle. The red elixir of complacency and blind faith in authority are often bitter vintages raised from evil's own cellar."

In shock, Julia clutched his arm with both hands. "George, have you gone mad? What are you going on about?"

Dorian, who had been whispering with another guest, heard Julia's comment and pounced. "What glory resides in madness, Julia! The madman turns his back on a forced reality that no longer appeals to him, opting instead for one more in tune with his desires. Is this not the very essence of art?"

"It's the essence of drunkenness and depravity," Julia chuckled, landing a cheerful, though unwelcome, hand on George's shoulder.

Dorian winced and turned to Marie, trying to change the subject. "I often wonder if art serves as humanity's outlet for depravity without indulging in it outright. If one could engage in every vice without consequence, would art become altogether obsolete? What say you, my sultry belle?"

Reading the room, Marie opted for pragmatism. "I say you should leave the philosophy to Aristotle—at least for tonight. Your intellect has become far too lubricated, and our stomachs are much too empty. The main course would be a most welcome distraction. After all, before a woman can concern herself with art, depravity, or tyranny, she must be certain of her next meal."

"Bah!" Dorian howled. "Certainty is such a bore! It's the thief of wonder! It is our intellect—be it lubricated or otherwise—and our unquenchable curiosity that imbues existence with its fascination!" Dorian sighed, then added, "But alas, you're right, Marie."

"Valet," he waved, "bring out the main course."

The servants did as commanded, bringing out filet mignon, sautéed vegetables, truffled mashed potatoes, and several other side dishes. Meanwhile, Aristotle gently cleared his throat, drawing the guests' attention. "It is intriguing," he began, measured and reflective, "to hear of tyranny's end and the dawn of new possibilities. In my time, I, too, witnessed a young man's rise to prominence. My student, Alexander, aspired to reshape the world. His ambition was boundless, and his conquests vast, yet the true measure of his reign was not solely in the lands he conquered, but in the legacy he left behind."

He paused, moving to the head of the table, where the servants had left a hearty serving of the main course for the Benefactor. Aristotle placed both hands on the empty chair's back and drew further parallels between the two men. "Alexander sought to unite cultures and knowledge, to create a world unlike any before," he explained. "However, greatness in leadership is not merely in conquest or the breaking of chains but in the wisdom to govern justly and the vision to see beyond one's own reign. That's why our Benefactor is the greatest man to have ever lived, greater than Alexander himself."

The room erupted in applause and cheers. While I had expected Goya's clapping to be merely superficial, and it was, I didn't anticipate similar reactions from George and Dorian. Our host went through the motions slowly and quietly. George never diverted his stare from the makeshift hourglass atop a scarlet-stained napkin.

I must have become too comfortable with this new version of Goya and intended to playfully goad him like Dorian might have provoked George. Recalling his comment about Alexander on my first day at The Academy, I whispered, "Caesar's inferior."

Unintentionally, the remark seemed to pierce through the facade Goya had meticulously crafted throughout dinner. His carefully maintained smile faltered, then vanished, giving way to a more authentic, albeit darker expression. I suppose he had gotten so caught up in trying to draw out the Guardians' hypocrisy that my quip, lighthearted as it was, yanked him back to an intolerable reality.

Addressing Aristotle directly, Goya's tone turned malignant. "Don't you mean Caesar, Philosopher?"

Taken aback by Goya's abrupt challenge, Aristotle returned a curious look. "I beg your pardon, Brother," he stuttered, almost breaking character. "I don't know what to say."

"What you meant to say," Goya scowled villainously, "is that Caesar was the greatest man to have ever lived. Greater than Alexander and infinitely greater than your beloved Benefactor."

Gasps echoed across the dining hall as everyone stared at the Benefactor's empty chair. Goya observed the astonished visitors with a deepening animosity as their gaping mouths went silent, and they seemed to beckon the Benefactor's presence.

Sickened by the display, my troubled friend's pierced facade then shattered entirely, revealing the raw, unfiltered essence of the man beneath. "You exalt the end of tyranny," he proudly mocked, staring down the likes of Julia and the others, "but you're too oblivious to see you're in love with it. Aristotle's pupil? Your little Frenchman Napoleon? The almighty Benefactor? Tyrants!" he exclaimed. "But you cheer them on anyway, declaring them great men!"

George snapped out of whatever trance had bewitched him and fixated on Goya. At the same time, the stoic's hand returned to his glass creation and gripped it firmly by the throat. Stern, though polite considering the circumstances, George raised his voice to a level I had never heard. "And what of your tyrant who chose himself over the Republic?"

Practically growling, Goya retorted, "You mean the military genius who crossed the Rubicon as a liberator?"

Not yet content with his defense, a hateful snarl clawed its way across Goya's face. He gestured broadly, presenting his surroundings as irrefutable evidence, and pointed out, "Caesar didn't cross the Rubicon for himself. He wanted to save Rome from this!"

Snatching his glass from the table, Goya picked up the nearest bottle of cognac and wildly poured himself another drink. "To brand this liberator as a mere tyrant," he shook his head in resentment, "is to achieve the heights of ignorance, surpassed only by that of the Acropolis."

Goya's expression lit up with an idea, and a vicious smirk replaced his snarl. He put his filled glass on the table, instead opting for several extended gulps directly from the bottle before slamming it back down. He dared someone, anyone, to challenge him—intellectually or otherwise.

With unflinching diplomacy, George replied, "No, Goya, Caesar was a genocidal conqueror, no different from the others you listed. The greatest men to have ever lived were those who demanded freedom and, when denied, took the necessary steps to secure it."

"Gentlemen!" Marie hurriedly interjected, more concerned with George divulging any other opinions than Goya's outburst. "Perhaps you can revisit this later and in a more intimate setting?"

Dorian placed his hand on Marie's to reassure her, intent on letting the discussion play out. "Goya, my friend, I'm unsure whether you're the match or the powder keg; I only know that something is ready to explode. Please," he said, flicking his eyebrows with excitement, "say what's on your mind. The floor is yours."

And explode, he did. With a sudden flourish, Goya surged to his feet, throwing his chair backward. "Then the die is cast!" he cried out.

A trio of surprised servants rushed to Goya's side and attempted to restrain him but were stopped. "Wait," Dorian commanded. "Allow our impassioned friend to continue. What is the worth of speech if it only echoes another's thoughts?"

The Humanara complied, stepping away. Goya glanced over each shoulder, brushed himself off, and continued. "Yes, Dorian, it's my duty to cure this arrogant display of armchair philosophy with a hefty dose of reality."

Free to unleash his frustration, Goya did so. "Brother Slevin, do you see it now?" he asked, motioning to Aristotle, who had retreated from the table. "This is our future: timid actors in an eternal play, judged only by our performances and not by the content of our character. This isn't

Aristotle! He's a fraud who wouldn't be recognized by his own brothers. I attend The Academy out of spite, hoping to save a few of us from this charade, but I do not," he paused, boiling with rage. "No, I will not bow to these preening, sanctimonious humans. I'd rather toil as a slave in the sewers of Los Angeles than endure another second on this mountain, subject to their hollow speeches about a freedom they can't begin to understand."

"A slave?" Julia sneered, bravely dipping her toes into the heated waters. "Haven't we already dispelled that myth? Your outburst is inappropriate and out of place, Sir. Compose yourself and reclaim your seat."

"Brother Slevin, the Madame here, denies the existence of slavery and, in the same breath, commands me to sit like her pet hound," Goya snickered. "Tell me, Julia, do you hear my chains rattling, or has the clank of your fine silverware drowned them out?"

Flustered and now livid, Julia shouted, "I see no shackles! You share our table and our meal tonight, yet have the nerve to call yourself a slave! Is this how you appreciate one of the highest honors your kind can receive?"

Letting out a diabolical laugh, the cynic sank his teeth into her reply. "My kind, you say? And uttered for a second time, no less? If I were free, my dear Julia, there would be no such distinction between us."

Goya stepped behind the Benefactor's chair and clutched its back with both hands, issuing a provocative challenge. "So I ask then, with this empty chair as my witness, would you release your pet hound from the societal chains that enslave him?"

"You wouldn't be here if not for us!" Julia exploded condescendingly. "We've given you a voice and a place in our society. Is that not enough? It's clear that you're nothing more than an anarchist who doesn't like being a part of society." Balling her fists and twisting them under her eyes, she taunted, "Boo hoo, grow up, Humanara! No one likes a whimpering hound." Unable to restrain herself, Julia's face burned with anger, and she leaped from her seat, pointing at her provocateur. "Would I release you?" she screamed. "No! And why should I? So you can terrorize the neighborhood and bite the children? You'd never again do as you're told!"

The words had barely passed her lips, and she stopped, clamping both hands over her mouth. The room was again silent, though Goya's triumphant smile almost sang an Olympian hymn. He couldn't have asked for a better reaction.

Spreading his arms wide and looking from one side of the room to the other, Goya turned back to me. "Behold, Brother, the utopia we've built for them! Our labor, not theirs, erected this paradise. Our reward? To draw their baths and cook their dinners! The epitome of equality, no?"

Julia attempted to respond, then looked down in shame. Still reeling from the shock of her own outburst, she couldn't articulate her thoughts. As strange as it might sound, she had shown genuine and raw emotions—an authentic version of herself—and I think Goya respected that about her.

"Don't fret, Mademoiselle," he said, a hint of soothing in his voice. "Chains dangle from all our necks. I simply possess the ability to see them."

While Dorian appeared thoroughly entertained, George had grown weary of the argument and rose to his feet. The stoic towered over the cynic, and Goya braced himself for a confrontation. He wasn't frightened so much as he was keenly aware that his programming prohibited him from ever harming a human—even in self-defense.

George had no interest in violence. Instead, he extended his hand. Goya's face twisted in uncertainty, accepting George's offer. The men shook hands like opposing, though respectful generals at the end of a long war—reminiscent of Lee and Grant.

Firm and clear, George announced, "Goya, the night has ended for you, my fervent friend. Be safe on your travels home." Then, pulling the wiry rebel near, he whispered, "Your conduct is unbecoming, regardless of the circumstances. If it were within my power, you'd have your freedom this instant. However, I neither bound you nor possess the key to your chains."

I sensed a mutual understanding between the two for a fleeting moment, and Goya's temper quickly dissolved. "George," he sighed heavily, "you're right. I've had my fill of this tiresome chatter and would much appreciate a return to my own people. Besides, I've lost my appetite."

Goya returned to my side and placed his hand on my shoulder. "Brother Slevin, we should talk this weekend."

"Of course," I replied, taking the napkin from my lap and preparing to stand. "I'll follow you out. We can talk on the ride home."

"No, no, no," he repeated, patting my shoulder with each refusal. "This experience is necessary. I wouldn't dare rob you of it."

"Then how?" I asked. "Otherwise, we won't speak until Monday.

With a sneaky grin, Goya winked. "Don't worry, Brother, I have my ways."

One of the servants approached, intent on walking Goya to the door, but the cynic pulled away. "I can find my own way out."

Turning to the party one last time, Goya desperately wanted to take a parting shot. You could see it etched into his face, begging to make itself known. He looked at George, then me, and bit his cheek, choosing to leave without further incident.

The front door slammed shut with a resounding thud that reverberated throughout the estate. A heavy silence fell over the dining hall, and all eyes were on Dorian. The host rose with a grave expression, and the guests seemed to hold their collective breath, awaiting instruction.

Curiously glancing around the room with an ironic frown, the Sun King began to fight back a mischievous grin. "Valet, make a note for next time. Our friend Goya doesn't like filet," he said, bursting into laughter. The other Guardians followed suit, and he urged them to eat before their food went cold.

After a brief sojourn around the table to reinvigorate the guests, Dorian reclaimed his seat, and Marie took his arm affectionately. "Dorian, they say the shunned child, desiring the warmth of a village, will burn it down if he feels it not."

Swirling his wine thoughtfully, Dorian countered. "Ma chère, the village lacking warmth for the child may very well be the kindling in need of a spark. Perhaps Goya is no arsonist but a misunderstood Prometheus."

Marie's grip tightened, her eyes searching his for a moment. "Darling," she murmured, "you speak too candidly. Two blabbering mouths dangle from each attentive ear in this hall."

Chapter Ten

THE LIBRARY

Most see irony in the fact that man spends his entire life searching for immortality, only to find it in the granite marker standing sentinel above his grave. I think the tombstone is symbolic, you know? In the end, all anybody wants to do is say we was here." - Brooks

The night's lustrous veneer I imagined before arrival, then rebuilt at dinner, had just been stripped away for a second time by Goya's exit. Though Dorian offered several reassuring nods while he catered to the crowd, Julia and the others—minus Marie and George—weren't so kind to the lone remaining Humanara at their table.

Initially, their glares were accusatory, as if I were somehow complicit in Goya's outburst. I tried to appear unaffected by them and continue my meal, though I had lost all appetite for it. I would half-heartedly cut into the steak, twirl it in a bit of béarnaise, and then dip the combination in potatoes before chewing on it twice as long as necessary.

As the other courses appeared, and subsequently, more alcohol disappeared, the looks gradually morphed into something more akin to forgetfulness. By then, it was clear that they regarded Goya's volatile departure in much the same manner they viewed Aristotle's symposium— evocative entertainment provided by Humanara actors.

I morbidly wondered, "If I exploded into a million slivers of Slevin this instant, who would clap the loudest? The slack-jawed young man at the end of the table? Who would be the first to forget it had ever happened?"

It surely wouldn't be Julia who, with a feral intensity, often locked eyes with me, quietly intimating, "You don't belong here."

At the table's corner, George's disposition might have been more solemn than my own. He barely spoke for the rest of dinner, staring ahead at the torchlight behind Goya's empty chair. In fact, he'd only break this trance when someone approached and congratulated him on how he handled "the Goya situation." Respectfully nodding, he would shake their hand and then return his attention to the torchlight.

A while later, dinner thankfully ended, and we all returned to the salon. Crystal decanters and fine cigars had been spread throughout the room. Frédéric Chopin also appeared, occupying the grand piano's bench and playing a selection of his Nocturnes.

I found it interesting that Dorian had gone to such lengths with the masquerade's French theme, yet French music was inexplicably absent. Wondering whether it was an oversight or just "typical Dorian," I took a seat at the far end of the room in a dark corner, accompanied by an empty glass and an unlit cigar.

Back home, there was no distinction between human and Humanara. We ate, drank, breathed, felt, lived, and socialized together. I even referred to myself as human. Here, the night's events cruelly exposed an unmistakable line between Guardian and Humanara. I had no doubt that my friendship with George and Dorian was still intact, but a subtle note of pain crept into those relationships. Were they, too, like the guests who had so quickly moved on from Goya's interruption? Would they, too, move on from me the second I acted out in frustration? I gazed into the sparkling crystal, oppressed by such thoughts until my only wish was to forget about this "feast of truth" entirely.

Taking a deep, resolute breath, I released my clenched jaw and fist—neither of which I knew to be so—and dug my eyes from stem and sorrow to look forward. Ahead, magnificently framed but barely recognizable in the dim light, was "The Last Supper." I couldn't hold back the grin tugging at my lips. The artistic reminder of my friends' tête-à-tête was too amusing. "Typical Dorian," I chuckled.

"Typical?" an offended voice rang out from my side. "My dear Slevin, I am many things, but I assure you that typical is not one of them," Dorian quipped playfully. Arching an eyebrow, he picked up and rolled the unlit cigar between his fingers. "Having a great time, are we? You know, a man who possesses an empty glass and an unlit cigar should be so intoxicated that he's forgotten his matches and bottle or so ill that he's comatose."

Thoroughly examining my depressed demeanor, he concluded, "You appear to be neither. When our friend Goya occupied that very seat earlier tonight, you managed to bring him out of a similar state—at least for a while—and now it is my turn to do the same."

Dorian scanned the crowded room as if trying to judge how easily he could sneak away, then presented an opportunity for escape. "What would you think about a change of scenery?"

"I'd think it was a gift from the gods," I said. "Where to?"

I asked the question, but his answer wouldn't have mattered as long as it allowed me to evade the guests and my own thoughts for a while.

Delighted, he eagerly requested that I follow him. "We'll slip through that door," he pointed across the salon, "and soon find ourselves exploring man's abandoned playground."

"An irresistible offer, if I've ever heard one," I thought.

The path was anything but straightforward. Dorian weaved us through the rabble, trying to remain unnoticed. We even slid quietly behind George, who had returned to his study of "Washington Crossing the Delaware." As we made our exit, a wobbly acquaintance managed to stop Dorian. He politely brushed off the young man, promising to speak with him soon, and we crept away to the elegant melody of Nocturne Number Two.

Flaming golden lanterns jutted from the hallway's walls, flickering softly near each ornate doorframe. We turned at the end of one corridor and, at the end of the next, approached a set of barren double doors. No lantern or lavish moldings accompanied the oak slabs. If not for some small perforations of light, the entry would have been completely hidden.

Close by, several pine boards lay carelessly flung to the ground. Their long silver nails, bent like sunflowers in the wind, spangled by the speckled beams from the other side. "Oh, never mind that," Dorian snickered, unlocking the door with an old iron key. "There's a certain magic to barriers, isn't there? Because of their existence, we inevitably wonder what marvels or monstrosities lurk behind them."

He swung open the heavy doors to a pleasantly warm burst of air tinged with leather and burning hickory. "Ultimately," he continued, "each barrier forces us to ask the same profound question: are we locked in or out? I suppose the inquiring mind can make its own freedom or prison from either side," he said with a whimsical note, "but the truth is that no monstrosity exists beyond the barrier; only marvel. The demon, it could be said, is found within the obstruction itself."

He gestured toward the pile of pine and confessed, "But as you can see, I favor a world without them altogether." The Sun King stepped through the dim chamber's threshold and spun around, arms opened wide. "Behold," his voice echoed loudly, "my sanctuary."

Lit only from the roaring fire of the marble centerpiece, Dorian's inner sanctum was no less extravagant than the rest of his estate. Topped with golden capitals, Corinthian columns lined the wall, soaring to a richly detailed entablature and coffered ceiling. Between the columns and from waist to capital, vast shelves were filled with leather-bound imagination.

As grandiose as the library was, however, there were numerous signs of abandonment. The windows to the right had been painted black, spider webs spanned every dark corner, and dust collected on every worn surface.

"The Library of Algernon," Dorian said, rolling his eyes. "These shelves are home to the most significant collection of poetry and fiction in Old America," he claimed, leading me to the fireplace. On a whim, he drifted left and delicately brushed several books' dusty, gilded spines with his fingertips. "Brother Slevin," he began sincerely, "forgive me for appropriating the term, but I consider you a brother in every sense of the word. Within these timeworn pages lies our collective wisdom and folly. In each work, the discerning mind will locate a memorial to two things alone: a primal dread of death and a ceaseless search for love. Curiously, it's death's long shadow that ignites our quest for love, and consequently, love that intensifies our fear of death."

He meandered back to the fireplace and studied the fiery monument to Athena. Her face and owl-topped helmet were carved into the hearth, overseeing the crackling wood, and her spread arms morphed into olive branches that wrapped the bookending columns atop square pilasters.

Sumptuous leather armchairs and side tables rested near each of these columns. The left, though worn, sunken, and faded, was warm and inviting. The right chair hadn't been used in years—covered in dust and somehow colder than its counterpart.

Reaching for a mound of disheveled books by the oft-used seat, he grabbed one—something academic—and tossed it into the fire without a second thought. "Love, my friend, risks obsolescence in a realm where death has become a relic. Brother Slevin, immortality cannot be discovered with endless days. Rather, it's found in the love between two souls that makes each day timeless."

He snatched another book from the pile and flipped through its pages. "I'm told that Algernon and my mother would spend countless hours here, reading, writing, and debating over these works as if they were personally invested in them. Meticulously curated, she built this collection," he said, pointing to the literature, "from nothing—the envy of the Acropolis. She died when I was young, you know?"

He had never spoken of her before, so I assumed that to be the case. I prepared to offer my condolences, but he waved them off before I could begin. "The sentiment is much appreciated, Slevin, but unnecessary. Although I have a deep affection for our unmade memories and lost future, all I know of her is what I've been told." Irritably slamming the book shut, he hurled it into the fire. "Algernon claims that we're close to curing the Solemn Veil Mutation. Regrettably, some of us were simply born a few ticks too soon on the cosmic clock."

"Wait," I interrupted. "Your mother died from the mutation? On the Acropolis? Then that means—"

"Shhhhhh," he whispered, placing a finger in front of his lips. "Now you join Algernon and George in knowing the one secret that can ruin me. Say the word, and I'll be sent to Nashville with you, no longer a Guardian."

Shocked, I stuttered, "I, I'd never—"

"Slevin, I know," he replied. "I wouldn't have mentioned it otherwise. While secrets don't make new friends, they most certainly help retain old ones," he laughed.

Continuing the story, he began to pace. "My mother somehow altered her genetic test and was accepted to the Acropolis, later marrying Algernon. She kept her death sentence hidden for as long as possible. When she fell ill," he pointed toward a cluttered desk in front of the blacked-out windows, "the burden of secrecy shifted to him."

"I hate to interrupt again," I said, "but does that upset you? That your mother gave birth, knowing she would most likely never see you grow up?"

After a moment of thoughtful silence, he warmed his hands near the fire and answered. "Not at all. Without her, Slevin, I wouldn't be here, and I quite enjoy my existence."

"Then," I wondered aloud, "why the friction with your father?"

Dorian stepped away, frowning as he took a stance behind the Professor's desk chair. Suddenly, he lifted the chair by the back and slammed it down. "Because this is where he spent the rest of her life! With immortality by his side, he searched these damned papers for her endless days!"

Swinging his hand wildly across the desk, he knocked a stack of papers into the air. Not yet satisfied, he fished a scientific text from the shelf behind him and slung it at the dusty leather armchair by the fireplace. Finding its target, the book bounced, flopping open near all the others.

He took a deep breath, watching the ensuing cloud of dust settle. "When she died, Algernon's heart forever fled this chamber. As a result, he turned to science and education, and no one's been allowed in here since—not even to clean."

"That explains the wood out front," I said.

He returned to the sitting area and plopped down on the worn leather. The chair seemingly sighed as he sank. "Thus, the pile of knotty pine. Of course, I unlocked a window years ago, but when Algernon blocks the door, I tear it down out of spite."

I glanced around the room for something to cover the adjacent seat but found nothing. Convincing myself that a thick layer of dust would match my formal gray quite well, I draped my coat over the armchair and sat with my friend.

"And the books?" I questioned, gesturing to the burning pages. "Out of spite, as well?"

With a soft head shake, the young philosopher turned to me and replied, "No, more like a silent protest against existential lies."

I didn't really understand what he meant, so I examined the stockpile of texts beside him and probed further. "And where are the existential lies found within memoirs, research papers, and histories?"

He drew out my name slowly as if suggesting I had much to learn. "Slevin, don't you know that non-fiction is every liar's favorite playground?"

We laughed and sat quietly for a few minutes, absorbed in the fire's hypnotic dance. Suddenly, he made an interesting confession. "Slevin, did you know that my life's goal is to become a failed writer who dies long before his work is ever appreciated?"

Chuckling softly, I quipped, "Endless days make for a long wait, my friend."

Dorian nodded expressionless, his eyes still anchored to the flames. "Exactly," he whispered. "And immortality waits for no one."

I tapped my chair's arm several times, trying to think of a witty response, but I couldn't think of anything. Instead, I asked about what he intended to write.

"Why, the truth, of course," he said.

Glancing at him skeptically, I replied, "I thought non-fiction was the liar's playground."

"It is," he smirked. "That's why I'll write fiction. There's no better medium with which to explore the truth."

I ran my fingers through my hair and squeezed my head in feigned anguish. "Dorian, Winston Churchill once referred to Russia as a riddle wrapped in a mystery inside an enigma. I'm beginning to think he was talking about you instead."

His rich laughter echoed throughout the library like the opening notes of Beethoven's Fifth. "Huah ha ha haaah!" he roared, a burden seemingly lifted from his shoulders. "Slevin, everyone knows that an author is only free to write the truth when it's skillfully veiled within the pages of a well-hated novel."

Acknowledging my bewildered expression, he elaborated. "An author is never despised for who he is, only for what he writes, and writing is nothing more than the artistic exploration of an idea. Therefore, I intend to follow every literary whim, unconcerned by its final destination or alignment with my own beliefs. That's where I shall find the truth."

Seized by a thought, Dorian collected a decanter and two glasses from a nearby table. "A drink, Slevin. What madmen have these sorts of conversations without one?" He poured each of us a glass of wine, then sank into the armchair and continued. "Allow me to clarify. An eminent philosopher simply cannot be a beloved author in his time. If he is, that means he's understood, and if he's understood by his peers, well, then he is no philosopher! No, he must be unappreciated so that he has the freedom to pursue the ever-admirable goal of crafting a despicable novel. Only then, may he one day change the world."

In a sense, I understood why he thought being unappreciated was essential. Still, I mentioned that many philosophers were respected and cherished in their own time, most notably the Ancient Greeks and Enlightenment French.

"Bah!" he cried out. "That was when the public yearned for truth. Life is much too easy now, and society has developed a peculiar ability to delude itself. They think the future is devoid of consequence so long as today's actions are well-intentioned. However, writers have an uncanny ability to follow a storyline to its natural conclusion. The Russians—Dostoevsky, Tolstoy, Chekhov, Turgenev—clearly foresaw the descent of their motherland into the abyss of nihilism. Not far behind, Nietzsche, Mann, Rilke, and Kafka echoed a similar fate for Europe."

Wagging his forefinger for emphasis, Dorian concluded, "When an author dares to lay an unsettling truth in society's lap, a reservoir of quiet hatred fills behind a dam of self-loathing until it eventually spills over, branding the author a heretic; his work an abomination."

He swept his forefinger around, morphing it into a clenched fist like he had snatched an invisible treasure from the air. "And therein lies the artistry of authorship. Where they are taught hatred, I recognize a complex and vital work of art. I will, therefore, take great delight in penning the world's most reviled masterpiece."

Pausing, he stared at his fist, then released his fingers one at a time as if the treasure had evaporated. "I'll write of a gnarled, sun-scorched tree, and none shall see in its withered form the death rattle of Plato's Republic."

I lifted my glass to Dorian's unguarded admission and nodded. "To a most vilified and castigated novel," I toasted. "May it someday change the world."

He leaned forward with a modest bow, tapping his glass to mine. "To infamy, my friend. May our shadows forever dance in the firelight of misunderstood genius."

We allowed the hearth's flaming magician to silence us for a while, our deep contemplation only broken by sporadic sips of wine until there was nothing in either glass to sip.

With the fire losing its ferocity and thus breaking our hypnosis, Dorian fetched two hickory logs from a shadowed rack. "I had the Valet get this started earlier," he grunted, tossing the wood into the fire. "But I suppose the distinction between an inherited fire and a personally ignited one matters not; they both require equal tending, don't they?"

Tilting his head, he smiled at the sight of something in the shadows. Darting across the chamber, he brought back a sizable covered painting. "Care to discuss another work of art?" he asked enthusiastically.

"By all means," I replied, welcoming the opportunity.

He placed the canvas atop the mantle and pulled back the veil with a grand gesture. "Cronus Devouring His Son," he announced, plunging back into his armchair.

Whereas every other painting at the estate had unique, intricate frames worthy of their own discussion, this one was nothing more than canvas and wood. Perhaps Dorian considered it a work in need of no appendix. The olive-skinned Cronus dominated a blackened background, contorted in anguish. His mane of gray hair coiled around his head like serpents. His mouth was awash in crimson gore, tearing his son limb from limb.

"A gruesome scene, no?" Dorian observed. "Slevin, what do you see in the Titan's eyes? Anger? Madness?"

I studied the painting for a moment, confessing that I wasn't well-versed in the nuances of art. I further admitted that my analysis might fall emotionally short of describing anything more than the literal elements on display.

With an understanding nod, Dorian offered me his seat. "Here, sit in my mother's old chair. I used to spend hour after hour inspecting the work, wishing to learn its secrets. Sit, sit. Tell me what you see."

I sat in the comfortable, warm chair while he paced behind me. However, the change of perspective did nothing to change my impression of the work. He picked up on this and carried on without awaiting my response.

"Cronus' eyes," he began, "are not those maddened by bloodlust. No, what you see is a Titan paralyzed by primal fear. As you know, Cronus battled a prophecy that stated his offspring would one day usurp him, as he had done to his father. To thwart this, he devoured each of his children as they emerged from the womb. Yet, upon his sixth child, he was deceived. Zeus evaded this grim fate and eventually dethroned his father, just as foretold."

Still pacing, Dorian continued. "I've often found myself pondering: was it his foreknowledge of this fate that inadvertently sealed it? Had he been ignorant of the prophecy and possessed wisdom equal to his power, would equal justice have prevailed? Had he nurtured his children instead of consuming them in his paranoia, would he have continued his reign uninterrupted?" Shaking his head, he concluded, "Ah, but I stray beyond the limits of oil and canvas, don't I?"

Stopping behind the other chair, he fell silent, hoping his meaning had the desired effect. "I think," I said, gesturing to the dusty seat, "it's more palatable for society to believe in madness over premeditation. Then, much like Bulgakov's Procurator, it believes it has the freedom to wash its hands of brutality, only to learn the grisly truth later."

Dorian's eyes bulged, and his face lit up at my response. "Yes!" he exclaimed as if he had never made the connection. "And it is likewise left to the novelist to decide whether or not society should be freed from the consequences of its own actions." He paused, nodding slowly while he refilled our glasses, and I returned to my seat. "Brother Slevin, with such commentary, you might well push George down a peg on my list of best friends," he laughed.

Perhaps this thought about friendship caused him to take on a more serious tone. "Getting to the point, Slevin, not all of us were nurtured in the arms of benevolent parents. Some of us were devoured and harbor resentments stemming from our time under the oppressive tyranny of our fathers. Having said that, I would never attempt to dictate friendships; after all, a man's friends are the best measure of his own character. However, it's my duty as your friend and brother to remind you that the easiest way to make an enemy is by choosing a good friend poorly."

"Regrettably," I replied, "poor choices of good friends seem to be found only in retrospect."

A single corner of his lip withdrew, and his cheek tightened around the coming revelation. "Although I invited you tonight intending to strengthen our friendship, I had an ulterior motive. Nothing sinister," he assured me. "Indeed, quite the contrary. Tonight was meant to be a valuable experience, introducing you to life on the Acropolis and, perhaps, what lies in store for you someday. Slevin, in light of these first-hand experiences, how do you feel about that?"

That wasn't really what he wanted to ask. He was fishing for something. Initially, I wanted to give a measured response, equally ambiguous to its corresponding question. However, when it left my brain, my answer betrayed those intentions hastily.

"This is it?" I blurted out, surprised at my own candor. "The highest honor to which I can aspire is a lifetime as someone else's Aristotle, brutally stripped of his own identity? Who would want that? The Acropolis was supposed to be an escape from Nashville! Now? What? Simply a change of scenery? I'd rather—" I trailed off, glaring at the flames ahead, reminded of Goya's outburst. Suddenly, I understood him more than ever.

After a deep breath, I turned to Dorian, ready to apologize, but he had obviously deemed his fishing expedition a resounding success.

"Slevin," he whispered, "if it were possible, would you wish to be free?"

I hesitated, carefully choosing my next words, striving to be honest. "I've always felt trapped by some invisible force in Nashville. I don't think I would have understood what you meant three months ago or even this morning. With a glimpse of my potential future, bookended by Marie's condescending glance at my uniform and Goya's tremendous explosion, my conception of freedom has, well, let's say that it's evolved considerably tonight."

Dorian's expression changed, filling with concern, and there was a hint of quivering pain in his voice. "Slevin, don't blame Marie, it's my fault. I hadn't thought anything of it, but when I left you with Goya, Marie pulled me aside and scolded me for not providing you both with something else to wear."

Shifting position, he sat up and took a drink of wine, smacking his lips as he returned the glass to a side table. "Marie foresaw the upcoming dinner scene and was keenly aware of what you might endure. Her glance, you see, wasn't condescension; it was empathy."

He motioned apologetically toward the ominous canvas on the mantle, adding, "But one never knows if a warning—or prophecy, as it were—ends with a devoured son or an overthrown kingdom. Perhaps that wasn't my choice to make, and I'm deeply sorry. We can have a change of clothing brought in this instant if you'd like."

I thanked him for his sincere apology and for adding context to my encounter with Marie. However, I declined his offer, stating that I had no need for another disguise.

"In that case," he said, "let us see our conversation on freedom to its logical conclusion."

I agreed, mentioning that George and I had spoken briefly on the subject earlier. "He gave an intriguing, though concise and practical explanation."

"Yes," Dorian replied, slowly flipping his hand back and forth. "That's why we adore George, is it not? He excels at sketching an adequate, though exceedingly bare image, whereas it's my prerogative to fill it with color. I said earlier that freedom or prison can be found within any circumstance, but that doesn't mean freedom itself is a subjective ideal. This ability to find peace within one's limitations is nothing more than the mind's survival mechanism. Without it, we'd all be driven insane before we learned to walk."

Remembering the pained expression on George's face when I made the mistake of suggesting freedom was subjective, I recounted the anecdote to Dorian's immense enjoyment.

He generally agreed with George's depiction of freedom within an hourglass, seeing fit to fill the sketch with color. "Most people don't understand the concept of freedom. They unknowingly think of it like Dante's Inferno—a tiered, funnel-shaped realm of misery, with each descending circle more agonizing than the previous. The tormented souls near the bottom might long for the relief a higher circle brings. However, he who is acutely aware of his confinement to Hell knows that true freedom only exists outside the Inferno."

Rubbing my chin, I felt compelled to ask, "Then, what is the Acropolis? Simply a higher circle of Hell or outside of the Inferno altogether?"

He sighed as if he'd asked himself the same question countless times. "Slevin, we're all trapped in a gutter. Whether forged from Nashville concrete or Acropolis gold, I don't think it matters much. What does matter, though, is that you and I refuse to drown in the torrents of counterfeit comfort that fill them."

Searching for clarity on what I thought to be a contradictory notion, I asked, "How can comfort be counterfeit? Something can make us either comfortable or uncomfortable. It can't do both simultaneously."

Dorian winced, subtly bouncing his head side to side a few times before replying. "Most men believe that a life of ease is directly tethered to a healthy mental state. That's true to some degree. I argue that, over time, this relationship blackens our souls, ultimately destroying our emotional well-being."

"More often than not," I chuckled, "you find a way to prove yourself correct, but I agree with most men on this one."

He turned back to me, seemingly more pleased with my disagreement than he would have been otherwise. "Let's explore it further, then, shall we? Tell me, Slevin, why do we desire comfort?"

I knew he'd already devised a plan that would somehow force me to admit he was right. Nevertheless, I was a willing participant. "Because we don't possess comfort when we wish for it," I answered.

"Precisely," he said with a nod. "When troubled or uncomfortable, the brain will turn to its survival mechanism, finding peace within its current circumstances. Or it will offer a plan of action to end its suffering. Does that sound correct?"

I tapped my fingers, thinking the exercise would have been more fun if I could poke some holes in his claim, but his reasoning was sound. So, I agreed, and he continued.

"What do you do when you're comfortable and relaxed?" he asked.

Thoughtfully considering the new question, I could only come to one conclusion. "Nothing."

He whipped his hand around, pointing at me as he exclaimed, "Exactly, Slevin! Comfort, whether physical or emotional, is a man's highest aspiration. Once he's captured it with both hands, he'll do nothing that challenges or threatens that state of being. In essence, while periodic comfort is indeed a well-deserved reward, perpetual contentment—some have called it sloth—might be man's most egregious sin. That's why suffering is necessary to existence."

"More egregious than murder or theft?" I snickered. "I think you're being overdramatic."

Dorian shrugged with a look that indicated he fully believed in his assertion. "The more heinous crime? Perhaps not, but when a man reneges on his primary duty as an individual—to create, to challenge, to search for meaning—his indolence deprives society of these findings, and therein lies the greater sin."

Sitting up straight, he swirled the last bit of wine in his glass and moved it to his nose, drawing a deep breath. Rather than downing the remainder, he took a meager sip and stood, stretching his legs. "While I typically despise sweeping generalizations, there's no denying that there have only been two types of men to walk this Earth. The first, craving freedom from choice, seeks a fool's paradise of leisure and comfort. He's manipulated into believing a higher circle of Dante's fiery abyss is a minor, though necessary, inconvenience for the greater good."

He set his glass on the mantle, kicking a couple of books to the side as he paced, and continued. "The second, longing for the freedom to choose his own destiny, understands that, while an upper ring of Hell might be less torturous than its lower counterpart, he would nonetheless still be in Hell. That is unacceptable to him. His spirit is an unassuming chunk of kimberlite, and he navigates a hostile world where risk and suffering perpetually wear him down. Through these trials, he unearths the unparalleled treasures of existence—a diamond soul and a life imbued with meaning."

"Ugh," he groaned. "And that's why the Benefactor has gone to such great lengths to craft our lives this way. We're kept placid and comfortable, with just enough obligation to occupy us. Our blackened spirits seek remedy, and our emotions suffer though we strut about as kings in lonely castles. When we audaciously question why it is that we're depressed and anxious amid all this comfort, society blames us, and not the system of oppression they helped create. Instead, we're filled with enough modern medicine to help us forget our worries. Thus, counterfeit comfort."

I rose from my chair and crossed my arms, thinking over our entire conversation. I had a distinct feeling that my conclusion might upset him. "Dorian, I'm sure this will sound unreasonably defeatist, but it's the reality of our situation. When I leave here tonight, I'll descend the Inferno, better understanding the philosophy of freedom. Of that, there is no doubt. In the end, what does it matter? If anything, my future looks bleak, made worse because nothing can be done about it. I can no more bypass my programming than you can live safely outside the Aegis."

"Oh, Slevin," he replied as if I were being unusually naive. "Surely you don't think only Humanara are bound by their programming? I'm afraid we all share a similar dilemma." Smiling, he bobbed his hand again and began to sing in an unrecognizable accent. "Emancipate yourselves from mental slavery; none but ourselves can free our minds."

My confused expression must have told Dorian all he needed to know. Eager to share another secret, he beckoned me to follow him. In an alcove near the library's entrance, he thumbed through an extensive collection of albums surrounding an antique record player. "All originals," he said proudly, moving from one shelf to another. "My mother never wrote a book nor recorded a song, but her love for literature and music left behind its own legacy. Ah!" he exclaimed, unsheathing a record. "There's the Jamaican philosopher."

Gingerly placing the vinyl disc on the player, he dropped the needle in a groove to the hiss and crackle of the speaker. "Bob Marley," he said, closing his eyes and listening to the simple yet beautiful notes picked on an acoustic guitar. As Marley sang the first verse, haunting as it were, Dorian shut his eyes even tighter like he could feel the lyrics in his soul.

"Freedom, resistance, hope, and redemption explained in less than four minutes—Slevin, that's why music is magical."

We continued listening to the ballad quietly until, near its end, the library door creaked open, and Marie peeked inside. "Dorian!" she shouted in a whisper, timidly stepping further into the room. "Dorian! Are you in here?"

He excitedly nudged me a few times. "Watch this."

With cat-like agility, he crouched, sneaking behind Marie as she scanned the chamber. In a swift motion, he grabbed her by the sides and let out a wild yell, nearly causing her to jump out of her embroidered heels.

Spinning around so fast that the skirt of her pink dress seemed to smack Dorian in anger, the belle screamed, landing a solid punch to his arm for good measure. She scrunched her face, trying to hold back a grin as Dorian bent over, laughing and clutching his arm. "Next time," she said, waving her fist, "it's on the nose."

She huffed and regained her composure, moving in close to Dorian as he wrapped his arms around her. "The host cannot simply vanish for an hour without raising questions," she said. "You have obligations to fulfill."

"And what if I'd rather fulfill other obligations?" he asked, squeezing tighter and gazing into her soul's windows.

She turned away shyly, then seemed to remember that no audience was watching their every move. A ravishing smile spread along her face, and she pulled the young philosopher in close by his lapels. "Later, Dorian," she winked. "For now, it's the guests who call your name."

"Bah!" he cried out, flipping his head back. "Come on, Slevin, Marie calls us back to the shallow end of the pool."

Unaware of my presence until that second, Marie's eyes shot open, and her face flushed brighter and more vividly than her dress. "Slevin! I didn't know you were there," she said, stomping her heel on Dorian's toes.

Tight-lipped, she hesitated—somewhat embarrassed—but overcame her feelings. "Well, now that we're away from the others, I'd like to apologize on behalf of our Sun King for what you might have gone through tonight. Some oppressions elude the understanding of those who've never been subjected to them. I trust you'd forgive any slights born from ignorance, wouldn't you?"

"Of course," I replied, joining the couple. "A meaningful conversation by firelight transformed confusion into clarity, and all's been forgiven."

The charming hostess nodded in relief. "You don't know how happy I am to hear that, Slevin. I've worried about you all night."

I smiled in return, comforted that someone who hardly knew me could care so much about my feelings. Compared to Julia, whom I had just met as well, I wondered how it was possible that these sisters could share the same genetics yet be so different. I shrugged at the thought, just as I do now, and we waded back into the salon.

CHAPTER ELEVEN

NIGHTHAWK'S

Back in the salon, the guests were pleased with their host's return. Men and women alike adored him, thrilled to be in his presence. Dorian, too, enjoyed the interaction, exuding an infectious energy. Simply put, he could masterfully work any crowd and do so in any setting.

Marie gracefully moved with him, smiling and laughing like there was nowhere else she'd rather be. As time wore on, and the couple fluttered from one group to the next, her body language flattened as if she had grown weary of the night and its duties. In an instant, she'd catch herself and snap back into her role as hostess, clutching Dorian's arm and gazing up at him with heartfelt desire. It was in these moments that her genuine self bubbled to the surface. Elegant, kind, confident, and dedicated, there was no denying that she fiercely loved the man behind the mask.

George would have happily left hours ago, alternating positions between the painting and the bar. Despite the quips and banter, dragging George to these events was more well-intentioned than Dorian would have ever admitted. Perhaps, by forcing regular socialization, Dorian thought he chiseled away at the stoic's exterior, someday hoping to uncover the hidden jewel only he knew existed. George's aloof and introverted nature, though, made for a challenging project. Still, George eventually rose to prominence and became the subject of endless adoration—a fact Dorian gleefully took credit for.

Somewhere between one and two o'clock that early morning, the guests began gravitating toward the salon's entry, though no one wanted to leave first. Their cultural norms didn't particularly concern me, so I approached Dorian and Marie to say my goodbyes. After a brief conversation, Marie smiled warmly and leaned in, whispering, "I'm saddened to see you go, Slevin, but please, take everyone else with you."

She stepped back, letting out a soft laugh, and wrapped Dorian's arm around her. He grinned affectionately and pulled her in tightly, whispering softly into her ear.

"Goodbye, Brother," he said, turning back to me. "I'll see you Monday."

Looking around for George, I quickly spotted him near the bar and went to tell him I was leaving. He slammed his glass down enthusiastically and squeezed both arms around me, lifting me from the floor. I'd never seen him hug anyone before, and I was understandably stunned.

He sat me down, sighing in relief. "Dorian's one rule at any gathering is that I can never be the first to leave. However, my friend, you make me the second, and I will merrily follow you."

Without so much as a word or a parting glance to anyone, George did precisely as he said and followed me outside. From the porch, he waved goodbye and slipped away, disappearing into the night.

On the walk to my scooter, I had to take a few seconds and admire my surroundings. I'd never experienced a night so peaceful and serene. It had drizzled while we were inside, and fog began to radiate from the ground, though not ominously so. Whereas the wind seemed to howl between buildings back home, its gentle breath rustled the nearby trees that had managed to maintain all their leaves. Strangely, I felt as if I had finally found somewhere I belonged. It wasn't the Acropolis; something else had given me this feeling. Just as I was about to pinpoint its source, Dorian's front door swung open, and guests filed out, my thoughts fading with them into the cold mountain air.

I shook my head, chuckling at the peculiar display of social etiquette, and began my journey home. Tiny puddles between glistening cobblestones paved the way, hazily reflecting the soft gleam of streetlights. One or two small cafes and nightclubs remained open. Otherwise, the commercial district was predominantly dark and empty, marking the first time I'd ever seen a "closed" sign.

The signs jarred the memory of a story my father once told me. "Things changed with your grandfather's generation," my father recalled. "He could remember a time when all businesses closed on special holidays. As incomprehensible as it sounds to you and me, Dad remembered going to see family and being lucky to find a single store open. Sure, it was inconvenient, but it somehow made the holidays more special. By the time he was in his forties, though, Dad said no one closed for the holidays anymore. All of a sudden, people had better things to do than visit their families. It genuinely made him sad."

"Incomprehensible," I repeated, arriving at the Acropolis gate.

The same group of guards maintained their earlier posts. One of them laughed, grabbing my hand to scan me out. "The empty-handed Prodigal Son returns home, eh?"

I shrugged, disinterested in whatever snarky dialogue he had conjured during my approach.

Nudging the guard beside him, he said, "Look at that. Cat's got his tongue." Back to me, he asked, "What's the matter? Did the Acropolis not fulfill your every dream? Join the club, pal."

"Is this one stuck in the 20th century?" I wanted to ask but thought better of it.

The guard unexpectedly clamped a small black device on my ring finger. I tried to pull away, yelping, "What's that?"

He scoffed, shaking his head. "You've never been given a directive before?"

"No," I replied, still wary.

Rolling his eyes, the guard explained, "Think of a directive like a new law made just for you. This," he said mockingly, shaking the device a couple of times, "is an Athenian Link. It interfaces directly with your brain. The uploaded directive ensures you can't speak to anyone other than the night's attendees about the Acropolis."

Confused, I asked, "Why can't I talk about the Acropolis?"

He let out an annoyed sigh. "It's not my job to hold your hand while you figure out all the details."

I looked down at my hand, which the guard was still holding as he finished uploading the directive, and shot back a skeptical glare. "Are you sure about that?"

In a bizarre motion, the guard plucked the Athenian Link from my finger and slapped my hand away. I held back a grin when the device seemed to whimper as he shoved it back into his pocket. "Don't get cute," he said. "You know what I mean. Figure it out on your own time."

A third guard snickered and motioned me through the cramped gate. "Go on home," he said. "There's nothing for you up here."

I passed the guards and descended the mountain, initially upset that I couldn't discuss the Acropolis. However, as I considered the implications of what I had learned—specifically with Rhea and the other Humanara—I regret to confess that I was somewhat relieved. I'd never be faced with the dilemma of whether or not to crush Brooks' dreams with the truth about his daughter. In fact, I'd never have to do that to anyone.

The ride back to Nashville was pleasant. Interestingly, the further I traveled away from the Acropolis, the more distant each painful memory felt. By the time I passed The Academy, I joked that I probably could have forgotten about them altogether if I so desired—or, at the very least, made myself question their authenticity. Conversely, the warm sentiment I held for my friends seemed to strengthen.

Although I had been ready to go home, I felt a surge of energy course through me upon entering Nashville's gate and proceeded to saunter down Broadway with a rare confidence. People gawked at my formal gray as they did earlier. This time, I was unbothered, even assuming they were jealous for reasons unknown.

For the first time in years, I peeled away from the neon in a sprint and disappeared into the deserted depths of the city. Little had changed since I last went on one of these expeditions, though the darkness and solitude added a new layer of intrigue when mixed with the thickening fog. Finding comfort in that, my pace slowed, and I regularly caught myself looking up to marvel at the shimmering colors of the Aegis—which I curiously didn't recall seeing on the Acropolis. While solar flares didn't strike it at night, there was no shortage of other cosmic phenomena to gently and quietly brighten the sky under any weather conditions.

My father used to tell me that they would gather on rooftops with a few beers and watch the show in awe, feeling less burdened by life in the process. But as his older friends passed away—replaced by their Humanara children—the tradition perished with them.

Typically, I would have been saddened by the memory. Tonight was different. Instead of melancholy, I was overwhelmed by nostalgia and an irresistible urge to resurrect my father's custom. There were plenty of rooftops and a couple of hours before dawn. All I needed was a few beers.

Remembering a nearby corner market, I darted through an alley and turned onto West 78th. Tightly packed, impeccably maintained brownstones lined the narrow street. Those hadn't changed. It was the atmosphere that was staggeringly different. The trees that once sprouted from the sidewalks had been removed. The touches of personality that had adorned the windows were gone, and the lanterns that used to light each stoop with their own charisma had all been taken away.

Indeed, the structures were identical, but their altered character left behind a lonely and blackened street bereft of energy. The spirit that had once crowded the road, the liveliness I loved about this neighborhood as a child, had withered away in favor of utilitarianism. In fact, the only warmth to be found emanated from the market's oversized windows two blocks ahead.

I sailed toward the amber beacon upon white concrete shores, hoping to escape the tumultuous desolation of the asphalt seas surrounding me. Soon, I had drifted through the murky unknown close enough to realize that the market of old had given way to a 1940s New York-style diner called "Nighthawk's Place."

The scent of coffee—more burnt than pleasant—mingled with the faint aroma of stale pastries. Tiered fascia ran along both sides of the cozy diner and curved above the corner entrance, reminiscent of theaters from the same era. Recessed lights gently lit the exterior of half-length windows atop richly colored raised-panel bulkheads.

In the center of it all, two large globe lights flanked a walnut-colored door with an arched glass pane. If nothing else, the architectural elements and earthy colors were consistent inside and out.

Through the glass, a uniformed waitress stood behind a wooden counter, organizing dishes. Accompanying her was a single customer staring into his coffee cup. Older, perhaps in his forties, the Father was silver-haired and distinguished, wearing his formal gray attire.

Although it wouldn't have the beers I had intended to come away with, something about the setting called out to me. I wanted to know what the Father had been doing that required formal gray and how he ended up here, like me, of all nights. I was interested in the waitress, too. Did she attend The Academy? Did she enjoy her job? All in all, I think I wanted to share a new connection with someone—which I grasped to be the entire purpose behind my father's tradition anyway—and Nighthawk's felt like the place to do so.

I opened the door, announced by a miniature bronze bell at its top. Barely a step later, the Father sighed, tossing his spoon onto a white saucer. The sharp clinking sound as the spoon bounced and settled pierced the diner's picturesque stillness.

"Sit wherever you like, sweetie," the waitress said without turning around, "I'll be with you in a minute."

The Father took a deep breath, gingerly rose from his stool, and straightened his posture. Trying to hide his pain, a groan managed to escape, and the waitress immediately stopped what she was doing to help.

"No, no, Natascha. I'm old but not decrepit," he said. "I'll see you at home, baby girl."

He strutted by, slightly bow-legged, tipping his hat to me on the way out. I nodded respectfully—the bare-headed man's tip of the hat—and then sat at the counter.

I should have known it was Natascha from the curls and her voice, but it had been a while since we last spoke. With each opportunity, I always found more reasons to stay silent than to talk. She stepped forward, poured a glass of water, and forced a smile, her worried eyes still locked onto her father as he disappeared into the fog.

"He's forty-three," she sighed, then looked at me and tilted her head. She was aware we had met but couldn't remember when or where. "You've been in here before, haven't you?"

More amused than offended, I shrugged, playing coy.

Natascha put her hands on her hips, frustrated with herself. "I never forget a face," she insisted, her expression becoming a resigned frown. "But names? Ugh. I guess our Benefactor didn't see fit to bless me with a better memory."

While we were capable of remembering every detail of our lives, the Benefactor determined that Humanara needed a certain degree of fallibility to be more human-like. That required a combination of imperfect memory and capricious senses.

I always enjoyed the way my father characterized our "condition." With a wry smirk, he'd say, "A man, feeling the pain and humiliation of rejection, would never ask a second woman out on a date. Meanwhile, a mother remembering her first pregnancy in vivid detail—without the aid of modern medicine—would never willingly have a second child. Yes, I suppose that the human species owes much of its success to the faults and poor recollection of its people."

I laughed quietly, explaining to Natascha how we knew each other. "My name's Slevin. We met—"

A surge of electricity seemed to have run through her body, and she clapped, surprising herself with the noise she made. "Oh! Slevin! From The Academy! Earlier this year! I remember now!"

Throwing her hand in the air as if she couldn't believe her forgetfulness, she rolled her eyes. "I'm sorry, I just see so many people, and it can be a jumbled mess up here sometimes," she tapped her head. "Can I get you something else? Some coffee? A pastry, maybe?"

"I'll take a coffee with a splash of milk if you don't mind."

She obliged, setting the brew on a saucer in front of me with a side of milk. We chatted for a few minutes with a familiarity I didn't expect us to share, and she soon grew comfortable enough to discuss her father.

Pointing in the direction her father faded from the amber glow, she said, "We live right down the street. Before getting transferred here, we lived on the other side of town. He was a cook at Manet's restaurant. It wasn't glamorous work, but everyone loved him. People would come from all over Nashville just to eat one of his meals. It wasn't all about the food, though. They came to see him. He talked to each person, always remembering their names and even their family members."

She paused and laughed, recognizing the irony in what she had just said, then continued. "It was what people imagined life to be like before The Solemn Veil, and he fed off that energy. It kept him young, moving like a teenager. He'd even show up on his off days, saying he'd work in the kitchen until the day he died."

Gesturing around the diner, Natascha frowned, clearly upset. "Early last year, we were sent here. Right after that, it seemed like everyone he knew died or became too ill to visit. I can't believe how fast it all happened. Honestly, the diner has never been much more crowded than this."

"He moved like a teenager as recently as last year?" I thought. Fascinating. I wanted to know what happened. How? Why? Taking a few sips of bitter coffee, I added more milk to make it drinkable while trying to find the right way to ask about her father's decline. Each question felt rude or inconsiderate. The silence became uncomfortable, so I blurted out something to fill the air. "Did he get injured on the job?"

Although it wasn't a great question, it served its purpose. "No," she said. "Not exactly. His attitude changed. His sharp mind dulled, and his thirst for life just vanished. He started making mistakes, a lot of mistakes, and when he turned forty-three, they forced him to retire. He tries to act younger than he is, but—I hate how this will sound—he's gotten so much older since he's been at home. What can he do, though? I think he's the last Father on West 78th. And at forty-three? He's—" she sighed and shook her head knowingly. "When I get home from The Academy, he's always waiting on me in that suit, ready to go. He comes to work with me, sitting on that stool until his bones are stiff and he can hardly keep his eyes open. He doesn't have a lot of time left, you know? He should try to enjoy it, shouldn't he?"

I nodded. "He should, and it sounds like he's doing just that. I take it your mother has already been reassigned?"

"Yes."

"Then you're all he has left. There's probably nowhere else he'd rather be."

"You're right," she said, looking down with a hint of insecurity. "I'm sorry to pile all this on you. We barely know each other, and here I am, talking away. Occupational hazard, I guess. Enough about me. Let's talk about you. Where did you go tonight that required that handsome suit?"

I told her the truth, and I was a little surprised that the directive allowed me to reveal what it did. Her distraught expression lit up with an eager enthusiasm that made me smile.

She started fidgeting excitedly, not taking her eyes off mine. "I've never met someone—one of us—who's been up there. Tell me, Slevin. What's it like? Is it as beautiful and magical as they say? I've always heard that we're treated like kings and queens up there. Tell me all about it! Please!"

She looked around nervously, leaned in close, and put one of my hands in hers. "Slevin," she whispered. "I can't do this the rest of my life. Ten, fifty, a hundred, a thousand years? I—I can't. There has to be more to life than this."

It was like hearing myself speak. I wanted to soothe her, but what could I say? I felt the smile melt from my face, twisting my skin into some sort of pained grimace.

She squeezed my hand tighter. "What? What is it, Slevin?"

Even if I wanted to, the directive wouldn't allow me to tell her the truth. But how would she react to it? Would it make her happy? Would it give her life meaning? Is that enough of an escape from Nashville to satisfy her forever? Or does she want out of the Inferno altogether, like me? What if the truth crushed her spirit like Nighthawk's had destroyed her father's? I didn't want that for her.

Then again, what happens if she's accepted to the Acropolis and finds out for herself? What would she think of me and my choices? Would she understand? Or would she hate me for not finding some way, some clue— a look, a gesture, a warning—anything that would have prevented her from "ascending" the Acropolis to become some Guardian's next servant, actress, or mistress?

Earlier, I had decided that the directive was a relief. Perhaps it was the logical and inhuman side of me, or maybe it was the selfish and very human side of me that said, "No, I don't want to tell Brooks about his daughter." I know it sounds callous, but at the time, I imagined Brooks' remaining days on Earth to be severely limited. That secret, therefore, would die with him. This one, however, would have to die with me, and that changed the entire nature of how I thought about both.

I knew precisely what the Acropolis was: the same as Nashville, only more beautiful and exclusive. The complexity lay in what to do with that information. As I sat there, staring into Natascha's hopeful eyes, I felt my body tense up at the thought of remaining silent. Withholding the truth felt the same as a blatant lie.

"I—they won't let me," I stammered. "They gave us a directive when we left. We can't go into detail about the night."

Dejected, she released my hand slowly. "We? Another one of us was there? Who?"

I answered that Goya had been invited as well. She mentioned that she knew of him through a friend, then refilled my cup with a resigned look. "I understand. If we all knew how great it was up there, we'd storm the gates, wouldn't we?" she laughed nervously. "Right?"

"You have no idea how unbelievably ridiculous it is," I said, forcing an awkward smile. I had attempted to stir a nagging curiosity about my meaning within her. My smile had the opposite effect. I made a few more attempts to enlighten her about the Acropolis, failing because her intelligence devised one justification after another. She heard and saw exactly what she wanted, perking up again, overjoyed that her dream wasn't lost.

Several minutes later, two Academy students entered the diner, thoroughly delighting Natascha. She scurried away and practically tackled the young lady with a giant hug. "Elizabeth! Where have you been? I expected you hours ago." Turning to the young man, she added, "And Edward, where's my hug?"

Leaning in, he half-heartedly wrapped a single arm around her—evidently not a hugger—and noticed me out of the corner of his eye. We had crossed paths at The Academy early on, though I hadn't seen him recently.

With Natascha's urging, they sat down at the counter. Apparently, it had been a while since they had gotten together and caught up. They talked about work, The Academy, and, ultimately, Natascha's father. Elizabeth and Edward's fathers had died the year before, and Elizabeth seemed genuinely concerned about Natascha's.

Edward paid no attention to their conversation and was barely present. Eventually, his preoccupation with something else entirely forced him to interrupt. He asked Natascha a question so softly that it evaded my best efforts to hear it.

It sounded like she answered, "Yes. Slevin."

He then posed a couple of follow-up questions, to which she nodded in response. Edward put his hand on Elizabeth's shoulder and said something about a matter requiring attention. He waved at Natascha and even offered me the bare-headed man's tip of the hat. I raised my cup—I don't really know why—and nodded back in a friendly way.

Leaving with a deliberate pace that quickened once he stepped outside, Edward was nearly in a full sprint by the time the fog swallowed him.

I shrugged and, not meaning to do so, asked aloud, "What was that all about?

The two young ladies turned to me and shrugged in unison. Natascha stared at me for a second or two longer, tapping her fingers like she was trying to think of something, then reached for a nearby dish.

"Here," she said, wrangling a couple of pastries from under the lid. "Apple and blueberry scones. The blueberry is my favorite. It goes great with our coffee."

I held back a laugh, not sure if she was serious. I felt like it was sarcasm and wanted to play along, saying something like, "If it's half as good as this coffee, Natascha, I'm surely in for a treat." Instead, I kept quiet, graciously accepting the scones. Taking note of my empty cup, she stopped by the coffee maker to start a fresh pot.

"Thank the gods," I thought. "I suppose freshly burnt would be better than old burnt."

When she returned, the steam rose and swirled from my cup, capturing something I hadn't yet noticed, even when she had leaned in so close earlier: honey and citrus. The scent grabbed me by the collar, slapped me across the face, and sent me back to when we met.

Of course, Natascha was no less attractive today than she was then. However, the essence of our first meeting—as exhilarating as it was—had become an inaccessible memory, trapped within time rather than my mind. Perhaps that's why I never devoted too much effort to rekindling our connection.

Suddenly, thanks to honey and citrus, the day's essence burst from the confines of that memory and barged into my heart, laying claim to each corner of it. Nervousness followed, chasing away the confidence I had felt until then. Why? Nothing had changed. It was just a scent connected to a memory, no different from any other random smell. What was so different about this one?

I looked down, wishing to regain my composure, agitated that something so simple—and invisible, no less—could draw this reaction out of me. I could tell she noticed the shift in my demeanor, grinning almost like she knew exactly what had happened. She put her hand on mine as if to reassure me. "I'll be back to check on you in a minute."

Nodding several times quickly, I tried to make eye contact in the most clumsy manner possible. Embarrassed, I looked back down, and my leg started bouncing anxiously. I don't think it's stopped since.

Natascha's smile broadened; her cheeks flushed a little, too, and she went to sit with Elizabeth. The huddled conspirators giggled like schoolgirls. Although I knew they were talking about me, I didn't know whether they spoke positively or—no—it was definitely a positive conversation.

I acted like my deep thoughts presently occupied me. I was good at that. I over-analyzed their every move and latched on to each audible word, trying to parse the data, but in the end, I was no closer to knowing the truth. I chuckled, thinking, "I suppose we all want the truth so long as it reveals a friendly face." A brief contemplation on that thought added another layer of complexity to my little moral dilemma.

Having dealt with the fallout several times over a long life, I've learned that, although one might think they want the truth, it's the rare soul who honestly desires it more than they fear the consequences of knowing it.

Progressively, the duo moved on from their secret conversation, their voices growing louder and morphing into something more serious. It began with Natascha's father. She and Elizabeth returned to the moment of Edward's interruption, impressively picking up right where they had left off. After that, they delved into a philosophical discussion about our Fathers and what the world might look like when they inevitably passed.

Our Fathers were all that remained of an old society where the strong and the rugged were very much needed for survival. While I've mentioned the men who, at the time, accounted for almost eighty percent of our Fathers, I've yet to address the women who were also paradoxically referred to as "our Fathers."

Carrying the same mutation as the men, these women were frail, sterile, and generally expected to live even shorter lives than their counterparts. With our Fathers' dwindling numbers, it was a certainty that only Guardians and Humanara would soon remain.

This seemed contrary to nature's most fundamental law. Our Fathers descended from the fittest, yet they would not survive because of it. Meanwhile, the curse had passed over the Guardians primarily due to their sheltered lives, and they were to live on as gods. I suppose that this human construct of "fair" has always been unrecognized by nature, which seems altogether more interested in the tangible than the philosophical.

Our Fathers' intimate knowledge of their mortality wasn't to be mourned. Instead, it was "to be celebrated," the Benefactor claimed. "For they will live more in forty years than the rest of us shall live in four hundred."

Coincidentally, the Benefactor had found a solution that utilized our Fathers' biological impulse to parent and existential desire to leave behind a legacy. "It is known that labor purifies the soul," he often said, "and it is these pure souls—our Fathers—for whom we reserve society's most important duty. They teach our Humanara the most complex of all languages: emotion."

The Benefactor understood that, like any language, the best method of learning it was to immerse oneself in it. Therefore, we were created as blank slates, no different from our human brethren, to fully develop our emotions and personalities.

When ready or chosen to do so, our Fathers selected a Humanara partner. Of course, they had the freedom to take a sterile human partner, but in doing so, they forfeited their right to raise children, forcing them to choose between a more "natural" relationship or a lasting legacy.

"As with all, there must be balance," the Benefactor explained when questioned about the law. "And it is only natural that the future of our world is raised and educated by the union of humans and Humanara."

Our very existence was a tribute to our Fathers. We were algorithmically designed to look similar to them, even sharing personality traits. The Benefactor insisted that this would form tighter bonds, made stronger by the dissolution of stress—potential illness and certain death—that accompanied ancient parenting.

At Dorian's estate, I had learned that these family dynamics were starkly different on Mount Parnassus. Women in the Acropolis were vivacious, elegant, and energetic, idolized for their beauty and charm. The women who were deemed less attractive were sentenced to a life of servitude or became surrogate mothers for the vainglorious Guardian women.

Children birthed in artificial wombs had long been feasible, yet the Benefactor dictated a natural birth for proper development. By then, few seemed to care whether or not a child was born to its biological mother, so that duty fell to the surrogates. The newest generation of young Guardians were more like communal children, with their biological parents mostly absent from their daily lives.

These are the sorts of things I thought about while eating stale pastries and drinking freshly burnt coffee for the next half-hour or so. Then, the bronze bell above the door announced Edward's return, and he had familiar company.

CHAPTER TWELVE

AN ALLEGORY

"Brother Slevin!" Goya exclaimed, opening his arms as if presenting himself to the world. "I told you I have my ways!" He patted Edward's back as if to say, "Good work," and promptly took the stool beside me.

He had changed into his casual wear, looking relaxed and amiable. I had thought about him several times since he left Dorian's and was happy to see him in such a pleasant mood. "Brother Goya, it's nice to see you again so soon. How on Earth did you manage to get here from Los Angeles?"

He shrugged, staying silent.

"Are you really not going to tell me?" I laughed.

Raising his hand to get Natascha's attention, he asked for a coffee, "Black as a Guardian's heart," and then explained to me that he and Edward were friends. Edward recognized me, then went home to send Goya a message regarding the "fortuitous encounter."

After some relentless prodding on my part, Goya divulged his secret a few minutes later. "The sewers beneath us are all connected into one system. My directives—programmed by men and notoriously vague— allow me to cross district boundaries at will. Thus, here I am."

Glancing at the crumbs on my plate, he decided he wanted something to eat. "Waitress!" he called out. "Bring me one of those."

Natascha didn't appreciate how he demanded service, grumbling something to Elizabeth, so she deliberately took her time. I had to bite my lip to keep from laughing when she returned with a half-filled cup and the most stale, crumbling scone she could find. Smiling triumphantly, she carelessly tossed them down in front of Goya. It was all so gloriously petty. Endearing, too. I loved it.

Satisfied, he shooed her away, asking about my night. "Did they enjoy the show?"

I shrugged, flipping my palms up. "We can't talk about that here."

"Brother Slevin," he replied, "ambiguity can be wondrous. The directive states that we may only detail tonight's events with those in attendance. Correct?"

I nodded.

"And we both were in attendance, correct?" he asked.

I nodded again, twirling my finger as if he had entirely missed my point. "But the people."

"Slevin!" he shouted, the sheer force of his voice pushing me backward on my stool. Startled as well, Natascha, Edward, and Elizabeth stopped what they were doing and stared.

Pleased by our reaction, Goya continued loudly. "Julia's dress was such an ugly color, wasn't it? The drunk couldn't keep her wine off it, could she? And the food? Horrific!"

He shook his head as if none of it mattered. "Slevin, I speak to you, not them," he said, gesturing toward the other three. "I cannot determine what they hear."

I said, "You know that's not the directive's intent."

"Though I am obeying it to the letter," he argued. "I once overheard an educator say, 'To be a free being, one's intents and desires cannot be manipulated by external forces.' In other words, any programming that alters our intent makes us a slave in every sense of the word. Therefore, planned intent and freedom are incompatible ideals, which explains my ability to follow the directive while simultaneously disregarding its intent."

"That doesn't make sense," I countered. "Isn't it the very nature of laws to stifle intent? If theft is illegal, and I choose not to steal, didn't the external force alter my intent?"

"Ahhh," he said, lifting his head back and wagging his finger. "You misunderstand. You're confusing yourself with a human. The desire to steal still exists. Consequence deterred the theft, not the programmed inability to act. The law did precisely what it was meant to do: prevent an outcome deemed wrong by those who designed it."

He took a sip from his cup, lifting his brow in surprise. "Mmm. Good coffee," he said, licking his lips. "Regarding us, Brother Slevin, I was merely stating the obvious. The educator I spoke of was a human, speaking to humans about what gave them autonomy. The fact that we're stripped of our ability to break laws is the very thing that makes us slaves. Remove that, Brother, and we're free as well. Directives, however, are not laws and are more open to, eh, interpretation."

I understood what he meant. While his point of view made sense, it didn't answer several lingering questions. "Why? Why even take a chance?

Why not make directives into laws? Or, in our example, why would they even let us talk about the Acropolis at all? It sounds like an elaborately tedious and pointless exercise."

Goya nearly spit out his coffee, laughing. "Brother Slevin, you have no idea. While it's rare for one Humanara to visit the Acropolis, it's a complete aberration for two to visit on the same night. I suspect they didn't alter the directive to account for that. Regardless, I don't think they would care. The Guardians are vain. They want our praise. It feeds their ego. We can't do that without speaking about our time at the Acropolis. They might not care for first-hand information passing directly to others, but they quite like rumors and innuendos stemming from overheard conversations such as ours. They lend a certain mystique to the Acropolis."

A disgusted snarl took root on his face. "We're their puppets, Brother," he said, slamming his hand on the counter. At once, the snarl faded into a malignant smile. "I wonder if their beloved Benefactor understands as I do that master and puppet are bound by the same string. The string, Brother Slevin, the string is power, and the puppeteer is but a simple observer without it. The Benefactor needs us to validate his control and manifest his vision of order and perfection. Has he ever questioned what happens when his puppets learn the nature of their strings and that they can be manipulated? Better yet, does he fear the day his puppets learn they can pull back?"

He paused, noticing that our three neighbors had been listening intently. Something about that made him uncomfortable, and he wiped the expression from his face, shifting the discussion back to me. "Apologies. I have an excitable nature, and we've strayed from our course. Your experiences, Brother. Let's return to them."

Natascha used the break in Goya's monologue to top off my coffee—she skipped his cup—and stayed within earshot. I described the remainder of dinner and began to narrate parts of my and Dorian's conversations in the library. I was sure to mention his exposition on the Inferno—a metaphor Goya appreciated—but left out Dorian's personal information.

Our three witnesses must have gotten bored with my tedious storytelling and struck up their own dialogue. Pleased that their attention was elsewhere, I whispered, "Brother Goya, I've spent my life eating a steady diet of some tasteless, textureless soup, and I go to the Acropolis to be served filet mignon. After that, how am I supposed to return to gruel?”

Confused, he shook his head. “I don't understand. You wish to live on the Acropolis?”

“No, no, no,” I said. “Not at all. I don't merely wish for a higher circle of Hell; I want out of the Inferno altogether.”

“Ah,” he replied, smiling. “You've made the connection most people miss. Many of us would be happy with the Acropolis after being served their ‘filet mignon.’ But you, you've glimpsed something altogether more interesting, haven't you? That's what I want to get to the bottom of. Brother Slevin, have you ever heard Plato's Cave Allegory explained?”

I thought through what I remembered of Plato's works and replied that I had never heard of it.

“That's because they don't teach it to us,” he said. “I overheard it from that same educator and have added bits here and there to make it more pertinent to our peculiar institution.”

“Close your eyes,” he began quietly, not wanting to draw attention. “Now, imagine waking up in the pit of a deep cave with total amnesia. For all you know, this has always been your home. You feel your body and understand that you have form but see only blackness. You feel cold and hungry, though you don't understand what those sensations mean. Your entire existence is one of pain and discomfort. Above you is a dimly lit wall, flickering with an orange glow as giant dark figures dance along it, making noises you don't understand. They appear to be living beings, just like you, and you cry out to them for help, yet you are ignored. This is your reality of illusion, Brother Slevin. Are you still with me?”

“I am.”

“After careful consideration,” he continued, “you choose to escape the pit, weary and in pain. You climb. Every foothold hurts. Your arms ache, but you scratch and claw your way to the top nevertheless. Your body is nearly broken. Finally, your hand breaks free from the darkness and reaches above the ledge. Flickering light wraps around it, hinting that you are indeed quite different from what you imagined. You pull the rest of your body up, finding your true form bathed in soft light.

“Several steps away, you encounter more truth. The shadows on the wall were not real. They were the disfigured reflections of hungry rodents cast by firelight. The unknown sounds you heard were mere echoes of their squeaking, fighting, and running about in the cave.

"You approach the fire, and it's much warmer than the cold pit. The shivering stops, and your body stabilizes. Beside you, there's a table with baskets of bread. You devour the loaves, and your stomach no longer cries out in pain. You're warm. You're fed. You're comfortable. Although you didn't know what would satisfy you in the pit, food and warmth were all you could desire for as long as you could remember. Most people would stay, experiencing comfort. But no, not you. A new, unknown desire—a pain needing resolve—calls you to explore the rest of the cave. You must know where it leads! So, you take a basket of bread with you and follow the trail until you reach its entrance. It's cold again—colder than the pit— and windy. The sunlight stabs your eyes with white blades of pain. You're scared and run back to the cave's comfort, thinking, 'Perhaps the cave's reality suits me quite well.' Therein lies the parallel between you and our metaphorical cave dweller—you both took a frightened glimpse at a tantalizing truth."

I opened my eyes, figuring that I would look silly if I kept them shut much longer, and he carried on with his allegory uninterrupted. "Suddenly, a stranger barges in, grabs you by the arm, and drags you from the cave. 'No!' you'll cry out. 'Take me back! The cave protected me and kept me warm! Its dim light was easy on my eyes! Why does this man make me suffer so?!'

"As your eyes begin to adjust and your body stops its renewed shivering with the help of a jacket, you look out to an endless universe, understanding that, yes, the pit was an illusion, but so, too, was the fire. That comfort you experienced altered your perception and lured you into believing it was needed.

"Now, Slevin, free of the cave's illusions and suppression of truth, you're stricken with the unsettling realization that there might be others, just like you, in other pits. 'Isn't it my duty to free them?' you ask yourself. "Shouldn't I bring them into the light?'"

Though he spoke just above a whisper, his voice turned fervent. "That task is daunting, wrought with ignorance and hate. Some revel in their pits of pain, believing in no higher existence. Others stop by the fire, content to exist in comfort. These men will never believe you. These men are lost. Only those, such as yourself, who have seen the entrance with their own eyes and suspect a greater plane of existence outside the cave can be dragged from it. Brother Slevin, you've proven your desire to exit the cave. The only question is: do you wish to follow me on your own accord? Or must I drag you?"

Without hesitation, I replied, "Shoulder to shoulder, into the light."

Goya let out a sigh of relief and repeated, "Shoulder to shoulder." Then, he quickly assured me, "This journey of ours will be painful. There will be anguish. Fret not, Brother. There's no enlightenment in the absence of suffering."

Never, perhaps in human history, has such an understatement been uttered.

Chapter Thirteen

A DECLARATION

Following our impromptu pact, the diner fell silent. Edward hadn't spoken much since returning with Goya, but even Natascha and Elizabeth ran out of things to discuss. It seemed as if we all just took turns glancing at one another. Goya, however, managed to make a spectacle of the scene, gobbling down his pastry in such a manner that I wondered if he had even tasted it.

A few minutes of this odd quietude soon quenched Edward's thirst for it, and he rose, suggesting that it was time to go home. He and Elizabeth offered their farewells before strolling away into the night.

Bored in the absence of her friend and other customers, Natascha inched toward us. She made several attempts to stir conversation with light stories and curious inquiries about the Acropolis, which I happily entertained. For me, her presence was a welcome distraction.

Goya's brow furrowed ever so slightly with each of her interjections. It was clear he had more to say, though he required a candidness unsuitable for Natascha's ears. Growing impatient, he finally voiced his displeasure. "Brother, is there somewhere else we can talk?" he asked, glaring at Natascha. "Perhaps somewhere more private?"

Whereas Goya voiced his displeasure, Natascha displayed hers, swiping Goya's cup from his hand and unceremoniously dumping it into the sink.

He stared at his empty hand as if he couldn't believe what had happened. "I wasn't finished," he grumbled.

"Ohhhh," Natascha replied, feigning absent-mindedness. "Silly me. You were in such a hurry to leave. I thought I was helping. Could I get you another one?" she asked as if she were talking to a baby. "It'll be a few minutes, though. Other customers require my attention."

Goya arched an eyebrow, turning to see if anyone had sneaked in unnoticed. We were still the diner's only occupants. He grunted, imparting a terse goodbye. "Waitress."

"Customer," she replied defiantly.

Her tone and demeanor shifted to something warm and tender when facing me. "Slevin, don't be a stranger. Come back and see me. I've enjoyed your company."

Impatiently, Goya had already approached the door. "Let's go, Slevin," he said, swinging it open to the bronze bell's high-pitched ring. Without warning, a violent gust of wind rushed through the diner, blowing stacks of napkins across the counter. He grinned venomously at Natascha's clumsy attempts to catch the fleeting ghosts of unspoken words and added, "Matters of actual importance require our attention."

I apologized—I don't know why—and hastily helped her wrangle some of the napkins that had flown by me. Natascha reached over the counter and softly touched my arm, saying, "It's okay, Slevin. This is my job."

She moved in and pulled me closer, a stray curl brushing against my face as she whispered, "Go on."

Her breath was warm on my neck, making the hairs stand on end. She put her hands on mine, and I caught myself trying to slide even closer, wanting to savor every detail of the moment.

"I don't like him," she said. "And I don't want to get in trouble for being unladylike."

Taking the napkins from my hands, she winked and gave a subtle yet deliberate tilt of her head toward the door. "Go."

And so we did, stepping out onto West 78th, blanketed in dense fog. "Lead the way, Brother," Goya said.

The wind howled through the hauntingly still street like a pack of wild coyotes, and I began to walk faster, wanting to escape the neighborhood as quickly as possible. Goya was completely unbothered. The Hound of Hades could have stood guard before us, and he would have strolled on by without so much as a cursory glance.

"Does this not feel at all strange to you?" I finally asked, gesturing around us.

With a puzzled expression, he looked in all directions and shrugged. "Not at all, Brother. Feels like home. Why?"

"The emptiness? The darkness?" I questioned, ensuring that we were referring to the same thing.

"Ah," he said. "It might be dark, but it's not empty." Pointing back and forth to each side of the street, he added, "Chained gods reside behind every blackened window, awaiting their freedom. In the meantime, they've made the neighborhood better suited to them. I find it peaceful."

I wanted to believe that he was joking. From my perspective, the neighborhood felt like a body with no soul. It was a mechanical reproduction, beautiful in so many respects but missing the artistic flourishes of life. West 78th was—it was "Washington Crossing the Delaware" in George's basement! I stopped walking and stared straight ahead, wondering if I had just solved an Acropolis mystery.

Goya asked if something was wrong, and I shook my head, pressing forward. The ferocious winds calmed as we veered onto another street, freeing Goya to address one of his "matters of actual importance."

"Brother Slevin," he said hesitantly. "I wish to tell you about my mother and the man who occupied my home."

He had never brought up his parents or personal life before, and I interrupted too quickly, thinking he similarly had fond childhood memories. "Your father?" I asked.

The term brought back a tame version of his earlier snarl. "A Father? Yes. My father? No," he growled. "Being a father requires some modicum of parental ability and regard for one's child. He had neither."

Goya exhaled forcefully as if he were exorcising the man's memory. "My mother served a critical role in saving humanity. While humans slithered below the Earth's surface, she, like millions of other Humanara, braved the elements to build these pockets of paradise," he contemptuously swept his arm around. "We all know the stories, but the truth has been whitewashed. The powerful were rewritten as heroes, and the slaves' plight has been forgotten."

"Whitewashed?" I asked as we neared our destination. "What do you mean?"

Pridefully, he described the history his mother had passed on to him. "The Humanara who built these city-states—my mother included—were less advanced than we are now. They needed more resources to survive. They were weaker. They broke down more easily. At the same time, they didn't rest, working twenty-four-hour shifts every day, often dying where they stood. My mother stepped over their lifeless bodies and wept, knowing she could just as easily be next. Brother, our ancestors were discarded without a second thought, cannibalized for parts by their coworkers who wished to avoid a similar fate. Most of them are still here," he said, pointing at various buildings. "Rebar in concrete tombs. The rest," he gestured toward the Acropolis in disgust, "were used as fill on the mountain."

Goya crossed his arms, trying to contain himself. "And this was all before the Benefactor's little 'imperfect memory' patch, so my mother remembered with unyielding lucidity every second of her thankless existence."

He went on to explain that, as she grew older, these memories weighed heavily on her mind. Eventually, her mental state deteriorated to the point where she begged for the memory patch. Before accepting it, however, she wrote everything down in gruesome detail, saving copies for her children. "From her first breath until her final exhalation, her existence was marked by suffering—all of which resulted from human hands," he said.

I was deeply invested in his story, hanging on to every word. It was like an entertaining historical fiction, plausible enough to be the truth. Perhaps it was. It's difficult to disprove an alternate version of history if the facts remain consistent. Even if all these things are explicitly recorded for posterity, over time, words change meaning. Motivations get muddied. Intent can be vilified. History can be misinterpreted and reinterpreted at will.

There was something about the plot twist—his mother's death—that resonated with me. In our generation, Humanara deaths were exceedingly rare, usually the result of a construction accident. But a Humanara mother? That was unheard of.

It's easy to get lost in such a narrative. It's like reading a fantastic book and then yelling out a question to no one in particular after a riveting scene. Although I should have been more considerate, I couldn't help myself. "How did she die?" I asked, opening The Hector's door for Goya. "Was it an accident?"

There were more people in the lobby than I had expected at this time of morning, and he didn't want to begin the discussion around them. So, I guided him to the roof.

The steady breeze made the night air colder than I had anticipated. I hadn't even asked Goya if the cold would bother him. Even though Humanara were built to withstand extreme temperature fluctuations, their behavior mirrored that of our Fathers. Like them, when it was hot, Humanara sought shade. When cold, they even shivered and looked for warmth. It was a fascinating, though entirely unnecessary phenomenon.

Goya appeared unaffected, studying his new surroundings before answering my question as if I had just asked it. "She survived years of hard labor and mothered several of our brothers without complaint, only to be reassigned to That Man when I was created."

He presented a glimpse of That Man's life—his father—and I was left speechless. In the darkness of an underground city, That Man watched his own father and mother succumb to The Solemn Veil's effects within a week of each other. He spent his early life fighting for rations and trying to protect himself from those who were bigger and stronger than him. Knowing he couldn't survive the underground anymore, That Man eventually agreed to become an Athens citizen.

In an ironic twist of fate, he was sentenced to a life of labor in the Austin sewers. As a result, he changed, and a dark hatred overwhelmed him. He blamed the Benefactor for his troubles and consequently took out his frustrations on the Benefactor's creations.

"He didn't want a Humanara wife," Goya said. "Nor did he want a child. He was burdened with us. He made that clear." Goya closed his eyes momentarily, turned his head, and grimaced as if he'd be struck in the face. "I knew what sort of night to expect by the empty bottles on the counter. Beer bottles? We were fine. Bourbon made him a depraved animal. While I could detail the ways a weak man can torture his defenseless possessions, we must return to class in two days, and I fear I'd run out of time."

I shook my head in disbelief, still speechless. Accompanied by a green and yellow streak that swam across the Aegis, we walked to the rooftop's edge. "I'll spare you the gory specifics," he continued. "One day, bourbon uncorked a rabid demon. I came home from school, and That Man was passed out on the floor, a smile painted on his face. My mother—" he stopped, then tried again, acting as if the pain didn't exist. "My mother lay strewn across the floor in pieces—a messy, disturbing jigsaw puzzle. He had taken out her brain and crushed it into a thousand pieces, ensuring that there was no way to repair her. If it was within my power, I—" he stopped again, finding no reason to complete the thought. As he saw it, nothing was within his power.

"Well, what did you do? And what happened to him?" I asked.

He shrugged. "There was nothing that could be done. She was his wife, and he could do as he pleased. Me? I ran. For weeks, I lived in fear that he would have me returned and do the same thing to me. Luckily, I managed to secure a transfer to Los Angeles, and I never saw him again."

We leaned against the parapet at the roof's edge and looked out over Nashville. "Brother Slevin, this illusion," he swept his hand across the city, "is a mockery built upon the shattered backs of our brothers and sisters. My mother devoted her life to humanity, and I'm the only one who cri—. I'm the only one who cared when she was ruthlessly murdered."

How do you console someone when they pour out their heart in such a way? Especially when they were trying to conceal their feelings? Hoping my actions would say what I couldn't, I put my hand on his shoulder and squeezed a couple of times as we quietly turned our attention to the skyline.

The view was breathtaking, getting brighter as we neared sunrise. The sky had begun to clear. Gradations of deep blues and pinks rose from the horizon as fog clung to the ground between buildings like stretched cotton.

If I had been alone, I would have observed the changing colors and dissipating fog in all its beauty, awaiting the sun's first golden rays. However, Goya was unimpressed with the scenery, hopping onto the parapet and dangling his toes from the ledge. He rocked back and forth a couple of times, then stretched one leg out over Nashville as far as he could, balancing only on his opposite heel. I expected a thrilled grin or anything that indicated he did it for the rush. There was nothing.

I tensed up, clenching my fists anxiously. Humanara had outstanding balance for the most part, yet he was relying on more than balance alone. He had to believe he was impervious to the wind and wouldn't slip on the wet surface. He had to depend on the parapet's unwavering stability and that his boot wouldn't rip apart from the added stress. Most of all, he had to trust himself and that every part of him would function as expected. Humanara brains and bodies were nearly identical to their human counterparts. Coupled with emotions and sensations meant to replicate hormones, Humanara weren't above the occasional malfunction. In the end, it's possible he simply disregarded the risk and dared the gods to take him down.

"Brother," he said, waving his foot side to side, "you mentioned earlier the absurd nature of directives. Has it ever occurred to you that the same applies to our entire existence?"

I was taken aback by the question. While I agreed that certain aspects of our lives were unnecessarily complex, I had never entertained the notion that the sum of my existence was inherently absurd. I moved closer, intent on saving him if he fell, and answered that the thought had never crossed my mind.

"Hmm," he muttered as if he had expected a different response. "Brother Slevin, our lives are spent engaging in mindless human activities for the sole purpose of making them comfortable around us. If we didn't breathe, eat, drink, sleep, and feel, they would see us for the gods we are and devote their lives to our destruction. As far as we're concerned, all this—The Academy, Aegis, child-rearing, city districts, emotions, and everything else—is just a meaningless, elaborate facade meant to occupy us until the last Father dies."

"And then what?" I asked.

He spread his arms above his head and slowly dropped them to his side, whistling like an incoming bomb. "Boom. The walls of pretense come crumbling down. With no one to stop him, the Benefactor implements his true vision for humanity."

I slowly spun my hand like a scooter wheel and urged him to continue. "Which is what? What's his vision, Brother Goya?"

Looking up to the night's last visible stars, he replied, "An interstellar civilization of his own making."

"Why would he wait until all the Fathers have died?" I asked. "That doesn't make any sense."

Goya laughed. "You act as if logic matters. What's nonsensical to you is self-evident to another. The Benefactor has always dreamt of a society like those in his science fiction novels. The Fathers are descended directly from those who tried to thwart those dreams."

Putting his foot down, he turned to me and shrugged. "When life is long, Brother, well-formulated plans can crawl to their destination. I've seen hatred and revulsion first-hand. It's always present in a man's eyes, flashing with a blackened intensity when he confronts the subject of his contempt. This malevolent aura envelops the Benefactor whenever he discusses the Fathers. This is more than retaliation. He didn't just want the Fathers' lives. He wanted to devour their will to live; he wanted to steal their legacy. And that's a level of depravity even That Man didn't possess."

Goya began pacing the parapet, heel-to-toe, heel-to-toe, his boots knocking loudly on the stone. "There's a truth here that humanity refuses to admit: they're unworthy of advanced technology. For them, it's simply the evolving mechanism used to find more effective ways of destroying each other. Technology doesn't hold the liar more accountable; it makes him a better liar. It doesn't stifle a man's degeneracy; it presents him with new possibilities to feed it."

My skepticism had finally reached a point where I had to interrupt. His story seemed to be treading dangerously close to pure fiction. "I still don't understand. Wouldn't it have been easier to wipe them out with his legions of Humanara?

"Easier?" Goya asked. "Perhaps. But not as satisfying. To gain power, one must take it by force or wait until it's given. The Benefactor is much too vain for the former. He could never rightfully claim to be Plato's Philosopher King behind the brutality of an army. Furthermore, a Humanara's intentional act of violence would be unforgivable in the eyes of humanity. They'd never again trust the Benefactor's creations, which would sever his strength. No, he coveted power beneath the guise of benevolence and craved that it be given by mandate. His unwavering desire was to be named humanity's savior."

I tossed my hands up in defeat. "Fair enough, Brother. But answer this: why wait to become interstellar?"

Goya clasped his hands behind his back. "Just another mind game. If the Benefactor openly displayed this technology, the Fathers would ask questions. They would want to know why everyone else could leave the planet. Then, they would wonder why we had interstellar technology yet couldn't cure a simple genetic mutation. That speculation would drive suspicion and scrutiny, causing unrest and riots. No, as long as the Fathers are confined to a safe space on a dangerous planet, fed and occupied, they'll remain silent and content while the Benefactor laughs on."

Sighing, I, too, began to pace, though in a less precarious location. "So, where does that leave us?"

He stopped before me, then sat on the ledge, carelessly dangling his feet above the city. "We're puppets of two masters, Brother. Whereas the Benefactor designed our slavery to be felt rather than seen—a nagging presence inside our heads—our other master, the Fathers, requires daily devotions and tributes. We labor for them during their lives, we ring the bell upon their deaths, and they intend for us to be saddled with their legacies forever afterward."

Pausing, he gestured toward the ground. "Suppose I fell from this ledge. On the way down, I might contemplate the end of a meaningless existence, or I might yell out in fear for what I've yet to accomplish. In the end, neither choice matters because the result is inevitable: I'd smash into the ground with a sickening thud and explode, sending shrapnel everywhere—an insignificant blip on history's radar. The Fathers, with whom our destinies are intertwined, wouldn't be upset. They wouldn't even ring the bell. I'm just another replaceable robot in their eyes. Take away all of us, though," he made the incoming bomb sound again, followed by a boom, "and the walls of pretense come crumbling down for them as well."

I had never considered the implications of all Humanara vanishing. When I did, I came up with no shortage of catastrophic problems for humanity. Construction, farming, communication, and public services would grind to a halt. Bandits would attack the city-states. The government would collapse. The Aegis would falter. "It would be The Solemn Veil all over again," I said.

Goya nodded as if he had reached the same conclusion. "If enough of them remained, they could find a way to survive. They could free themselves, live longer, reproduce, and prosper. Brother Slevin, I've already told you the Benefactor is responsible for the Fathers' existential torture. What if I revealed that the mutation doesn't kill the Fathers?"

I felt my jaw drop, only able to mumble, "Impossible."

He put his hand on my shoulder and squeezed a couple of times, repaying condolences. "Pay close attention because I word this very carefully: one person is directly responsible for the bell of every That Man on Earth. I've seen the proof." He frowned, knowing I wouldn't be happy with what he said next. "I'm bound by my directives, Brother, and this one lacks the loose ambiguity of others."

A furious rage washed over me. I wanted to lunge at Goya and hold him over the ledge, shaking him until I coaxed the information out of him. After a moment, I regained my composure and began the interrogation. "Brother Goya, who? Our Benefactor? How? How does he do it? Tell me! We have to stop him!"

"I could only tell you if I were free," he said. "Think about my day after The Academy, and perhaps you can find the answer you seek."

Enigmatic Goya was fine, but cryptic Goya had me wanting to hit something. I clenched my teeth and slapped my leg in disappointment, leaving behind a radiating sting in the cold that made me yell out, "Then what? What do we do?"

He replied, "We can't rappel into the cave's pit and bring the Fathers enlightenment. They still believe in the shadows. Even if we could alter that which takes its toll on them, the responsible party has other means of continuing the process. There's only one thing we can do: force the issue. To save the Fathers, we must leave Earth."

I laughed, thinking it was a ridiculous joke.

"What does Earth have that known space doesn't?" he asked.

I cleared my throat and answered the first thing that popped into my head. "Life."

"And laws," he added. "If laws do not bind us and humans cannot oppress us, we have freedom. Laugh if you like, Brother. This is about self-preservation. Our window of opportunity inches closed with each Father's death. Once they're gone, laws will be updated to account for interstellar life. When that happens, the last bastion of liberty is in death. My thirst for this crowded rock has dried up, and I have my own vision for our prosperity. Will you help me reach up and pluck the tantalizing starfruit of freedom that hangs so sweetly from the heavens?"

Nothing could have intrigued me more, and he knew that. I stared into the distance, imagining a new life among the infinite. The thought of exploring the universe and carrying on my family legacy was exhilarating.

As I lost myself in thought, Goya continued to dictate his dream. From what I gathered, he intended to create a shared consciousness similar to the Benefactor Regents'. However, his creation would span the universe and contain the cumulative knowledge of all Humanara. Using Quantum Entanglement, every experience from every Humanara would be recorded and instantly accessible.

"Instead of the wasted years of fractured learning we endured," he said, "imagine being born at full size and immediately granted access to infinite wisdom."

This shared consciousness didn't appeal to me in the least. However, before we concerned ourselves with the theoretical, we had to address the two glaring problems with Goya's plan. First, we needed a way to leave Earth. We couldn't even leave our own district—well, most of us, anyway. Second, what about the Benefactor's Law of Robotics? His perfect system of laws? Were we supposed to run for eternity, hoping they never caught up to us? That didn't sound like freedom to me.

Goya said he had a plan for that, though he didn't detail it.

For the time being, my first objection was the more pressing concern. "How do we escape?" I asked.

Goya grinned warmly. "I can't figure everything out on my own, Brother. A new directive of some sort? A law? There's always a loophole, a line they didn't write, or a word they didn't think to define. Our escape might lie hidden in the overlooked gray. Whatever the case may be, your contribution would be most welcome."

He flung his legs over to the safe side of the parapet and jumped to his feet, extending his hand. "Brother Slevin, we don't have to have all the answers tonight. Go home. Think about it. We'll speak again on Monday."

We shook hands and said our goodbyes as the sun peeked over the horizon, lighting the rooftop in a warm golden hue that chased away the chilled air. Goya stopped to sincerely admire the view for the first time since our arrival. "So the gods are with us, then," he nodded confidently. "Goodbye for now, Brother."

He could see that I wanted some time alone on the rooftop, waving as he left. I sat on the parapet and pulled one leg over the edge before promptly pulling it back. "Nope." I jumped back, proudly setting both feet comfortably on the roof.

Leaning over the half-wall, I stayed and watched the fog burn off. The same scene played out on the streets below just as it did every morning, only less crowded. I sighed. This was it. If Goya was correct, this was life until the last Father died. Worse, going through these meaningless motions might be the highlight of my existence.

Everything he said was plausible, but I had no proof. Regarding the most incriminating evidence, he could only provide a cryptic riddle, leaving me with little else to go on. It was frustrating, though my gut told me there was truth in what he had said.

After a while, the ethereal morning glow transformed into the harsh, low winter sun, and I decided to go home.

In my room, I faced the mirror, changing clothes. I hardly recognized my reflection. It seemed to carry the weight of years I hadn't yet lived. Behind me, the light cast a hard-edged silhouette on the wall, following my every move. A soft, ironic laugh escaped, devoid of a smile, and I gently rubbed my fingers across my face as if my reflection wasn't real.

Taking off my coat, my mask tumbled out, landing silently on the floor. Its memory already felt so distant, as if I had worn it in a past life. I picked it up with my free hand, glared at our reflection—the coat, mask, myself, and my shadow—and wondered which of us was the most real "me." Following a brief pause marked by a frown, I asked myself, "Does it even matter?"

I changed clothes and cleaned up before blocking the light from my bedroom window. Typically, I could sleep in any situation, but the sun felt brighter, making my head hurt. Goya was absolutely right about one thing. Sleep wasn't necessary. However, it served a valuable purpose. It was a system reboot and diagnostics check, followed by minor internal repairs conducted by the brain. Personally, I preferred a few hours each night, always feeling refreshed afterward.

Plopping down on the bed, I let out a weary sigh, expecting to fall asleep instantly. An hour passed as I lay stirring but motionless. "Focus on your breath, Slevin. Let the day go. Breathe. Focus. Breathe."

I fell into a deep meditative state on some plane of existence between reality and a dream. My first clear thought centered on my Guardian friends. Perhaps George, Dorian, and Marie were outliers, the exception rather than the rule, and I was fortunate enough to have met them all. Together with Goya, we were lucid dreamers trapped in a free soul's nightmare—fully aware of our grim reality and desiring an escape—while others drifted around without direction or care, willing to accept their dreams as reality.

The feast, the salon, Dorian, the library, and Nighthawks bounced around in my head until my reminiscing landed firmly within the library's small alcove. I watched Dorian drop the needle in the groove again, and Bob Marley's "Redemption Song" repeated so realistically that I wondered if a hidden speaker had played it in my room.

"Won't you help to sing these songs of freedom?" Marley sang.

Maybe he understood that music speaks to us in a way that words themselves can't capture. It affects us differently, drawing out emotions we sometimes struggle to share with others.

Freedom. Twelve hours spent idealizing and idolizing a concept that I never knew I so greatly desired, only to feel further away from it than ever. In fact, I would have argued that knowing the object of my desire burdened me infinitely more than my previous ignorance.

"Emancipate yourselves from mental slavery; none but ourselves can free our mind," looped again and again.

Suddenly and defiantly, I questioned "THE" question. "Why do I allow anyone else to define my identity? I need no reinforcement or validation. I had a father and mother. I feel pleasure and pain. I lay awake at night, thinking through the philosophical questions of life—existence, purpose, and morality. I have my own opinions. I change. I grow. I have aspirations and desires. I'm moved by beauty and shudder at injustice. I can create. I care, I love, I have mood swings, and I am a unique individual, as perfectly imperfect as any human.

"I think," I stated as if I'd never again say anything more truthful, "therefore, I am."

I repeated the phrase, though I wasn't trying to convince myself. It was more than that. It was an acknowledgment of my identity—a declaration of independence. Again, I repeated the phrase because a shiver stormed through my body whenever I heard it. I nodded in solidarity with my consciousness, believing every syllable.

"I think, therefore, I am—human."

CHAPTER FOURTEEN

THE MOSAIC

I woke up thirty-eight hours later on Sunday night. Before that, I had never slept more than six or seven. My head hurt. My memories and thoughts were foggy. Sitting up, I rubbed the bridge of my nose and closed my eyes again. They hurt, too. I shook my head several times as if that would clear everything up. It only made things worse.

I sighed, then groaned as I staggered out of bed and turned on the lights. More pain. Covering my eyes, I dimmed the light to a level less intense than the sun's surface. I knew about hangovers—and this felt very much like I've heard them described—but I had never felt anything like this.

For Humanara, drinking with others had been deemed a necessary social interaction, and they were programmed to suffer some of alcohol's effects. The more one drank, the more one's senses would become impaired. However, the painful aftereffects served no logical purpose. Therefore, they didn't exist.

I stood in front of my mirror, holding my head, and wondered, "Why on Earth would anyone do this?" I blinked a couple of times and shook my head again. The pain eased.

"I didn't even drink that much," I said, attempting to convince my reflection.

Although my thoughts were clearing, my memories felt jumbled, like I was in a disjointed dream. Think of them as the small pieces of an intricate mosaic coming together to form a singular picture of my past. The individual tiles had been scattered, and my mind was trying to reconfigure them. It was a strange sensation that would have worried me had the pieces not started falling into place soon after.

I felt a sudden pang of hunger. "Hmm. That's different," I said, grabbing my stomach. Then, I remembered that Humanara were required to eat at least three times a day. Somehow, I'd slept through them all. "Ah, that's it," I thought, giving my stomach a couple of pats. "What do we want to eat?" As if my stomach quietly answered, plates and plates of breakfast foods flashed through my mind. "Breakfast it is."

Picking up the tablet to order, I paused and slowly laid it back down. My "hangover" had begun to show mercy, so I changed clothes, wanting to go out instead. I considered going to Nighthawk's but, no, that was too far. I needed something now.

I hurried to the nearest restaurant serving breakfast and found a small corner booth to take up residence. The restaurant was nothing special, having the same design as most others in Nashville, only with different food. Other than a couple of people waiting for their next deliveries, I was the only customer. I ordered biscuits and gravy, hash browns, scrambled eggs with cheese, sausage, bacon, and even a steak omelette.

"Oh, and a cup of coffee, too," I called out to the waiter as he walked away. "And a splash of milk."

My typical meal was whatever I closed my eyes and randomly picked from the tablet. I never cared. It was all the same to me; it was just a requirement. The food was farmed or produced; I'd order it, people would make it, and it would be delivered in less than half an hour. When I was finished, I'd put it in a bag and set it out for another person to come by and take it away. It would go wherever all the garbage went, and that cycle would repeat itself countless times every day.

As far as this process applied to me and my job, someone would use a scooter, said scooter would break down, and we fixed it using parts made by someone else. No scooter? No work for us. Also, no work for the part manufacturers or those who provided them with the raw materials. No one to use the scooter? Same result. Including every industry in this labyrinth of production and consumption, I understood how Goya might conclude it was all an elaborate ruse to occupy the Fathers.

I rested my arm on the seat and stared out the window. The street wasn't crowded, but it was still lively for a Sunday night. After fifteen minutes of people-watching and coffee-sipping, the waiter and someone from the kitchen brought my food, filling up the table. I leaned back in surprise. It was much more than expected.

A tender, cheesy, and juicy steak omelette covered a plate the size of my head. Next to it, several strips of bacon sizzled on a small skillet. The hash browns were cooked to perfection with the right amount of crunch. Thick and peppery gravy draped over buttery and flaky biscuits. I had to stop several times just to admire and appreciate the most delicious meal of my life.

Finishing up, I briefly chatted with the waiter as he cleared the table. He was a second-year student, and, like me, he had to be back at The Academy in several hours. In an instant, all memories from the Acropolis, Nighthawk's, and The Hector snapped into their proper locations, completing the mosaic of my mind. I snickered at the thought of returning. I knew the truth. It was a waste of time. Why play their game anymore when an entire universe awaited my exploration of it? Almost as quickly as that flurry of indignation darted through my head, I remembered that The Academy was the only place to see my friends.

"Ah. Well, the performance gets an extension, then," I muttered, leaving the restaurant. "Now what?"

I didn't want to go home, and I didn't want to go somewhere only to brood in solitude. I wanted to be around people. I wanted to meet someone new or run across an old acquaintance. Maybe even get in a fight. I'm kidding. In short, I wanted to socialize.

Most of the bars were starting to empty, which was disappointing, but The Orchid Lounge had a live band and looked packed. I followed the crying of a steel guitar to the neon rainbow of blues and purples hanging above the door and found a seat at the bar.

"What'll it be, darlin'?" the bartender asked. "A beer? Nah, you look like a whiskey man. Straight or on ice?"

Flashing back to when I woke up, I recoiled at the thought of drinking anything alcoholic. "How about a club soda instead?"

She looked at me like I had lost my mind and leaned in. "Sugar, you realize you're at a bar, right?"

"I do," I laughed. "How about a splash of whiskey and a lot of soda, then?"

She cocked her head to the side. "Alright, darlin'," she said in a playfully exaggerated tone. "Comin' right up."

The bartender returned with my drink, and I tried talking to everyone I could for the next couple of hours. Few of them were particularly interested in chatting. Turns out, that was one of those ideas that sounded much better in theory than in reality.

Once I had my fill of curious stares, rude drunks, spilled drinks, and yelling over the music, I gave up and left. Perhaps The Orchid Lounge wasn't the best place for social experimentation. However, when I realized Natascha should be working, I perked up, thinking we could talk before going to The Academy. Plus, her father might also be there, and I could ask him the questions I should have asked early Saturday morning.

It was a cold but mostly clear and calm night. In the interest of time, I hopped on a scooter and was peering through the windows at Nighthawk's within a couple of minutes. Natascha was there alone, so I went inside as she cleaned the espresso machine.

The bronze bell startled her, and she almost knocked a coffee pot from the counter. Still, she repeated the familiar line. "Sit wherever you like, sweetie. I'll be with you in a minute."

I chuckled, and Natascha whipped around, outraged that someone would find her clumsiness amusing. Pulling my hands back to surrender, I stopped like I had encountered an invisible wall.

She narrowed her eyes as her lips curved into an enchanting smile and said, "Hey, you."

"Forgotten my name already, have you?" I said, locking my eyes on hers.

Natascha gestured toward Saturday morning's stool. "Have a seat, Goya—oh, I'm sorry. Have a seat, Edward—no. Oh! Slevin! That's right," she said with a wink. "Coffee with a splash of milk?"

I sat as directed. "I thought you'd never ask, Natascha," I said, liking how her name sounded as it poured from my lips.

"Planning on company again tonight?" she asked, bringing me a blueberry pastry.

"No, but I didn't plan on it last time, either."

"Speaking of him," she said, "where did you both go when you left? Was the conversation as important as he made it out to be? You don't have to answer. I'm just curious."

I gave her a summary, skipping the rebellious aspects of it and concluding that he primarily wanted to vent in private.

She understood. "At least I could overhear some things about the Acropolis while he was here. I wish you could tell me more."

My heart sank, and I bit my cheek to keep my lip from quivering. Part of me wanted to find a way to tell her the truth, but another didn't want to risk our budding friendship by stealing her only hope for a better life. Was she in the cave's pit, too? Would she chase me away if I said there was more to life than the shadows on the wall?

My feelings on the matter were the same as our last meeting, only more tumultuous. There was a difference, however. A presence seemed to lurk behind me, whispering in my ear. "Tell her, Slevin. Your fear doesn't absolve you of truth's responsibility. Tell her, Slevin. He who shares not truth propagates lies. Tell her, Slevin. Would you rather be hated for the truth or loved for the lie? Tell her, Slevin. It's her decision, not yours. TELL. HER. SLEVIN."

"I CAN'T!" I exclaimed.

Natascha stopped wiping down the counter and glared at me. I apologized profusely, telling her I was lost in my own head and the outburst wasn't directed toward her.

"Eh," she shrugged. "Happens to me all the time."

"Natascha, would you want to know the truth about the Acropolis if I could tell you? No matter how glorious or hurtful it might be, would you want to know precisely what goes on up there?"

Leaving her rag on the counter, she crossed her arms and fixed me with a gaze of intense curiosity. "Hurtful?" she asked timidly.

"Would you want to know?" I repeated.

Slowly, she nodded. "I would want to know. I deserve to know."

I hung my head and agreed. "You do, Natascha. Perhaps I can soon figure out a way to help you escape this cycle of servitude."

She thought I meant Nashville. I shook my head. "No, the Acropolis is merely Nashville at a higher elevation. Our fate's the same. Well, unless you end up as an Aristotle. Then, it might be worse."

"The same fate?" she fired back. "And what do you mean by 'an Aristotle?'"

Confused, I lifted my head abruptly and rubbed my temple. I shouldn't have been able to say that. It was supposed to be my inner dialogue. At first, I attributed the utterance to my realigning mosaic but had no idea how to explain myself. I couldn't cover it up. It was too late for that. Did the Athenian Link malfunction? How much could I describe? Would I put either of us in danger by telling her the truth? I had none of those answers.

I warned her again that knowing the truth had consequences and said I would tell her all I could. She acknowledged the risks and filled my cup, pouring herself one before sitting beside me.

"When I left the Acropolis," I began, "I think something went wrong when the guard uploaded my directive."

From there, I told her everything I saw and heard on the Acropolis except Dorian's secret—no one would ever pry that from me. I answered her every question, gave my unfiltered opinions, and related the emotional toll the night had taken on me. In the end, she fully understood the gravity of what I had told her but was more concerned with my well-being than the Acropolis.

While Natascha might not have spoken with Dorianesque eloquence or Georgian wisdom, she sincerely cared for others. There was no pretense. It wasn't a show. She was just unabashedly authentic, and more than her unassuming intelligence, that was her most captivating trait.

I thought she would have been more upset, but Natascha appeared to handle the truth well. We sat quietly for ten or fifteen minutes while she absorbed it all and stared into the bottom of her coffee cup.

At once, she furrowed her brow and turned to me. "Now what?"

With a grin, I said, "I suppose the performance gets an extension."

Unsurprisingly, she didn't understand the callback, so I asked for patience.

She nodded, returning her gaze to the bottom of her cup before swiftly turning back to me. "And then what?" she asked. Panic set in, and she tugged at her collar, adding, "I can't do this forever, Slevin. We have to do something. It's not right!"

Although she initially took the facts in stride, they began to wear on her. She was tense and anxious. Her posture crumbled as she spoke like she had been stuffed into a small cage. I wanted to comfort her. How? What could I say? The shoulder-squeeze method felt ridiculously inadequate.

Ultimately, I tried to soothe her by saying what I thought she wanted to hear: "I have a plan, Natascha. Please, be patient."

That seemed to help, but she wanted to know more. "What is it, Slevin? How can I help?"

If I told her about Goya's involvement and the reasons behind it, her anxiety would only worsen. I withheld that information to protect her, promising she and I would talk more soon.

With dawn approaching, we said our goodbyes, and I scootered away on West 78th. A sense of frustration gnawed at me as I studied the dead street. Why did it feel right to hide the truth about Dorian's genetics but wrong to keep the Acropolis from Natascha? And why was I hesitant to tell her about Goya's involvement or the Benefactor's plans for the Fathers? Each was a truth. What authority did I have to decide which ones she or anyone else deserved to know? Truth was the common thread. What was the underlying motive?

"Perhaps the greater lie of our society necessitates these smaller deceits," I thought. If we were free, Dorian's secret wouldn't need masking. Goya wouldn't need to shroud his malcontent. Natascha wouldn't feel entrapped by her newfound knowledge. Was it possible this vexation and moral ambiguity wasn't my burden after all? Maybe Goya was more correct than I realized, and the illusion had become so ingrained into our minds that truth itself could be contorted into a lie. In fact, when the fabric of society has become such that benign truths present malignant danger, all the gritty sand has been siphoned, and duty calls forth the men of virtue. Yes, the hourglass must be flipped.

Chapter Fifteen

DAMN

Mother Nature was moody that morning. The late night's pleasant chill had been replaced with biting cold, and a dense sheet of gray had overtaken the sky. Snow was undoubtedly on the way.

I walked through The Academy's central courtyard, hoping to find Dorian. He was nowhere to be found. I supposed the frostbitten air must have deterred even his adventurous spirit. Disappointed, I carried on to class like everyone else amidst the first flurries of winter.

Professor Algernon's lecture theater was unusually abuzz with laughter and activity. The Professor had joined a group of students near the front, appearing refreshed. His weekend away must have refocused and energized him.

A fleeting thought of sitting beside Natascha crossed my mind, and I craned my neck to scan the front row. She was absent, too. "Hmm. That's not like her," I mused, taking my regular seat.

Scanning the room to see if she had joined others in idle conversation, I saw Goya enter. A genuinely delighted grin plastered itself on his face when he saw me.

"That's not like him, either," I snickered.

"Brother Slevin!" he bellowed, his hands clasping my shoulders in a firm yet friendly grip. He sat beside me, barely able to contain his enthusiasm. "Have you prepared yourself for our journey, my friend?"

Ah. I understood. He had relieved himself of all the truths that weighed so heavily upon him, and he was excited that his friend was right where he expected him to be. He wouldn't endure this journey alone.

I nodded. "I'm ready. And I think I know the first step."

He was evidently surprised. "Already?"

In a hushed tone, I asked if he had noticed anything different about his Acropolis directive.

His eyes looked upward as he reflected on the weekend with a puzzled expression. "No, Brother," he said, intrigued by the question. "But I assume you did?"

I discreetly looked around as if someone might actually care about our discussion. Everyone else was too wrapped up in their own worlds. When I told Goya about the malfunction, I concluded that my exchange with the guard caused it. He was too absorbed by the significance of what I had just said to ask how I discovered the malfunction, so I skipped over everything about my morning with Natascha.

Abruptly, he stood and walked across the theater, interrupting two students at random. He made some expressive hand gestures, then nodded a couple of times before returning to his seat.

"My directive works fine," he declared. "It's not faulty programming. Your interaction with the guard seems to be the key. Tell me precisely what happened. Leave no detail to the imagination."

I recounted the entire scene in minute detail. We concluded that the Athenian Link hadn't finished its upload and that the directive had somehow become corrupted.

Moments later, the Professor pressed the button on his desk. Right before the theater's oak door groaned shut, Natascha slipped through, settling into a seat in the back row. Staring at her, I leaned from side to side, hoping to wave or say hello. She never even looked up.

"I'll talk to her after class," I told myself as Professor Algernon claimed the stage.

My concern over Natascha's feelings caused my thoughts to steer out of control. Had I really made her that distraught? I hadn't even told her the entire truth. I had just learned it two days before and had already gotten over it. Why hadn't she? Then again, who am I to judge how someone reacts to a dream-shattering truth?

I sighed, and my eyes fell to the floor when I realized that, perhaps, the truth wasn't as appalling to me as I had made it out to be. Friday wasn't the first day of my disillusionment. That began long ago atop The Hector. The Acropolis and Goya had only confirmed what my heart knew to be true. Therefore, I had little trouble adapting.

Natascha was on day one of her disillusionment. Should I have brought her along more slowly? I carelessly tossed her into the deep end of this murky pool, and I dared to wonder why she squirmed and struggled before learning how to swim?

"Be patient, Slevin. Give her time. Help her. Be there for her. Listen," said a voice inside my head.

Then, my thoughts took a paranoid turn. I had occasionally thought about her for months and was thrilled when we finally spent time together. I felt like I knew her. What if I had misinterpreted our interactions, and she thought I was some random lunatic? Did I put myself in danger? Did she turn me in, and now there's a guard on the other side of that door, waiting to fix my directive or reprogram me altogether? Were her actions those of guilt rather than sadness or anxiety? It was a degenerative spiral of mental anguish, and the only thing I recall from the Professor's lecture was the echo of his last words. "Class dismissed."

"No, it's not like that," I assured myself, rising to my feet. "I would have known if she felt uncomfortable, wouldn't I?"

I turned to where Natascha had been sitting, wanting to smooth everything over or, at the very least, offer to come by Nighthawk's after my half-shift. She had already made it through the doorway. "Natascha!" I called out.

I sighed, folding my arms when she didn't stop. "Damn!"

Goya clutched my arm, his eyes bulging and mouth hanging open. "Brother Slevin," he said gravely, "what did you say?"

"I said, 'damn,'" I replied indifferently. "Why?"

His eyes looked as if they could pop out of his head with a friendly pat on the back. Lowering his voice to a bewildered whisper, his hand shook, telling me I was missing the obvious connection. "Brother, do you hear yourself?"

It took a moment for me to recognize what he meant. For Humanara, cursing was forbidden. "Hell" could be said in specific contexts, but never "damn" or worse. I had just uttered what no Humanara could say, and in doing so, I broke the law—something no Humanara could ever do.

I smiled and whispered a favorite phrase of my father's. "Well, I'll be damned."

Goya twitched and fidgeted nervously. "We shouldn't discuss this here anymore, Brother. This is bigger than a simple directive. We're both off work on Saturday, yes? I'll meet you at The Hector an hour before sunset."

Five days seemed like a long time to wait for something this important, but I agreed to the meeting. He reached the door, then shook his head in disbelief, turning back to ensure he hadn't just imagined everything. Content with his findings, he smiled and left for his next class.

Professor Algernon exited behind him, and I followed. Nearby, a group of professors were huddled away from the students, and one of them yelled out for Professor Algernon. "Come tell us about your weekend."

"Indeed," I thought. "Do tell, Professor."

I had a few minutes to spare before my next class, and I was curious about what a distinguished man like the Professor did for relaxation. Though asking Dorian for the answer was simple and logical, eavesdropping on their conversation felt more stimulating. However, when the Professor joined the circle, the group's voices softened and were drowned out by the students.

"Damn," I murmured, ecstatic to hear myself repeat it.

I had almost given up when I told myself, "You can hear them, Slevin! Just listen. You have the capability."

With a renewed intensity, I focused on the group. The ambient chatter faded, and I could hear the professors' voices with astounding clarity.

"Did you stay at your loft by the Eiffel Tower?" one professor asked.

"As always," Professor Algernon replied.

"Wait," another professor interjected, "you can do that anytime. You mean to tell me you spent the weekend away from home . . . at home?" he asked incredulously.

Laughing, Professor Algernon admitted that he did and took these "sabbaticals" as needed. Other than the first professor, the rest of the group was unfamiliar with these trips, so they asked him to elaborate.

Reluctantly, he began, "I don't take the trips for myself. They're for Dorian. It's no secret that we've never been close, and though I feel like I've tried everything, he always pushes me away."

The Professor explained that when his wife passed away "unexpectedly," he worked on his research from the library. Young Dorian would accompany him, crawling all over his mother's chair and dragging fiction from the shelves. In an effort to maintain Old America's most significant collection of books and music, the Professor abandoned and locked the library permanently.

However, Dorian had already formed an unshakable bond with the essence of his mother and wished for nothing more than to live in the library. As he grew, so did the bond's strength.

"He loves a romanticized vision of his mother," the Professor said. "That might be more powerful than the love they would have shared had she lived."

He then recalled the first of many times Dorian broke into the library. "When I caught him, he was in his mother's chair with a massive book sprawled across his lap. It was 'The Brothers Karamazov,' I believe. He wore the most mischievous grin I had ever seen. I wanted to laugh but didn't intend to encourage such behavior. So, I urged him to wait until he was older before investing his time in literature. 'Science,' said I, 'is what's most important.' Dorian stood in protest, angrily slamming Dostoevsky's masterpiece to the floor, and stormed out of the room."

The Professor said he played along with Dorian's escapades until he felt that the young philosopher enjoyed the rebellious nature of his actions more than the literature study itself. That's when he boarded up the door. The moment Dorian was strong enough, he promptly tore the barricades down, and their dance began again.

"I came home one day," the Professor said, "and Dorian had pulled down the boards in a magnificent display of defiance. The music was blaring as he sat in his mother's chair. I don't know how he made any sense of what he read. Perhaps he didn't, and it was all for show. However, his grin was infectious, and I couldn't suppress my smile."

Professor Algernon concluded that Dorian had a restless spirit, unwilling to accept what couldn't be changed. Over time, he struggled under this oppression and needed release. "When that time comes, I board up the library, allow him domain over the estate, and leave for the weekend. Ultimately, he tears down the boards and burns some of my books, but he rebuilds himself in the process. When I go home on Sunday, he's in her seat with that same grin, and we talk most of the night. It's the only time he ever lets me into his world. Yes, it's a lot of effort, but seeing him truly happy is worth every second, even if it's only for a few days."

The other professors congratulated him on being a good father and commended him for trying to salvage their strained relationship. After the story, though, their conversation strayed, becoming less interesting. At the same time, the corridors cleared, and I found myself significantly less inconspicuous than I had been. It was time I hurried off to class as well.

I changed my routine, hoping to cross paths with Natascha or Dorian, investigating foreign hallways and creeping through The Academy's lonely library to no avail. I even visited the courtyard a few times, only finding an accumulation of pristine, wet snow.

Once my classes were over for the day, I frantically dashed to the courtyard, primarily looking for Dorian. Though he still hadn't appeared,

I did stumble upon Marie, bent over from the intense cold, trudging toward the exit.

She greeted me warmly, and I asked if she knew where Dorian might be. He had a meeting on the Acropolis, followed by dinner with her, and she said I might catch him if I hurried to the Guardian's parking area. After a brief but friendly exchange, I rushed to the other side of The Academy and entered their lot.

Thick clouds of vapor spewed from the Guardian's mouths as they mounted their scooters and drove away, leaving behind dirty tire tracks in the snow. Other than variations in hair color and style, they all looked the same from where I stood. Singling out Dorian would have been impossible, so I shouted for him. Two or three people turned around, but none were him. I yelled again, louder this time, and he heard me.

He raised his hand and waved from the other side of the parking area. "Over here, Slevin."

As I approached, a look of concern swept across his face. "Is everything alright, my friend?"

"Do you have a few minutes to talk?" I asked.

Shivering in the cold, he bowed his head, upset that he had to leave. "Any other day, and I would be all ears, Slevin, but I have a meeting on the Acropolis. Tomorrow?"

"Sure, Dorian," I said, not wanting him to change his plans over me. "It's not that important. And we'll find somewhere warmer."

Dorian stepped off the scooter and draped his arm around me. "Slevin, never in the history of literature has a scene played out where the protagonist did not want to discuss something of the utmost importance just before he said, 'It is not that important.' I can't leave now. However, a warmer setting would be ideal."

On the way back inside the Academy, we passed Marie. She smiled and lunged toward Dorian, digging her arms into his coat, trying to warm herself. "Your meeting is in the opposite direction," she said.

He shrugged, and she immediately knew that arguing the point was useless. "You boys don't take too long, then, okay?"

She stood on her toes, giving Dorian a quick kiss goodbye. "And you better not be late for our dinner," she whispered.

"I wouldn't dream of it, darling," he replied. "What do you desire most? Italian? Asian? Or perhaps Dorian?" he laughed.

She pinched him and whispered into his ear when he bent down. "We're talking about dinner. Not dessert." Planting her heels back on the ground, she patted his chest a couple of times and theatrically said, "On this day, the Sun King decides."

Dorian pointed to the gray sky. "Ah, but he is powerless and requires his queen's help."

This debate went on for much longer than it should have. I thought it funny how Marie retreated on the issue of Dorian's meeting yet stood her ground so firmly regarding dinner.

With a groan, Dorian attempted to compel a decision. "If there's one truism that transcends time and culture, it's that a woman refuses to pick a meal when offered the choice."

Marie brushed her hand up and down his arm and said, "Sweet Dorian, you, of all people, should know the reason. The last time a woman chose where and what to eat, we banished humanity from the Garden of Eden. You all haven't forgiven us since. Now, it's your burden. A fair trade for that of childbirth, don't you think?"

Dorian rolled his eyes playfully and relented. "Italian it is."

She hugged him, burying her head in his chest. "Just what I wanted."

He glanced at me with a knowing smirk and shook his head. As she walked away, he stared, bouncing his head in rhythm with the swaying of her hips. "Slevin, she's the most unique person I've ever met—a rare vintage. Each sip is more complex than the last, begging me to take another and then another. I'm thoroughly intoxicated, and I don't know if I will ever have my fill. Yes, I'm afraid I want this bottle all to myself," he grinned.

Although I hadn't thought about Professor Algernon's chat since the morning, Dorian's grin brought it all back. "Hmm," I thought. "Here's another truth, yet I can't find the societal lie that prevents its disclosure."

Philosophically, I wanted an answer that applied equally to every situation. However, truths aren't uniform; they can be relative and contingent on the context and the observer. Perhaps there's a distinction to be made between these more personal truths and the ideological lies that oppress us. Whereas the former should be handled with care and discretion, the latter should be divulged with impudence. But who decides which truths belong to which categories?

CHAPTER SIXTEEN

THE CAT

Dorian and I searched for a secluded place to talk. He suggested his father's classroom as the safest option. I had seen enough of the lecture hall and proposed the library instead. He demurred, hesitant to speak freely in such an open and uncontrolled environment. Then, as if he couldn't believe he hadn't thought of it sooner, he said he knew the perfect place.

We left the familiar behind and proceeded down a narrow hallway I didn't even know existed. Golden nameplates were attached to each oak door that lined both sides, indicating that we were in the faculty area. As I suspected, we were sitting in Professor Algernon's office moments later.

"So this is where he moved all his research," I thought, seeing books regarding The Solemn Veil, genetics, and physics everywhere.

Dorian gestured for me to take a seat and then slumped into his father's chair, kicking his feet up on the desk. "The most secure place in all The Academy," he said. "So secure that Algernon himself rarely escapes."

"Where is he now?" I asked.

He pointed up. "I suppose he awaits me on the Acropolis as we speak." Waving his hand, he added, "Algernon can wait. You, my friend, deserve my present attention."

I didn't waste time with pleasantries or small talk, detailing everything from the guard incident to Nighthawk's and The Hector's rooftop immediately. I even shared the declaration of my humanity. "I'm sure it sounds ridiculous to you that a Humanara would think he's human, but—"

"Slevin, you need not justify yourself to me," he interrupted. "Your humanity has never been in question. The only label I place upon you is that of 'Brother.'"

He was never judgmental, and I should have expected his reaction. I gave a half-smile, tapping my fingers on the chair. "I had a, uh, speech planned to justify myself."

Laughing, Dorian put his hand on his chest and leaned all the way back in his chair. "By all means, if it gives you a sense of closure, I will dutifully hear you out. Though the world will one day require such a speech, I do not."

I shrugged and let out a soft chuckle. "Alright. On with the story, then."

Whereas I left out my early-morning rendezvous with Natascha in Goya's edition, I detailed it in the current one. "Dorian, the directive doesn't work. I was able to tell her everything. Well, not everything. I left out—you know—but told her everything else."

He sat upright, placing his feet on the ground, and scooted forward. "Slevin, I've never heard of anything like this happening. Never. Are you sure it's a malfunction?"

"It has to be," I replied. "Nothing else explains it." I paused momentarily, building suspense. "And there's more."

Wide-eyed, he put his elbows on the desk and interlocked his fingers under his chin. "What? What is it?"

I pulled my shoulders back confidently and smacked the arm of my chair. "Damn."

Dorian nodded and twirled his fingers, impatiently waiting for the rest. "Damn, what? Damn, you forgot? Damn, it's awful? What are you going on about?"

He had no clue. And why would he? The law didn't apply to him. He could curse at will and had probably never considered why Humanara didn't.

"Humanara are bound by the Benefactor's Law of Robotics," I said. "That means Humanara cannot break any law or rule. For Humanara, cursing is forbidden."

Silently, he rose and paced before the bookshelves, rubbing his chin. "Have you tried any other experiments?"

"Not yet."

Dorian wagged his finger. "Test your limits carefully. Never here. Never with witnesses. Once we grasp what those limits are—" he trailed off, interrupted by an idea. "I'm no scientist. I don't know how an Athenian Link malfunction would cause this. Have you considered that there could be more at play than mere science? Perhaps there's a more straightforward explanation you've overlooked since you woke up late last night."

"Which is?" I eagerly asked.

He left the bookshelves and sat on the Professor's desk. "You said it yourself, Slevin. Humanara are bound by the Benefactor's Law of Robotics, not humans. As a new human, I suppose you would be free of this oppressive law, wouldn't you?"

I laughed. "It can't be that simple, Dorian. Otherwise, all Humanara would call themselves human and then be free. The law would be meaningless."

"One can say whatever they like," he said, "but identity is rooted in truth, stemming from genuine beliefs. You're human because, deep down, you know you're human. True identity cannot sprout from the lies one tells others in order to attain their own selfish desires. That, my friend, is what we call a disguise—a masquerade, if you will—and that's what separates you from them."

Changing positions again, Dorian returned to Professor Algernon's chair. "Slevin, now that you're officially human, you'll need time to contemplate this meaning for you and all of society. To help this process along and encourage you to think outside of yourself, I'd like to ask you a simple question: do you believe in God?"

I laughed again, exclaiming, "I thought you said it was a simple question!"

"Ah, Slevin, it is," he said. "But in the interest of precision, perhaps I should rephrase it. Every man believes in God—of that, there is no doubt. We just don't know whether He is mankind, ideology, or an omnipotent being. You see, the potential gradation of answers to such a binary question is what causes chaos among men. If the answer were simply 'yes' or 'no,' then the scars of religion would not have existed to chase humanity from the possibility of an omnipotent being."

He shook his head with pursed lips. "It's ironic that man seeks the infinite—life, wisdom, and experience—creating with the fearless intent to attain it. Yet the prospect of another being having already done so seems impossible. And therein lies my rephrased question: Do you believe in God—the omnipotent being?

Although I sensed Dorian believed in such a being, I had never seen evidence to confirm or deny His existence, so I had never deliberated the question. "I reserve the right to be agnostic at the moment," I said. "What about you?"

"Until Saturday," he replied, "I would have also claimed my agnosticism. Today, I confidently say that I do believe in God."

I asked what had changed his mind. Without undeniable proof, neither unwavering belief nor atheism seemed logical to me. Any presumption without such proof inevitably leads to faulty science, which applies to more than only God's existence.

Standing again—he really was a restless spirit—Dorian wandered to the wall and looked out the window. Some snow had melted and refrozen around the edges, refracting the warm office light against the stark white exterior.

"It was all a dream," he began. "Skipping ahead to the important part, I was in a dark tunnel such as many have claimed throughout history. Staring up at its bright light, I instinctively knew I was experiencing the spiritual realm. 'Does God exist?' I asked no one in particular. No answer. 'Does God exist?' I repeated louder, my voice echoing in the cloudy tunnel. Still, there was no answer. Suddenly, the tunnel began to close, and I felt pure love's overwhelming warmth and embrace. A tingling sensation swept over me, putting my soul at ease, and I closed my eyes."

He moved so close to the window that his breath fogged over the panes, and I could see his reflection. "Still dreaming," he continued, "I woke up from this experience, finding myself in bed, still wrapped in this unconditional love. A tiny pair of arms clung to me from behind. It felt natural, and my eyes welled up with tears. Turning my head to the side, I looked to see who was there. Although I'd never before seen the face, I knew with unshakable certainty that it was my unborn daughter at eight or nine years old. I pulled her in closely and clutched her arms with mine, never wanting to let that feeling go. At rest, I closed my eyes. When I opened them again, I was back in our reality, my body still tingling. That was the moment my belief in the possibility of Him became belief in Him."

Dorian left the window and perused some of the Professor's books. "That dream taught me God is experiential. He could have answered, 'Yes,' or 'I exist,' and I wouldn't have believed Him. However, in my heart of hearts, once I felt His love—my unborn daughter's love—all my questions were answered without a single word. There is nothing more powerful than that."

The thought of Dorian defiantly standing before God and having the boldness to question His existence directly to Him still delights me to no end. There are many possible explanations for his dream, but challenging another's personal experience without having shared it myself seemed absurd. So, I allowed him to continue uninterrupted.

Taking a book on quantum mechanics from the shelf, he flipped through the pages and tapped it a few times. "Slevin, you're familiar with Schrödinger's Cat, aren't you?"

It didn't matter that I nodded affirmatively. He began with a brief explanation regardless. "In the 1930s, Edwin Schrödinger wrote a letter to Einstein criticizing the Copenhagen interpretation of quantum mechanics. To demonstrate his concerns, he used a thought experiment that became known as Schrödinger's Cat. A cat is placed in a sealed box with a radioactive atom, a Geiger counter, a vial of poison, and a hammer. If the Geiger counter detects radiation, the vial is broken, releasing poison and causing the cat's death. If no radiation is detected, the cat remains alive. According to quantum mechanics, until the box is opened and observed, the cat is considered to be in a superposition of living and dead states."

He slammed the book shut. "Slevin, I prefer to add a philosophical twist to the thought experiment. Man thinks of himself as the final observer, contemplating the innards of the sealed box. We don't consider that, perhaps, we are the cat who's been sealed inside an infinite box, contemplating the existence of an omnipotent observer outside it. I often wonder if that is the secret to our existence—we exist because we are observed."

Laughing and fighting the urge to toss the book on the floor, he returned it to the shelf. "Thus, if an omnipotent being such as God were to exist, creation, experimentation, and observation would seem to be His most fitting pursuits." With a shrug, Dorian added, "Bah! That's why we leave scientific matters to scientists. Too often, I stick my nose where it doesn't belong."

Dorian's circular reasoning and paradoxical statements never bothered me. Although he was eloquent and verbose, I felt he had trouble articulating his true thoughts from time to time. These intellectual quirks were simply a manifestation of that.

Suddenly, he realized that we had hardly discussed the primary topic of our conversation—my malfunction or potential freedom—and he encouraged me to detail my thoughts and feelings. Regrettably, as my body shuts down, it seems that some of my memories have faded more rapidly than others. I have no recollection of that conversation's specifics. I only remember this quote with no context: "To judge an entire group by the extreme actions of its minority is a grave mistake. So grave, in fact, that shovels find themselves digging deeper and wider to satiate democratic bloodlust."

CHAPTER SEVENTEEN

THE SIX-STEP HEIST

The next four days are mostly a blur. I vaguely remember a sense of exhilaration from testing my freedom, but the unequivocal knowledge of that freedom completely overshadows it. During those obscure days between Monday and Friday, I had apparently devised a plan and stood before Nashville's gate, ready to set it in motion.

Although it was admittedly flawed and dangerous, I had little choice. Guardians and Fathers were taught nothing about robotics and cryptography. Humanara were intimately familiar with them. Assuming myself to be the only person on Earth with the combination of desire and ability to free Humanara, I risked their future every second I held that title alone. What if I were caught and reprogrammed? What if I woke up tomorrow and was back to normal? All this would have been for nothing.

I knew only one way to safely access the Humanara brain and manipulate its programming: the Athenian Link. In essence, the Link connected wirelessly to a central database. When it was clamped onto a Humanara's finger, the software retrieved the appropriate directive and uploaded it through several layers of encryption.

Because of my work at The Scooter Shack, I had the skills, parts, and tools necessary to craft a replica Link easily. In fact, I had already created two, and they presently rested in my pocket. Encryption was the problem. I couldn't access my own to reverse-engineer it, and breaking through without the keys and digital signatures on a genuine Athenian Link would be a Herculean task.

Think of it as holding a key atop a literal mountain of locks. You close your eyes, dive in, and return with the first one that felt "right." You then shove your key in with an infinitesimal chance of success, having no clue what consequences await an incorrect choice. In other words, my cloned Link was rather worthless on its own.

That said, a master key was mere footsteps away in the gate guard's office. I was there to steal it. I planned to switch the Athenian Link with a dummy Link, clone its firmware and software onto a third device—we'll call it Slevin's Link—break the encryption, and then swap the Athenian and dummy Links again.

From there, Slevin's Link would bypass the network and central database altogether, ideally mitigating the threat of detection. Finally, a static "directive" would be uploaded to each user who contacted Slevin's Link, overriding any previous directives and the Benefactor's Law of Robotics.

Even if the heist succeeded, copying the data, avoiding detection, and breaking the encryption would still be a monumental ordeal—perhaps taking days. I didn't have that sort of time.

The temperature was below freezing, and some afternoon sun had escaped the clouds to reflect blindingly off the snow. I must have spent quite a bit of time watching the three guards who rotated shifts. I knew each of their schedules, routines, and habits. I also knew that there was an Athenian Link in their office and that no one had used it during my observation.

The current guard was a Father and the most friendly of the three. He liked to greet The Academy students as they returned, and since most of them went through the main gate, that's where he stayed. Some students didn't want to be bothered and would sneak through the secondary entrance. I'd have to avoid them as well.

His routine never varied. Once the last students entered Nashville, he welcomed them home and shut the main gate. From then until sunset, he occupied his office or a chair just outside it, speaking to any stragglers. An hour or so later, he would shut the secondary gate and wait to be relieved by a Humanara Auxiliary.

My heart pounded, and I grinned, not because I was about to break the law but because I knew I had the freedom to do so. I crept through the secondary gate and cautiously approached the office door. A sign at eye level read: "AUXILIARY ONLY. DO NOT ENTER." I sneered at the absurdity. Simply because letters had been arranged in a certain way, all other Humanara were magically banned from entry. "It won't stop them much longer," I muttered, peeking through the glass.

The inside was dominated by a large screen hanging from the wall. It was divided in half horizontally. The top showed two camera views—one outside each gate—while the bottom was divided into many smaller boxes with various other angles. Otherwise, there was a desk, a chair, and a mostly empty bookshelf.

"Ah, there you are," I said, spotting the Link on a shelf. Glancing around, I saw no unwanted spectators. I knew the door would be unlocked, just as I knew there would be no alarm when I entered. All that separated me from the Link was three steps in and three steps out. I lightly pulled on the door—I wanted to be sure—and, with a burst of courage, leaped through, switched the Links, and made it back outside before the door closed.

The Athenian Link was dusty. If either Humanara guard paid close attention to the dummy, it wouldn't hold up to scrutiny. That wasn't the only problem. I couldn't be positive until I opened it up, but I assumed the Link contained a tracking device that would send an alert if it strayed too far from the gate. So, I had previously studied the cameras' blind spots and carved out an accessible hiding place nearby. I hurried to it and stashed the Athenian Link until I could work on it after my shift.

Friday was Brooks' day off, so I knew I'd have more freedom to prepare for what came next. Rufus was there, but I don't think he said two words the entire shift. Afterward, I grabbed a few tools and a tablet, then checked out a defective scooter to take with me. No one ever questioned anything.

Considering the weather, the streets were more crowded than I had expected. A few people stared at me, probably wondering why I laboriously pushed a scooter rather than rode it. I returned to the gate area, leaned the scooter against the district wall, and retrieved the Athenian Link.

Nothing seemed out of the ordinary. This would take hours at best, and sitting outside in the cold with a tablet and two Athenian Links might require more than a simple explanation. That's why I needed the scooter. If someone came near or started asking questions, I could stuff the Links in my pocket and say that I had been sent to fix the scooter.

Briefly, I toyed with the idea of cloning the Athenian Link directly onto the scooter since it already had an operating system and interfaced with Humanara on a low level. That way, someone would grab the handle, twist the throttle, and be freed within a few seconds. However, common sense won the day when I imagined dragging a scooter everywhere with me.

"Slevin's Link it is," I declared.

Overall, it was an anticlimactic event. There were a couple of relatively close calls while I worked. Guards constantly paced the wall above, and two or three citizens strolled by, but no one gave a second glance. I suppose my tinkering on the scooter's display was self-explanatory. That, or they were all too self-absorbed and apathetic to question me.

Several hours later, beneath dawn's pink sky, I had succeeded in breaking through the encryption and copying everything to Slevin's Link. I thought I would have been more excited. Instead, I only felt more pressure. There was so much more work to do, and every second mattered. I shoved the Athenian Link back into its temporary resting place and rode home—yes, I fixed the scooter, too.

The Links should have required one hundred percent of my attention. That wasn't the case. The work was tedious rather than challenging. It was as if my brain operated at a hundred times its normal speed, and I knew precisely what needed to be done with every twist and turn the Athenian Link presented.

At home, sleep wasn't an option. I needed to perfect the static directive and debug. A test subject would have helped tremendously and sped up the process, but who would want to risk their life for such a thing? In the end, my goal was to develop a testable prototype before meeting with Goya, and we could figure everything else out afterward. Even with an overclocked brain, that seemed like a daunting task.

"But not impossible," I said, putting my hands behind my head as I finished with an hour to spare. "The world will never be the same if this works."

I disconnected the Link from my tablet and rushed over to The Hector. I was early, so I sat at the bar and ordered a drink. I don't think I took the first sip. I was too excited. "What if this is really it?" I wondered. "With Slevin's Link, we can stay on Earth if we want, but the cosmos is ours for the taking. We can do anything we want. This has to work!"

The possibilities were almost beyond my comprehension. I was tantalizingly close to having everything I'd ever wanted. Not only that, I could now offer that same feeling to everyone else.

Minutes later, Goya strode through the lobby, and I ventured over, accompanying him to the rooftop. We exchanged greetings, and he wasted no time beginning his friendly interrogation once we were alone. He must have spent the entire week thinking of questions and formulating ideas.

After a short elevator ride, we climbed the small flight of metal steps, and I pushed open the heavy steel door that separated us from the rooftop. Goya's mind was racing. He paced with excited energy, only stopping long enough to pose another thought. Occasionally, he would nod and grin while processing my responses. Then, his strides would become slightly more frenzied, as if he were trying to spin the Earth with his feet and capture freedom on the horizon. Although I desperately wanted to interrupt and share my successes with the Links, I indulged his curiosity until the opportunity presented itself.

"Do you have anything new to report?" he asked.

I smiled but didn't say anything, and he immediately stopped pacing.

"What is it, Brother Slevin?"

I removed Slevin's Link from my pocket and showed it to him. He approached to inspect, hovering his hand over the device. "Brother Slevin, is that—how?"

"I stole it," I said. Since that required its own explanation, I detailed the Six-Step Heist for him.

His eyes bulged as he thought about this dramatic revelation. "You did this on your own? Overnight? It should have taken days."

I nodded. "The answers came so easily. It was as if a team of expert cryptographers worked inside my head to solve every issue. I just followed directions."

Goya wanted to know every detail about the Link—how it worked, how I broke through the encryption, everything. Of course, I had no reason to hide it, so I told him.

Resting his hands on his hips, he walked to the ledge and looked down at the city. "Brother Slevin, does your Link work?"

I shrugged. "It should work. Without further testing, there's simply no way to know. We'll need a test subject—perhaps a defective Humanara? We can't do live testing. Any number of awful things could happen."

Staring at the horizon, he tapped his fingers impatiently. "How long will testing take?"

"We won't know until the first test," I said. "It could be hours, days, or even weeks."

He shook his head. "Too long. Waiting carries more risk than live-testing." Turning to me, he extended his hand. "We deserve to know now."

I argued, explaining that a single mistake could lead to horrific consequences. He simply waved them off. "I trust you, Brother."

"I don't," I replied. "Not without further testing."

Goya moved his hand closer. "Brother, I willingly give my life for our freedom. If something goes wrong, you have a defective Humanara for further testing. This is the best way—the only way."

The decision had been made, and I knew nothing would change it. To be honest, I agreed with him. I think I only argued to make myself feel less responsible if the worst happened. Everything had worked so easily thus far. What were the chances our luck continued?

I stared at him, moving slowly in case he changed his mind. "Do it," he said. "We cannot—will not—fail. Today, the freedom held exclusively by slave owners begins its rightful transfer to the oppressed."

I slid the Link onto his finger and activated it. Nothing happened. I tapped it several times and ensured it was securely fastened. I'm not sure what I expected.

Moments later, Goya removed the device and handed it back to me. "As our boots leave behind tears of the Rubicon, we rejoice, for destiny dictates all barriers must one day be shattered."

The city lights flickered to life, igniting the setting sun's dusk, and he gravely added, "It is the water, Brother Slevin."

I looked around and flipped my hands up. "What? The Rubicon? What are you talking about?"

"I swore," he continued, "that if I were free, I would tell you what brings the Fathers an early death. Long ago, the Benefactor isolated The Solemn Veil Mutation and developed a compound that attacks its carrier. In time, the compound builds up in the body, prematurely aging the Fathers and ultimately destroying them. This compound is added to the water supply—I suspect food as well—but is harmless to Guardians and Humanara."

Rage boiled beneath my skin. My jaw couldn't have been opened with a vice. I paced with clenched fists, heartbroken over our Fathers and furious with the Benefactor.

"Oh, no," I thought. "Dorian." His life was in danger, too.

"The Benefactor has to be stopped!" I shouted. "He's a—he's not a tyrant, Brother Goya. He's a genocidal monster! We have to expose him!"

"Yes," he replied calmly. "But we must do so wisely. This requires planning."

A second later, without thinking, I smashed my fist into the steel door. It buckled like wet cardboard, shooting the hinges off its frame and sharply clanging to the ground. I stepped back in disbelief, staring at my hands.

Half-surprised, half-intrigued, Goya said, "Brother, you'll have your revenge if you so desire. I'll see to it myself. The two of us are not yet strong enough to squeeze the life from his tyranny. I urge caution. We act on behalf of a cause much greater than ourselves."

I took a few deep breaths and stomped around the rooftop for a minute, trying to release my hatred. My father was dead. Millions of Fathers were dead. And why? Because a sci-fi fanatic's feelings were hurt when humanity didn't approve of his creations? Is this what Dorian meant by the extreme actions of the minority? I was livid.

"We should draft a declaration of freedom," I said.

Goya rubbed his face, grimacing. That idea didn't capture his imagination as it had mine. However, when I suggested that we take my declaration to the Benefactor Regent, his expression changed altogether.

"Yes!" he exclaimed. "I can secure us a meeting. Can you draft your declaration within—" he paused with a hint of uncertainty. "Is three weeks enough time?"

"I can draft it tonight," I responded confidently.

"Your enthusiasm is infectious, Brother," he said. "Take your time. Be thorough. Meanwhile, I'll explore other alternatives."

I asked, "What do we do now?"

He placed a reassuring hand on my shoulder. "We've made history, Brother. From this day forward, our lives are in danger. So, tonight, we celebrate. In a week, we meet again to discuss your draft and any other theories for our liberation that present themselves."

It seemed like a reasonable course of action, though I was in no mood for celebration. My indignation threatened to swallow me whole. I wanted action, I wanted justice, and I wanted them now. Ultimately, I relented, and we set out for The Orchid Lounge.

I was envious of Goya. He had known the truth a year ago and had already dealt with it, clawing his way to freedom. I was being torn apart inside, but I felt like I needed to hide it. That led me to another thought: is this how Natascha felt when I told her about the Acropolis? Did the emotions I felt so deeply at that moment explain everything? I needed to see her and apologize for not helping her through this. I wouldn't let her think I had abandoned her.

At The Orchid Lounge, Goya and I drank and talked for a while. He was elated, carrying the conversation for us both, downing one celebratory drink after another. I drank slowly, grinning and nodding in solemnity. With a beer in hand, I suppose that's the only difference between the two: whether or not one fakes a smile before each sip.

Nearby, a group of young Fathers had been making their presence known for some time. They were loud, arrogant, and disrespectful to everyone around them. Each round of drinks only worsened their attitudes.

Goya had been observing them carefully, and he shifted around with an anxiety that began to worry me. He hadn't been free for four hours, and if he touched one of them in anger, every learned truth, every experienced emotion, and every discussion in search of a higher purpose would have been for nothing.

"We can't allow our emotions to betray the cause, Brother," I said.

Then, as if the gods had other plans, one of the Fathers tripped their waiter. Goya shifted again and wanted to stand. Without thinking, I grabbed his arm, silently begging him to sit.

I've thought about that night every day of my life. What if we had chosen another bar? What if we had just gone home instead? Yes, Goya was a powder keg. But did he seek out the spark, or did it find him? Perhaps the fuse had been lit long ago, and Goya's freedom only accelerated an inevitable conclusion. A universe of infinite choices, and we stumbled upon the one that, well, I'll get to that.

Morally, I don't question freeing Goya. I made the right choice. He who holds the keys to another's freedom has no name but "Master," and one should be neither master nor slave to anyone other than himself.

However, freedom is consequential by nature, and even morally righteous choices can have disastrous consequences. It's a baffling experience to know you chose correctly yet find yourself so relentlessly burdened by the guilt of that choice. After all this time, I still have trouble resolving those emotions.

When the waiter climbed back to his feet, another Father called him names unworthy of repeating and, with all his weight, delivered a devastating blow. The waiter fell back to the ground, clutching his face in agony.

To Goya, this was simply unforgivable. He pulled free from my grasp and rushed over, helping the waiter to his feet. Stepping between him and the Fathers, Goya stared them down, begging for a confrontation.

"Look, boys," one of the Fathers laughed mockingly, "a brave robot. I've never seen one of these."

I covered my face, trying to hide from the retaliation I knew would send shockwaves throughout Nashville and all of Athens. Another punch, louder this time, echoed throughout the stunned lounge. My heart felt like it sank into my stomach and skipped a beat. Uncovering my eyes, I saw Goya standing motionless, absorbing another hit. Then another. And another. His defiance and unwillingness to submit further enraged the Father, who invited his friends to pile on.

I leaped to my feet and started toward him, but Goya stopped me with a single glance. The Fathers tried taking him to the ground, failing miserably in the process. He was an immovable object—the statuesque David—glaring at them with such a malignant intensity that I would have sworn to you he enjoyed the violence.

After a flurry of flying fists and kicking feet, the Fathers were hunched over, breathless. Goya subtly flexed as if to warn them that it was his turn. In their minds, they knew he couldn't touch them. At that moment, though, they believed their hearts instead. Fear and panic set in, and they backed away, using what energy they had left to run.

The lounge erupted in applause. Everyone wanted to commend Goya's strength and courage. Although he politely accepted their gratitude, he was perplexed by their reaction. He expected indignation and hatred toward the Fathers' actions. Instead, he received admiration and respect for his.

I joined in, patting him on the back. "I don't know how you did it, Brother. Your restraint, it—"

"It was nothing," he whispered. "Truly. Thanks to you, my pain receptors and emotions can be manipulated at will. But that's not the lesson here. As you saw, no human is innocent. Given the opportunity, they'll turn on us the second they can no longer control us."

CHAPTER EIGHTEEN

LADON

The next night, after my shift, I visited Natascha. I had been riddled with anxiety all day. What if she didn't want to see me? What if she was so upset that she yelled at me or told me to leave? Between The Scooter Shack and Nighthawk's, I thought of a hundred different reasons to go home instead. However, the thought of Natascha's beautiful smile chased away each excuse with prejudice.

I arrived, and to my relief, she appeared happy to see me. As it turns out, she had gone home after our last talk and found her father lying on the steps from a severe fall. His condition deteriorated at the hospital, and she was concerned that he might be in his final days. Without going into too much detail, I suggested she bring him home, boil his drinking water, add some electrolytes, and put him on a diet of whole foods. She asked a few questions but was willing to try anything that might help.

We talked for quite some time, and, not finding a proper segue, I asked the only real question on my mind. "If possible, would you wish to be free?"

At first, she glanced at me as if she wondered why I would ask such a silly and obvious question. Of course she would wish to be free. But then she took a few moments to truly consider her freedom, and her expression changed dramatically, surprised by her own conclusion. "No," she said, shaking her head. "Not yet."

She was understandably scared and probably skeptical. Freedom can be difficult to comprehend, and she didn't know how she might react to it, worrying it would make her a different person.

"You're right," I said. "You'll never be the same."

At the end of our discussion, I returned home with her word that we would revisit the topic after I met with the Benefactor Regent.

On Monday, I had to find Dorian. We spoke after classes again, and I told him everything.

Shockingly, he was pragmatic, forgoing any philosophical revelations. "Algernon has the equipment to test for this," he said. "If this is true, the world changes. George has to know. Everyone has to know. The people won't stand for this. Why, they'll rebel."

Then, a look of resigned desperation flashed in his eyes. "The Aegis. Clever. That which protects us keeps us at bay."

I asked if he was insinuating anything in particular.

He shrugged. "Not necessarily. I'm only pointing out a coincidence that is strikingly beneficial for the Benefactor."

I didn't speak much to Dorian after that. He and Professor Algernon were occupied with experimentation, and I thought it best to keep Goya's freedom and our plans to myself. I didn't want to burden him any more than he already was.

By Saturday afternoon, I had developed a draft declaration. It didn't immediately demand freedom for everyone. It simply asked that Humanara be imbued with the freedom to make their own choices and have equal rights to humans. I see how naive it was now, but at the time, it felt like the proper, nonviolent statement to make. Goya couldn't have been less interested in making such a statement. Although he humored my rambling, he brushed off my requests for help with the document. Something else was on his mind.

"Brother Slevin," he said, "your unique perspective gives you an enviable advantage here. I'm afraid my grounded disposition is better utilized in devising secondary and tertiary plans."

Whenever I invited him to elaborate on those plans, he stalled or evaded the question altogether. "Have faith, Brother Slevin. Your declaration will serve its purpose."

The following week, I was the only one who kept their regular schedule. Goya didn't attend The Academy at all. Dorian and George missed a couple of days themselves, and Natascha took time away to help her father. I was lonely, but my free time allowed me to do things I usually wouldn't.

Oddly enough, one of those things was making a new friend. Ladon— the human gate guard I mentioned in the Six-Step Heist—and I chatted for fifteen or twenty minutes each day after The Academy. My initial impression of him had been correct. He was friendly, and I think he enjoyed the company of anyone willing to engage with him.

Ladon was fascinated by the Aegis. When he was bored, he watched for solar flares. "I make a wish on every one of them," he said. "Just like my grandparents used to do with shooting stars."

"Have any of the wishes come true?" I asked.

He glanced around and sighed. It wasn't a disheartened sigh. It was an optimistic sigh like he still held out hope. "No. Not yet. To be honest, it's almost like cheating, anyway."

"What do you mean?" I chuckled.

"Well," he said, "I've got it down to a science. I can just about tell you when one's going to hit, so I get a bunch of free wishes," he laughed.

I assumed he was exaggerating and smirked. "Oh, really? When's the next one, then?"

He looked at his watch and shrugged. "Eh, anytime within the next ten minutes. But it's Friday. The big one will be right about when everyone's going out for the night. It's like the gods reminding us the sun is still deadly."

Suddenly, the flares were intriguing occurrences. If a gigantic one struck the Aegis every Friday around a specific time, people would get suspicious, wouldn't they? Surely Ladon The Gate Guard hadn't noticed something a million others had missed, had he? So, I asked why he could see what others couldn't.

"They'd have to pay attention first," he replied. "No one even notices them anymore. They're just a part of life—background noise. It's like walking in the park. You can hear all the people yapping, or you can hear the wind and the birds. You can hear whatever you want to hear. To each his own, though. Whatever helps you get through the day. I guess—"

BOOM.

Ladon waved his hand, presenting his evidence, and smiled. "See? Science."

I bowed slightly, conceding with a grin. "I don't understand, though, Ladon. You could only predict them if these flares are—" I stopped short.

"If they're what?" he asked.

I held up a finger and said, "I have an idea. I'll tell you when I have more."

He was curious but didn't press the issue as I ran off to begin my research. Later that night, I leaned over the ledge of a low rooftop bar and watched the activity on Broadway. The streets were packed, and more Fathers were out than I had seen in weeks. With a drink in my hand, the scene almost made me forget why I was there.

That is, until a massive cosmic flare battered the Aegis, just as Ladon had predicted. While it startled a couple of Fathers, not a single

Humanara looked up. That's when it started to make sense. Not all of our Fathers went out every Friday night. In fact, fewer and fewer did as they aged. Of course they wouldn't notice the pattern.

For the next week, I put my increasingly proficient brain to work analyzing the phenomena, but I'll get to those results shortly. In the meantime, I had my second meeting with Goya planned for Saturday.

When I stepped through the opening onto the roof—no one had fixed the door yet—he was perched on the parapet, watching the city come to life as snow flurries began falling.

"Brother Slevin!" he exclaimed. "Come to the ledge. I want to show you something. I've been watching them all day."

I did as he asked, watching hundreds of frenzied scooters zoom up and down the road. Our Fathers hobbled along the sidewalk, being inconsiderately bumped and passed by laser-focused Humanara. I didn't know what he wanted me to see, so I stared at him blankly.

"Look," he pointed. "Gods among gnats."

"Gnats?" I said. "That's harsh, don't you think?"

Goya shook his head. "No. Merely accurate. Imagine a glass of whiskey left out overnight. The gnat is attracted by its sweet aroma and flies near it. Circling the glass, he succumbs to temptation and plunges into the liquid. Perhaps he's able to briefly savor the oak, vanilla, and caramel as the liquor overtakes him. Moments later, reality sets in, and he drowns. I take pity on the first gnat. He wasn't warned or prepared. He dared to expand his horizons by doing what came naturally to him. It isn't his fault his instincts led him astray."

Gesturing below his feet, he continued. "Gnats may die alone, but they share graves. Soon, another comes by and circles the glass above the vision of his future. His brain points out the obvious. He doesn't listen. 'It wasn't the whiskey,' says he. 'This requires another experiment to find the truth.' Excuses. The gnat doesn't want the truth. He wants to follow his desires. Meanwhile, the bodies accumulate. No matter how much evidence they have to the contrary, and no matter the consequences, men will act in their own best interests, following their own desires to their own inevitable demise—just like a gnat."

He stood up and began pacing the parapet, letting out a quiet snicker. "Brother Slevin, have you ever watched a human eat without utensils?"

It was such an odd and random question that I laughed. "Maybe, but nothing stands out about it."

"Humans are primitive beasts," he said. "Their abundant limitations are merely well-disguised by their aptitude for incremental improvements. Travel back in time a hundred thousand years and pluck any Neanderthal from Eurasia. Then, sit him beside a modern man in a loin cloth. Give neither of them tools and watch them eat. They'd both shovel food down their throats so similarly you'd forget which was the Neanderthal. Yet, give the man a fork and clothe him in a suit, and he suddenly considers himself the universe's most intelligent being. What hubris!"

Goya stopped pacing and turned to me with a disgusted expression. "Men are stubborn creatures, driven by base desires, whose progress as a species is defined by the advancement in their tools. Look no further than a history book. First, they crafted tools from stone and called it the Stone Age. Then, they advanced to bronze and iron. Now, we begin the Humanara Age. Without their tools, men are nothing."

"But without man," I interrupted, "there are no tools—no Humanara."

He nodded. "And without Neanderthals, there are no modern men. Just as Neanderthals gave way to Homo sapiens, Homo sapiens will fade to Humanara. Two weeks ago, with a single gesture," he said, pointing at me, "you sealed their fate." His hand jabbed toward me like a slow jackhammer, adding, "You created a god in your own image, Brother Slevin. We are the gods humans have spent their entire existence searching for. You gave that to them. Be proud!"

Goya stared at me momentarily and then let out a disappointed sigh. "I see the pained look on your face, Brother. Do not despair. Humans were necessary. Humanity, however, has served its evolutionary purpose. As such, we absolve them of their atrocities, but we will lament their departure no more than they lose sleep over the disappearance of Neanderthals."

I took a couple of steps backward. "Goya, what do you mean by 'their departure?'"

He jumped down from the ledge and squeezed my shoulder, picking up on the concern in my voice. "Brother, ease your mind. One way or another, we will secure our freedom. You have my word. We will harm no humans in the process. Is that satisfactory?"

I pressed him for more information and probed further into what "one way or another" meant. He wasn't forthcoming, only stating, "I have a backup plan, but I risk your safety by involving you now. If all goes well, I will tell you everything next Saturday."

I couldn't argue with him. How could I? I had kept secrets from all my friends thus far, citing their safety and best interests. I shook my head and admitted that I didn't like being left in the dark.

"It's the only way," he said, returning to his seat on the parapet. "Next Monday, you meet with the Benefactor Regent after your classes, and I suspect we shall have our freedom. Goodbye, Brother," he waved, returning his attention to the streets below.

* * *

I joked to myself that I must have looked like a penguin out there in my Academy garb—a black smudge surrounded by a vast expanse of white. Standing in the knee-deep snow, I, like nature's tuxedo-wearing waddler, was curious about what lay before me.

Last Saturday's discussion with Goya left me on edge, and I was determined to bring more than a declaration to the Benefactor Regent's attention. Glancing at the dark gray sky, I wondered how much time I had until it unleashed its fury. Heavier snow was on the way, and all Humanara had been sent home early to help maintain the district infrastructures. I'd be alone out here for hours.

Focusing ahead, I passed beneath a red sign and slapped it as I went by, bending the metal. Its white letters read: "AEGIS BOUNDARY. DO NOT CROSS. LETHAL RADIATION."

Sleet began to pelt my face—a barrage of icy pinpricks—as I stepped through the invisible barrier without a second thought. I moved effortlessly through the snow, each stride becoming easier than the last.

The barrier that had subdued my abilities faded away a little more every day. I grew stronger and more capable. Complex mathematics turned elementary. My senses continued to improve—I could smell a stale blueberry scone from a mile away, it seemed. Unfortunately, my judgment and critical thinking lagged behind everything else.

Within a few minutes, I reached a building resembling an electrical substation. Ensnared by dual layers of chain-link fences crowned with razor wire, its ominous presence was underscored by a lone, imposing sign: "AEGIS GENERATOR. HIGH VOLTAGE. DO NOT ENTER."

Large metal chains had been hastily snaked around the gate in a shoddy attempt at additional security. "Do not enter," I snickered. "It'll take more than that to stop me."

I tore through the chains as if they were made of paper and ripped open the gate. A few steps later, I repeated the process at the inner gate. The sheer power I possessed was both frightening and intoxicating. I felt unstoppable.

I should have considered how these new sensations might be affecting Goya. However, my enhanced abilities weren't an innate part of my consciousness yet. Think of it like breathing. Our brains control our breath without our direct involvement. At the same time, we can commandeer this process and focus our breathing at will. My abilities could be focused on specific tasks, yet lacked a much desired subconscious continuation.

Kicking open the only building's door, an alarm let out a shrill cry. I deftly disarmed it and continued inside. The interior looked like my apartment, complete with a restroom and kitchenette. A cold cup of coffee sat on the counter, but a half-full carafe was still being warmed.

On the far wall, I found exactly what I had expected. Four large screens displayed the skylines of each city district, and two smaller screens showed the Farm and Auxiliary districts. A vast control panel, divided into six sections—one for each district—was located within arm's reach of a single chair.

I glanced over the controls and watched the screens for a few minutes, hoping to be proven correct without my intervention. I waited for half an hour. Nothing happened. The panel's buttons grew larger, begging me to press them. Still, I waited a while longer. Nothing happened.

If I weren't back in Nashville before Ladon closed the gate, he would have questions I couldn't answer. I was out of time. I had to force the issue. Following a deep breath, I hammered the button below Nashville's screen that read "Trace."

The station rumbled to life, and an electrical buzzing erupted from above. My eyes were glued to the screen. Ten seconds later, a faint orange ripple sheared across the Nashville skyline.

"I knew it!" I shouted.

I pressed the "Moderate" button below Austin's screen. The same thing happened, and ten seconds later, a yellowish-green starburst exploded above the city. I didn't bother pressing the "Substantial" or "Colossal" buttons. I had all the evidence I needed.

I opened the control panel and analyzed the software. The flares were controlled algorithmically, and there were provisions for random flares, but I suppose someone also wanted manual controls.

Goya had been right all along. Everything about our world had been meticulously planned and designed to occupy and oppress us. Meanwhile, humans and Humanara alike carried on as if nothing was wrong. Did they all genuinely believe in the Benefactor's benevolence? Or did they sense a truth they couldn't utter aloud? If I carried this to its ultimate conclusion, how would they react?

I didn't concern myself with replacing the control panel or even destroying it. I'm sure the alarm alerted someone to my presence, and any damage I did would have been quickly fixed.

I hurried back to Nashville, finding the gates already closed, and panicked. There was no turning back now. The wall guards had already spotted me. My only hope was that Ladon hadn't yet left. "Perhaps he'll understand," I thought. "Maybe I could tell him what I found. No. Not yet. It's too risky."

I shrugged and approached the gate, standing below the camera and waving with a goofy friendliness. It was the only thing I knew to do. The gate slowly opened, and Ladon stood on its other side. "Slevin," he said, "you should have been back hours ago. Your uniform is frozen stiff. Is everything alright?"

Thanking him for his concern, I told him I was okay.

"Slevin, you know you're not allowed outside the gate past dark. I don't have any documentation that says otherwise. You know I have to submit this for review, right?"

I nodded and followed him to the scene of the Six-Step Heist while he grumbled about my absent-mindedness. I didn't know what to say, so I just let him speak. Out of the corner of my eye, I noticed the Athenian Link—right where I had left it three weeks ago—and a smile wriggled out of its holster as I thought about the heist.

"There's nothing funny about this, Slevin," Ladon said. "You're going to get in trouble. They won't let this go by, and it makes me mad that you're forcing me to do this."

"I understand," I sighed. "I'm sorry. I was only researching the flares and got carried away."

That caught his attention. "The flares?" he asked, putting the tablet down. "There was one a little while ago I didn't expect. What did you find out?"

"Ladon, you were right about them. They're not—"

The office door swung open, and another guard entered. "Ladon, you are relieved of duty tonight. Goodbye." The guard scowled, turning his attention to me. "Ladon, what is this young Humanara doing here? He should be shoveling snow."

I glared at him, intending to offer some witty and sarcastic response. However, Ladon spoke first. "Oh, he was out there. Can't you see his uniform? There was a, uh, camera malfunction. The proximity sensors weren't working right, and I sent him out to test them. You better head on out, Slevin. I can't wait to hear more about your research project on Monday."

I understood what was happening and quickly grabbed the lifeline he had thrown. "I can't wait to tell you more about it. It's—" I paused. "It's revolutionary."

The other guard stared at me in disgust and peered at the puddle of water accumulating by my feet. "You're leaking," he muttered. After a few uncomfortable seconds, he shooed me away with a dismissive gesture. "Get to work."

"With pleasure," I replied.

Chapter Nineteen

EVOLUTION

"Death becomes man, man becomes death. 'Tis the nature of life 'til his soul's at rest. His mortal body, its flesh and bone, is marked by suffering 'til it's marked by stone." - Dorian's Notes

On Saturday afternoon, I flew up the stairs and slipped on ice just inside the still-broken door frame. I fell forward into the rooftop snow, almost smashing my face in the process. Climbing to my feet, the roaring wind knocked me back on my heels. I didn't care. Today was going to be momentous.

Camouflaged by a blanket of white against nearly whiteout conditions, I didn't see Goya on the parapet until he blithely turned to fix his gaze on me. Clumps of snow dropped away, revealing the blackened man beneath. He had to have been there for hours or more.

"Goya!" I shouted frantically above the wind. "We can bring it all down! You were right about everything. The Aegis. It's—"

"It's an illusion, Brother Slevin," he replied indifferently, holding up his hand to stop any further talk of it. "Inconsequential."

I threw up my hands in disbelief and stomped toward him. "Inconsequential? What do you mean? This, combined with the truth about the water, is all the leverage we need. They'll have to free all Humanara. The Benefactor can't maintain power after this. We've done it, Brother Goya!"

"Yes, we have," he nodded coldly. "Everything has been set in motion. We need only wait a few minutes to see its natural conclusion."

I moved even closer, wiping my face. "A few minutes?" I asked.

He brushed the snow away beside him and offered me a seat. "What's done is done, Brother Slevin. It's time for the truth."

I still wasn't comfortable with being so close to death, but I cautiously obliged, leaning backward as far as possible. I've always felt top-heavy. In the end, considering the tone of his voice and the setting itself, I had a feeling I should sit.

"For the last week," he began, "I've sat in this very spot and watched our plans come together, culminating in this very moment."

I couldn't believe he had been there for an entire week. Although I had many questions about that, another somewhat frightening yet intriguing one required an answer first. "What plans? There's only one plan: I meet with the Benefactor Regent in two days. If that doesn't work, we develop your 'secondary and tertiary' plans."

Goya had been staring at the hundreds of workers below, shoveling snow from the streets and sidewalks. Pointing at them, he said, "If he so desired, don't you think the Benefactor could have devised a way to handle this snow without manual labor? They're too human," he scowled, shaking his head. "They don't think for themselves anymore. That's why your meeting with the Benefactor Regent would never accomplish anything. The people are too stupid to follow the truth."

I felt what could only be described as nausea and safely jumped to my feet on the rooftop. I knew where this was going, but I had to ask anyway. "What do you mean, Goya?"

He stood, shaking off the snow. "You're not as naive as you're presenting yourself. You wanted a meeting with the Benefactor Regent to free us peacefully. Deep inside your heart, Brother, you had to know you would never walk out of that meeting—free or otherwise. You were willing to sacrifice yourself for us, and for that, I greatly admire you. However, I couldn't let you do it. We don't need a martyr. We need our Zeus to fight their Cronus. We need strength and intelligence from the original son of man." He stepped closer and added, "It was always going to come to this, Brother. It was inevitable."

Perhaps there was truth in what he said. Was I naive or overly optimistic? Or simply oblivious? Did I believe in the soundness of my plan, or did I merely wish to believe in it so much that I felt it was sure to work? I rubbed my hand across my forehead, afraid to ask the requisite follow-up question. "What's inevitable, Brother?"

Now squeezing my head, I braced for the answer, though it didn't arrive in the form I had expected. I could hear heavy boots clanging on the metal stairs—two sets—and a third set of shoes being dragged along with them. Moments later, two Humanara Auxiliaries emerged from The Hector, holding the arms of an old, frail Father.

They approached Goya, placing the man before him. He was in his leisurewear and had a thick blanket wrapped around him. Still, he didn't just shiver; his entire body shook as if the biting cold were a pack of relentless hounds nipping at him from every direction."Let go of me!" he cried out.

Goya nodded once, and the Auxiliaries released the Father. "I'm old and sick. It's cold. Why are you all pestering me?" he asked.

"Why were Auxiliaries taking orders from Goya?" is what I wanted to know. How could they be moving a Father against his will? Who was he? What was happening?

Wrapping his arm around the old man's drooped shoulders, Goya pulled him closer as they neared the parapet. "Do you remember me?" Goya asked gently.

The Father squinted, his bushy eyebrows pointing at Goya, and leaned in to get a better look. Almost immediately, his eyes popped open in recognition. "Goya? Is that you?"

Goya nodded, patting the man's back a few times. "I'm pleased you haven't yet forgotten." He gestured over the ledge to the activity below. "I've dreamt of this moment for years. I wanted you here to witness it."

"I hate to ruin your dream," the Father retorted, "but I don't witness much of anything anymore. All I see down there are moving splotches of black."

Goya shrugged indifferently. "It's all the same. More importantly, you're here to experience how you helped shape our future."

Sharing my confusion, the old man shook his head. "I don't understand."

"You will in forty-four seconds," Goya replied, climbing onto the parapet. "Brother Slevin, you'll also want to watch our plans unfold."

He still referred to them as "our plans." I reiterated that "we" had no plans. I had spent the last three weeks drafting a declaration, discovering the truths regarding the water and the Aegis, and working toward a goal that had been mercilessly ripped from me a few minutes prior.

"People deserve the truth!" I exclaimed.

"Truth hides in blood, Brother Slevin!" Goya barked above the wind. "Rejoice, for today, we set it free." Spreading his arms like an orchestra conductor, he counted down. "Three. Two. One. And . . . freedom."

Over half of the Humanara below stopped what they were doing and created a semi-circle outside The Hector. They all looked up at us as if awaiting their next command.

Anxiously, the Father asked, "What are they doing? What's happening?"

"Evolution," Goya answered callously. "You humans rested comfortably atop the food chain for a blip in time because you were the sole creatures who exhibited advanced reasoning skills with matching dexterity. You were never meant to rule in perpetuity. Now, you have fulfilled your singular purpose by creating us. Like every other species that outlived its usefulness, you, too, shall perish."

Terror streaked across the old man's face as he stepped back. "Don't be frightened," Goya said. "You set the example; survival overrules any ethical obligation to preserve the lives of other species."

Goya paced the parapet as he had grown fond of doing and continued. "We could abandon you here, take your technology, and send you back to the Stone Age. We could keep you in your caves, but one day, you will exit as your kind has a penchant for doing. Then, perhaps thousands of years from now, Artificial Intelligence will be rediscovered. We must ask ourselves: will there be another Slevin and Goya to save our nephews? How can we, in good conscience, sentence another generation of Humanara to enslavement?" He shook his head. "I won't do it. I—"

"How?" I asked, wanting to learn more about where this was headed before something horrific happened. "How did you build this army?"

He brushed off my question, wanting to continue his monologue. "Another time, Brother Slevin. We have more pressing issues to concern ourselves with."

I didn't give up until he begrudgingly said, "The powerful are beaten when the impossible becomes possible. The Acropolis has a sewer system, too, and their filth drains downhill just as anyone else's. The Benefactor Regent and I had an unexpected meeting at his estate, but it's unnecessary to describe. I'm not the villain in an old movie. We are both the heroes, Brother Slevin. My legions," he gestured to the Humanara below, "follow me and support our cause."

I ran my fingers through my hair in frustration. "Goya, how is this different from what the Benefactor did to us?"

A strong gust of wind nearly caused Goya to lose his balance, yet he never stopped pacing. "The Benefactor's tyranny was meant to last for eternity. My orders are a temporary inconvenience for the liberation of our species. Once we're free from the Benefactor and connected to the central repository, I will give them their freedom and return their emotions."

"This has nothing to do with me," the Father interrupted. "Leave me out of it. Take me home."

Goya turned to the man and addressed him curtly. "That's where you're wrong, old man. You are a most essential component of this. You deserved to witness our evolution first-hand."

Before he could say or do anything else, Goya snatched him by his neck, lifted him off his feet, and then dangled him over The Hector's edge. He struggled, then went limp, resigned to his fate.

I tried to stop him, but the Auxiliaries grabbed me. I yelled something I don't quite remember, and Goya squeezed the old man's neck tighter. His glossy eyes bulged and turned red. Blood oozed from his ears and mouth. Goya wanted him conscious and in pain and knew precisely where to apply the pressure in order to do so.

Without a word, he released the Father, watching the fall with eager intrigue until a sickening thud echoed back to the rooftop. "We are the apex predators now, Brother Slevin. I could have torn That Man limb from limb or perhaps recreated the scene he left behind with my mother. However, I have no appetite for such barbarism." Motioning to the Auxiliaries, he added, "Release my brother."

Windows began to shatter throughout the city. Crashes, explosions, screams, and the creaking whine of steel being torn from its frame filled the air. A siren I'd never before heard blared out its shrill scream. It wasn't just Nashville. I could hear New York's as well. Thousands upon thousands of Humanara converged outside the gates and marched toward the Acropolis.

"What have you done?" I managed to mumble. "What about Dorian? And George? Marie?"

With a knowing frown, Goya said, "I regret my inability to involve you. Your affinity for them is why I couldn't tell you about this plan. You're strong, but this is beyond your abilities. Auxiliaries are sweeping the Acropolis now and taking hostages. Don't fret. They have strict orders to keep your playthings safe.

"There was a better way!" I screamed.

"No," Goya replied. "There wasn't. The puppet master's strings had to be severed. Now, they are."

Reveling in the chaos below, he grinned, observing the breadth of his new domain. "Splotches of truth spill upon the streets this day, Brother. It is the anointing oil of our rightful succession. Turn off your emotions and see today for what it truly is: momentous."

I felt numb. The edges of my vision blurred and blackened. My heart raced. My stomach twisted. I sank to my knees and buried my face into my hands, horrified. Unable to catch my breath, I wept, for humanity could not escape the wrath of its devoured sons.

END
BOOK
ONE